All of a Sudden Being Alone in the Parking Garage Was Making Paula Nervous . . .

This wasn't the first time she'd been there at night by herself. But tonight the combination of the rain and the eeriness of the fog made her particularly edgy.

Then she heard a thud, the sound of a shoe pressing against the concrete floor. She swiveled around. Was someone in the garage with her? She heard the noise again. Now there was no denying it. It was a footstep! Her skin felt prickly, as if tiny knives were jabbing her. She tried to tell herself there was nothing to get alarmed about, but the footsteps persisted. They were coming from somewhere above her. No one should have been on the roof at this hour, in this weather! *But someone was there.* And the person had not come in after her. The person had already been up there. Watching her. Waiting for her . . .

By Duffy Stein

THE OWLSFANE HORROR
GHOST CHILD
OUT OF THE SHADOWS

QUANTITY SALES

Most Dell Books are available at special quantity discounts when purchased in bulk by corporations, organizations, and special-interest groups. Custom imprinting or excerpting can also be done to fit special needs. For details write: Dell Publishing Co., Inc., 1 Dag Hammarskjold Plaza, New York, NY 10017, Attn.: Special Sales Dept., or phone: (212) 605-3319.

INDIVIDUAL SALES

Are there any Dell Books you want but cannot find in your local stores? If so, you can order them directly from us. You can get any Dell book in print. Simply include the book's title, author, and ISBN number, if you have it, along with a check or money order (no cash can be accepted) for the full retail price plus 75¢ per copy to cover shipping and handling. Mail to: Dell Readers Service, Dept. FM, P.O. Box 1000, Pine Brook, NJ 07058.

Through the Flames

Duffy Stein

A DELL BOOK

Published by
Dell Publishing Co., Inc.
1 Dag Hammarskjold Plaza
New York, New York 10017

Copyright © 1986 by Duffy Stein
All rights reserved. No part of this book may be reproduced or transmitted in any form or by any means, electronic or mechanical, including photocopying, recording or by any information storage and retrieval system, without the written permission of the Publisher, except where permitted by law.
Dell ® TM 681510, Dell Publishing Co., Inc.
ISBN: 0-440-18671-4
Printed in the United States of America
May 1986
10 9 8 7 6 5 4 3 2 1
WFH

for Lillian Cominsky

Prologue

IT WAS A LATE SEPTEMBER DAY IN BOSTON. THE FOLIAGE was at its most colorful, kingly displays of reds and oranges, rusts and burnt umbers. Leaves poised in time and posed in individual brilliance. A fall turning the way only a New England one can be.

Paula Weller, a woman in her early thirties, was sitting on a bench in Boston Common, breathing in the crisp fall air and watching her children—Michelle, her strawberry-blond, freckled six-year-old, and Jeremy, at nine, mature for his age, as he manfully led his little sister through the wind-swirled piles of fallen leaves. It was a week before her wedding. She was about to marry Hugh Tolson, best-selling author and screenwriter. But more important, a man filled with life and laughter, a man radically different from her first husband, a staid, ambitious lawyer who was unable to communicate his feelings and emotions. It was a day of beauty and serenity and anticipation. She had so much to look forward to.

Paula first sensed the eyes on her and she squirmed with the crawling feeling people sometimes get when they are being watched. She shifted around to see a woman in the shadows of the trees. The woman could have been looking at any of the scores of people enjoying the fall day. But she wasn't, Paula saw. The other woman was looking at her. Then coming toward her, and Paula stiffened defensively.

"I'm Judith," the other woman said simply, but instinct told Paula there was nothing simple about the words or the woman's sudden appearance.

Hugh had talked only briefly about his ex-wife. She was the same age as Paula, once a beautiful woman, now practically a skeleton of a person, looking a decade older than she was. Her face was pale and drawn, her eyes sunken. Wrinkles lined her face prematurely where her skin was dry and tight. Paula also saw a slight tremor in the woman's hand. Her life had changed after her children had died in a fire eighteen months before. Judith had taken the children to their Cape Cod vacation home to decide upon a separation from Hugh. That very night there had been the fire.

"What do you want?" Paula asked.

The woman's eyes darkened and seemed to flare, becoming more pronounced against her skin, which was tinged with the pallor of death. "I have to warn you about Hugh," she cried. "He set the fire. He killed the children. He tried to kill me too."

Paula stared at Judith, trying to comprehend what she was saying. She remembered the little Hugh had told her about his ex-wife, how she had gone completely to pieces after the fire. She had been in the house with the children and had been unable to save them. Her mind had snapped. The divorce had come soon afterward, at her insistence.

The woman was sick, but what she was saying now was wrong, evil.

"You're mad," Paula gasped.

"Forget Hugh. Get away from him. If you marry him, you'll be in danger. And your children. He'll kill you all too!" The warning croaked shakily from deep in Judith's throat, as if she hadn't spoken in some time.

Both women looked toward Jeremy and Michelle, who were busy throwing leaves at each other.

"No," Paula whispered hoarsely as she weakly shook her head and got up from the bench. Her legs quivered. "Stay away from me."

"You'd better listen to me," Judith warned. "I saw him that night. Watching from the woods. I'm not sick. If he told you I was, he lied to protect himself."

All Paula could think of was the soothsayer telling Julius Caesar to beware the ides of March. She stared at the woman, for one moment trying to discern the symptoms of insanity, then decided this was not a time for observation. She shook her head more vigorously, her strength returning. "No—I won't listen to you. Don't bother me again." Her voice was snappish. "I don't want to hear you say these things."

Then she quickly gathered up her children and ushered them toward the edge of the Commons. A glance over her shoulder told her Judith was still watching her. The other woman's eyes bored coldly into Paula's back where perspiration was causing her blouse to mat against her skin. Her words echoed in warning in Paula's ears. *If you marry Hugh Tolson you'll be in danger. He set the fire. He killed the children. He'll kill you all too. . . .*

Chapter 1

ELEVATOR DOORS OPENED ONTO THE SECOND FLOOR OF Boston's Copley Plaza Hotel. People filed out and lined up at long tables to give their names and secure their reservations for the evening's seminar. Beyond the open double doors leading into one of the ballrooms, chairs were arranged in rows and the room was filling.

Paula Weller stepped out of the elevator and let an older woman and two young men, casually dressed in open collars, step past her. Hesitantly she surveyed the crowd and suddenly felt very silly and embarrassed. A perfect case, she thought, of something that seemed like a good idea at the time. *The good idea* was attending a writer's seminar on how to write and sell a novel. It was part of Boston University's adult education program, and here Paula was, surrounded by several hundred other would-be writers attending the lecture. *The time* was three weeks ago when she had bought the ticket. But now as she searched the people's faces and saw in every one of them the same hope of one day producing a best-selling book, she knew that like all of them she had the same slim chance. She should just cash in her ticket and go home to her children, admit she wasn't yet a novelist, and be content in knowing she was an expert advertising copywriter.

While she was trying to make up her mind she felt someone

looking at her and spun around. The man was standing in a corner of the hallway, partially hidden by a large potted plant. He smiled at her and Paula walked over to him and returned the smile wanly.

"This is probably a waste of time," she groaned. "I'm thinking of selling my ticket and going home."

"Don't," the man urged. "I hear Tolson's a pretty good lecturer." He shrugged. "Who knows? You may pick up something useful tonight."

"I guess as long as I'm here," Paula agreed.

Her decision made, she took her seat in the ballroom along with the other hopeful writers. She was surprised and amused to see that the man who had talked to her outside was the master of ceremonies, novelist Hugh Tolson, who would be introducing a guest editor and agent to speak about various aspects of the publishing business. When he took the podium he searched her out in the front of the room and smiled in her direction. Paula returned the smile, then settled back to enjoy the lecture and the handsome author in front of her.

As the young female agent from the William Morris Agency made her prepared remarks, Paula scanned the program she had picked up on the way in and read the brief biographical notes about Hugh Tolson. He was the author of eight internationally published suspense novels; two of them had been made into movies and another three were under option to major studios. All had reached the best-seller list. She tried to focus on the speaker but kept drawing back to Hugh, who she saw was also watching her from his straight-backed chair on the panel.

For his part Hugh was having trouble keeping his mind on the evening's program and his eyes off Paula. He had noticed her as soon as she came off the elevator. She was just over thirty, he estimated, with loosely curled brown hair that touched her shoulders. Her eyes were bright and winning, a light forest green, with a hint of jade-colored mystery behind them.

She was someone he wanted to get to know better.

After the lecture he brushed through the crowd of people who waited to ask questions of the speakers and caught up with Paula.

"Was it a waste of time?" He grinned.

She smiled wryly. "That was another case of 'open mouth,

change foot?' wasn't it? But I'm glad you got me to stay. Everyone was quite good."

"Including me?"

"Of course."

"Although I'm sure it was a waste of time for most of the people here tonight," Hugh whispered confidentially. "They probably have no talent to begin with." He eyed Paula up and down, a playfully critical glance in his eyes. "I'm just guessing of course, but I'd say you have a fair amount."

Paula cleared her throat to show she was enjoying his humor, but she was also enjoying the moment that passed between them.

"Can I buy you a drink to discuss it?" Hugh asked.

Paula thought about her children at home and hesitated. But her mother was baby-sitting and an extra hour wouldn't make a difference. Besides, she was intrigued by Hugh Tolson and, she had to admit, a little attracted to him as well. She liked the way his dark hair fell boyishly over his eyes, which were soft pools of brown. But there was also a pointed masculinity about his face, a chiseled look to his features, like a sculptor had shaped his angular jaw and Roman nose. His face held determination and strength. She smiled.

It had started to rain. A fine mist sprinkled the early summer air and iridescent halos adorned the streetlamps. Paula and Hugh darted into a restaurant at the end of the block.

Hugh gave their order to the waitress and Paula went to call her mother to tell her she'd be home late. As she weaved through the tables Hugh watched appreciatively, admiring her long legs, her graceful movement and posture.

When she returned their drinks were on the table.

Hugh raised his glass. "Shall we toast to successful writing and chance meeting?" She nodded and they clinked glasses.

"Now clichéd as it might sound," Hugh said, "especially coming from someone who makes his living from words, but as you know all about me from the program, tell me all about yourself, Paula Weller."

"Let's see." She smiled. "A bio about me might say I went through college in the late sixties, wrote poetry, and actually had some of it published in BU's literary magazines. To date the high point of my fledgling writing career. Then right after graduation I married Michael—tall, handsome, member of Harvard

Law Review, workaholic Michael Weller. From whom I am since divorced," she added quickly. "With two children."

Hugh smiled grudgingly. "He doesn't sound like a terrible catch."

Paula flip-flopped her hand, leaving it open to discussion. "He was hired as an associate at one of Boston's prestigious law firms and there was no question of his rapid ascent. But that unfortunately carried its price. He was always working—*always*—and I rarely saw him."

Hugh laughed. "I know the type."

"I wanted more attention from him. Respect, too, because I sometimes felt he wasn't taking me seriously enough. Or anything I did—my poetry, my ad writing. That particularly hurt because I was good at it.

"It all came to an end when he accepted a partnership in a Wall Street firm and planned on moving us to New York without having first discussed it with me. I then knew where I stood in his scheme of things. So we divorced."

"Do you ever see him?"

She shook her head. "Practically never. Only when I'm in New York or he's in Boston and it's convenient. The children see him once in a while but there's nothing between us anymore except child support." She shrugged and looked down at her glass, shaking off memories of her early days with Michael, the times before their marriage and his job. There had been picnics by the Charles River, football games at Harvard where they had sat huddled under one blanket. She had always seen the aggressiveness in him, the constant drive, and had admired him for it. But she had never anticipated the consequences or the kind of person he was going to become. She looked up at Hugh and opened her arms theatrically. "That's Paula Weller in a nutshell. Now you tell me. From the program I know all about the professional Hugh Tolson. As long as we're trading intimacies, how about it?"

"I don't want just to get to know you in a nutshell," Hugh said, then asked, "Are you bitter at all?"

"No. The marriage didn't work out but I have two lovely children who mean the world to me, so I can never be bitter. Rather, I guess I'm thankful."

A candle flickered in its urn-shaped holder in the center of the table, caressing Paula's gentle features in contours of light and shadow. "He was cruel to you," Hugh said.

Paula shrugged. "He doesn't think so. He saw himself making a good living for me and the children. In a way he's right, but I never needed a six-figure salary to be happy. And I know he was doing it more for himself than for us." She trailed off and Hugh sensed her reluctance to continue. He signaled the waitress for a refill.

"Tell me about your advertising work," he asked to change the subject, and the time passed as Paula talked about her copywriting work at Taplinger & Witt, some of the campaigns she'd been involved in—the successes as well as the disasters. She continued writing poetry for her own pleasure and had never seriously considered writing a novel until a conversation with a stranger at a party had given her the germ of an idea for a saga. She had started the following day with a burst of energy but soon realized how difficult and time-consuming the writing actually was. "I'm really only into chapter two of my book and don't get that much of a chance to work on it. Occasionally on a weekend, but *very* occasionally. And during the week, forget it. It's the office all day and I've got to be mother and father at night. Between dinner and helping with the new math and sewing costumes for school plays I barely have time to watch the news. Then by eleven-thirty I'm exhausted. You know," she joked, "I'm probably the only person in the country never to have seen Johnny Carson."

The words made her look at her watch, and Paula was startled to see that it was close to midnight. They had been chatting for almost two hours.

"I wasn't aware of how late it is," she said, genuinely surprised. "I really should get going."

"Let me see you to your car," Hugh said as he signaled for the check.

As Paula got into her car in the hotel garage, Hugh smiled. "Perhaps I write suspense novels, but right now I'm smitten like a character in a romance novel. Can we get together again?"

"I'd like that."

"I'll call you." Hugh closed her car door and leaned against the window frame. A moment passed between them and Hugh fought the sudden urge to lean inside and kiss her. Instead he pushed himself away from the car. "Drive home safely. We don't want next year's Book Award winner to get into an accident."

He watched as her car accelerated up the ramp and out of sight, sensing with pleasure her eyes looking at him through the rearview mirror. Then he gave his check to the attendant and waited until his Mercedes was brought up from the depths of the garage.

As he listened to the squeal of tires on the concrete ramp, he whistled. He felt good. Excited. In fact he hadn't felt this excited about a woman since he had first met Judith.

He drove up the ramp into the quiet midnight Boston street, flipped on his directional signal, and headed toward his home in nearby Wellesley.

He was unaware of the woman who was standing across the street watching his car pull away from the garage.

She had been at the lecture and had seen who Hugh was hurrying to afterward—the attractive woman sitting at the front of the room. She had watched them go into the elevator together. Then, catching the next elevator, she had arrived in the lobby in time to see them leave through the hotel's revolving door. She had followed them to the restaurant, where she had stood in a doorway for the past two hours as they talked and laughed. Then she'd trailed them back to the hotel garage where they had finally parted.

A cool, rain-swept breeze gusted through the air. The woman shivered and drew her sweater tightly around her.

Chapter 2

THE SUMMER SUN HAD BURNED AWAY THE FOG AND RAIN and the morning rose bright and clear. Paula was assaulted simultaneously by the clock radio, which burst alive with an annoyingly cheery song, and a ray of light forcing its way under the drawn shades of her Boston town house. She groaned and pulled her pillow over her head to escape the sun and music but suddenly two playful little hands yanked away the pillow and exposed her to the daylight. Paula felt Michelle's excitement. It was the last week of school and she knew the six-year-old sensed freedom.

When she came downstairs the children were finishing breakfast. Jeremy was dressed in chino pants and a light cotton shirt. Blond hair covered his forehead and slipped over his eyes. He kissed Paula, grabbed his baseball mitt, and started for the door. "See ya," he said and was gone.

"Yeah, see ya," Paula called after him. He was nine, almost ten, and was already on the run. But Michelle was still hers, and as she watched the little girl pull open the door to the dishwasher and carefully stack her plate on the rack, a wave of love crested over her. All the times she thought she never would have had children had she anticipated Michael's lack of interest in them dissolved as she watched these precious everyday moments in her children's lives, each one folded into her memory along with a million other similar images of both Michelle and Jeremy as they kaleidoscoped into one another, a living, shifting photo album of the people who meant the most to her in the world. How could Michael have given this up? And for what?

Michelle sensed Paula's eyes on her and turned. "What are you looking at, Mommy?" the little girl demanded. Her hands were on her hips and her head was cocked slightly to the side, giving her an almost statuesque pose. The morning sun caught her hair, which Paula suspected would soon deepen into a glorious red. Freckles danced from cheek to cheek.

"Nothing, dear." Paula smiled. "Let's get ready."

They walked upstairs together and Paula went into the bathroom to put on her makeup and prepare for work. She blow-dried her hair and looked at herself in the full-length mirror, pleased at her reflection. Her waist was still slender, her legs still firm and muscular from a lunch-hour dance class she took twice a week. She had no complaints about herself, nothing she would change. She knew why she was feeling so good this morning, and the thought of Hugh Tolson made her smile.

When she got to the office no one was smiling. She smelled the tension as soon as she walked into the reception area. Secretaries were scurrying about, assistants were carrying storyboards and folders. Everything had been under control the night before. "What happened?" she asked Amanda, the secretary of her creative group.

"The ogre," the young blond woman said. Two words that sent fear throughout the entire company.

Paula sighed and asked weakly, "Not the new campaign?" Not the new campaign they had just spent weeks putting together.

Amanda nodded.

"Does Glenn need me?" she asked.

"Not yet." Amanda grinned. "But he will."

Glenn Adams was the creative director of the firm. *The ogre* was Dwight Hempster, wunderkind president of Hempster Industries, a giant hardware manufacturing company headquartered outside of Boston that was Taplinger & Witt's biggest client.

"He hates it, Paula."

Arthur Witt, the agency's president, stuck his head into Paula's office. "He's rejected it all. Finds the whole concept boring. Not sexy enough." He shrugged helplessly. "*Sexy* he wants. Remember—we're talking hardware here."

"I thought he approved the concept," Paula said.

"Of course he approved it. But now he's saying he thought we had something else in mind."

"And he's threatening to take his business somewhere else if we don't come up with something new," they said in unison.

Then Witt added, "More than just threatening. He's asked another agency to prepare a presentation."

"That stinks!" Paula flared. "He knew exactly what we had in mind!"

"I know." Arthur held up his hand to calm her down. "And this is not the first time he's pulled this on us either. I think he purposely does it to show who's boss. Anyway"—he exhaled in a tone of voice that Paula recognized as his questioning the futility of everything—if they lost the Hempster account there would have to be layoffs, something the firm prided itself for never having had to do—"we've got a meeting set up with him on Monday to try to hold this thing together. Glenn has some back-up ideas to talk to you about."

"I know all about the back-up ideas." Paula smiled. "We rejected them, remember?"

Arthur rolled his eyes. "Believe me when I say that my fantasy is to one day tell Mr. Dwight Hempster of Hempster Hardware where to stick his nuts—"

"That's good, Arthur," Paula said encouragingly. "Never lose your sense of humor."

Arthur winked at her and at least some of the tension dissipated. If the head of the company was smiling, things couldn't be too out of control.

Paula liked Arthur Witt. He was her boss but he was also a friend. He had hired her right out of school as a copywriter trainee but he gave her a chance almost immediately. Her first campaign was only a small one but it was for an important client. Arthur had shown faith in her ability and she had come through for him. He had very readily taken her back after Michelle started nursery school two years ago and she was breaking up with Michael. She had been a full-time mother for seven years, and as much as she had liked it, found herself with hours to fill up and nothing to do. She had wanted to go back to work and Arthur was pleased to have her again. He liked her work and had helped her advance rapidly to senior copywriter with more and more responsibility.

"We've got a meeting at four," he said. "Bring your ideas and sanity, although today I'll settle for one out of two." He winked at her, turned to leave the office, and almost collided with Joan Lassiter, the director of media, who was hurrying through the doorway.

"I'll say this much," Joan said. "If we ever took on an automobile account we could advertise that we can accelerate hysteria from zero to sixty in no time at all."

"I love you both," Arthur said. "See you at four."

When he was out of earshot Joan said, "So to get away from the craziness around here for a moment and into some other craziness—remember that guy I met at the gym—the almost cute one?"

"I remember him," Paula said, smiling. "Almost cute."

"Married."

"Oh, Joan. I'm so sorry."

Joan was a petite woman in her mid-thirties, with dark hair and warm, friendly eyes. It was only too large a nose that stopped her from being really pretty. She had never married and had absolutely no luck in the romance department.

She shrugged philosophically. "I should have known. Somehow the almost cute ones always are. And the *cute ones* are gay."

They laughed as Amanda came into the office with a box of flowers. "Just delivered for you, Paula."

Surprised, Paula opened the box of flowers. There were a dozen long-stemmed roses. The card read "To chance meeting."

Then, as if Hugh had known she had gotten the flowers, the phone rang.

"How about lunch?" he asked.

"I'd love that," Paula readily answered, deciding to forgo her dance class today and trying to suppress her budding smile in front of Joan's broad one. "But can we make it a little later than usual? There's chaos here and I've got to get some new ideas together. How about one-thirty?"

"No problem. I'll meet you in your lobby."

As she hung up the phone she said to Joan quickly, "His

name is Hugh Tolson, the author. I just met him last night. And so far there's nothing."

Joan shrugged and feigned disinterest. "So who was asking?"

Paula laughed. "Oh. You . . ." She arranged the roses in a tall vase on her windowsill.

Joan looked over her shoulder and frowned. "Hey, there are only eleven here."

Paula quickly counted and confirmed the number. She shrugged. "You know, I'll take the loss."

She picked up her pencil and prepared to work. Her morning's activity was to make Hempster's bolts and screws seem more sexy. It went easily, because without a doubt that was exactly how she was feeling.

Hugh was standing in the lobby holding a rose when Paula came downstairs.

"For you." He smiled. "It fell out of the box and I didn't want you to feel cheated."

Paula took the rose and, with a lopsided smile, shook her head at Hugh. "Believe me, I wouldn't have." She waved the flower under her nose and laughed, flattered that Hugh had arranged to have the last rose to give to her. "You are too much. And thank you for rescuing me today. I'm so glad to get out of there. If you hadn't called me I'd probably be working through lunch like everyone else."

"I didn't take you away from anything important, did I?" he asked.

"Yes, but believe me, that's what I'm grateful for," Paula said as they pushed through the revolving doors and out into the June sun, which shimmered off the glass and chrome of the downtown office buildings. It was the peak of the lunch hour and people were streaming along the street, window-shopping, munching on food bought at corner pushcarts, enjoying the summer day. "It's one of our accounts," Paula continued. "He goes through the crazies periodically and he's having an attack right now. He thinks he has the right to make everyone else crazy too."

"He doesn't have the right to make you crazy," Hugh said, and his tone made Paula look at him. There was sincerity and concern in his voice; he wasn't being flip with her.

The Traditional Cape was a seafood restaurant with Colonial

decor. An exposed brick wall was decorated with clocks, weather vanes, and toys from Revolutionary times. In the winter a fire blazed in a corner hearth beneath a mantel filled with antique artifacts.

After they ordered Hugh reached across the table and lightly touched the top of Paula's hand. The sudden gesture startled her and she found herself staring into Hugh's deep expressive eyes, which no longer seemed as boyish as they had last night.

Hugh smiled. "I wanted to tell you again how much I enjoyed our evening together."

"I did too," Paula said softly. She was feeling excited. A tremor played in her chest and a blush crossed her face.

"I couldn't sleep," Hugh said. "So I stayed up and worked all night on a romantic scene I'd been having trouble with. I think having that drink with you put me in the proper mood. And instead of being tired today, I'm higher than ever."

The waiter arrived and put the plates down in front of them.

"What timing," Hugh groaned. "My big moment of passion and our lamb chops are upon us."

They ate in silence for a moment, then Paula spoke in a mock serious tone. "You know, last night you let me go on and on about myself and you didn't tell me anything about yourself. So now it's your turn, Hugh Tolson. All the vital statistics, and I don't want anything left out."

Paula was surprised at Hugh's reaction. She saw him swallow and pause thoughtfully, as if trying to decide what to say. No— even more than that, she considered for a moment—rather, *if* he wanted to say anything to her at all. Then she had her confirmation and understood his reluctance to talk.

His personal life was tragic.

Hugh's mother had left his father when Hugh was only four years old. Then when he was eight he had been in an accident with his father and aunt. Their car had skidded out of control and into a ditch where it overturned. Miraculously, Hugh had been thrown free, but his father and aunt were killed.

He taught English at Boston College and married a former student he met again five years after her graduation. They were married for six years and had two children. But Judith wanted something more out of life and asked for a trial separation. She took the children away with her to their Cape Cod vacation house to consider her future.

That night a fire raged through the cottage and killed their twins, John and Danielle, barely four years old.

Hugh spoke quietly about the fire, his voice even and dry, his tone seemingly emotionless, but Paula still heard the terrible pain and hurt that broke through his dispassionate mask. Throughout his story she kept shaking her head, leaving her lunch untouched and cold on the plate, horrified by what she was hearing. One part of her did not believe it, but of course she knew it was true. She simultaneously tried to shield herself from Hugh's words, but was drawn to them as well in an odd, voyeuristic way she would feel guilty about later.

After the funeral they tried to continue their marriage, but it was over, Hugh said sadly, and they divorced. He spoke about how he had put his life together afterward, although Judith had never been able to. A portion of her mind was permanently gone, destroyed by the horror of that night.

When he was finished Paula could scarcely move and she couldn't remember when last she had taken a breath. It was as if time had been suspended. What Hugh had just said had affected her deeply, as it would any parent, *anyone*, although she could conjure no emotion to even approximate what she knew they must have felt. And the awful, awful time afterward, the guilt, the blame. She shook her head weakly.

"It was a terrible accident," she whispered hoarsely, struggling for words. And suddenly Dwight Hempster and the hardware account seemed so unimportant. What she felt like doing —*right then*—was to rush home and gather Jeremy and Michelle close to her.

As if Hugh could read her mind, he smiled and said, "I'd like very much to meet your children, Paula." The smile widened on his face and Paula saw he didn't want to speak about the past anymore. He had told her and now it was over. "How about a picnic this Saturday. All four of us. We can go up to Cape Ann, maybe see a witch museum or two, dunk some toes in the water and watch them turn blue. How about it?"

Paula looked at Hugh's hopeful face, grateful he had led her away from the tragedy. There was life in his eyes again.

And her answer made them sparkle all the more.

She was preparing for the four o'clock meeting when Joan came rushing into her office. "It's all set," she said. "I spoke with Maggie at the bookshop and she's reserved a copy of each of his books for us. By a week from Tuesday we'll all have read one book each and be able to give you a complete report on the guy."

"Joan, I've only seen him twice now. Let's not make too much out of this." But she didn't believe her words, nor did Joan.

Paula, Joan, and other friends met in a women's group modeled after the one in the film *An Unmarried Woman*. It was formed when Maggie was divorced three years before, and Paula and Joan had closed ranks around her to see her through the first weeks and months. Others had since joined them for their evenings twice a month.

"What if we don't talk about Hugh just yet?" Paula asked. Something told her this wasn't something to gossip about. This was special.

Late that night, in a small apartment across the Charles River in Cambridge, Judith suffered through a recurrent, torturous dream. She was standing outside the Cape Cod beach house helplessly watching the fire that raged inside. And through the flames she heard her children screaming for help. She cried out their names—*John! Danielle!*—and reached out desperately for them, her arms entering the searing fire to try to save them.

She burst awake, in pain from the fire. She was lathered in a cold sweat, the echoes of her children's cries evaporating as the first light of dawn slanted in through the window.

It was only a dream, she told herself, only *another* dream, like so many before. Although a dream that mirrored reality. She breathed deeply to calm herself, then covered her eyes with her palm to try once again to blot out the terrors that constantly plagued her, haunted her days, drove her screaming from sleep, incessantly reminding her of what had happened that terrible night.

But she knew she could never forget.

The vacation house was set on a secluded half acre on a side road near the beach at Eastham. Judith had been alone with the children when the explosion had awakened her. But by then it was already too late. She jumped out of bed and raged toward the children's rooms on the other side of the house, but was blocked by a wall of fire that beat her back, scorched her hands. From behind the blazing door she heard their cries for help. Desperately, she ran outside to try to reach John and Danielle from the ground-level window but she could not get near the house, which was engulfed now by fire. The children were trapped inside and Judith could only watch them helplessly through the flames, their mouths open in terror, their tiny arms pounding futilely against the glass until they were completely swallowed up by the billowing smoke.

And out of the corner of her eye, at the very edge of her peripheral vision, there had been a shadow, a shrouded figure watching from the line where the woods began.

"Help me, please!" she had cried imploringly to the figure, who didn't come forward to help. It had turned and disappeared into the night.

Hugh.

Chapter 3

THEY ALL VOTED TO SKIP THE SIGHT-SEEING AND GO RIGHT to the beach. Hugh knew of an out-of-the-way spot that had more sand than rocks along the jagged Cape Ann coastline—which a lot of others seemed to know about as well—and all four of them shared in the lugging of the blanket, towels, and picnic basket to a spot on the sand where they defensively staked out their territory in the event the area managed to get even more crowded later in the day.

Sun glimmered off the sandy beach, dazzling the eyes with pinpoints of colored lights. They ran down to the water but at the end of June the Atlantic was still bone-chilling cold. Only a few bathers had actually ventured into the water as far as their knees, and fewer still—staunch polar bears—were swimming the cresting waves.

"Too much for me," Paula said, flapping her arms in an exaggerated gesture to get warm. "You three can stay here. I'll get lunch ready."

She weaved back to their blanket, threw on her top, lathered suntan lotion over the exposed skin, and started to unwrap the sandwiches. She watched Hugh and the children as they conducted a scavenger hunt for colored stones and seashells, then explored a jetty, scrambling over the smoothed rocks. Paula instinctively wanted to cry out to them to be careful, but she trusted Hugh to look after the children and she could see his excitement even from a distance. His children would have been Michelle's age, if they had lived, Paula knew. A shock of sadness surged through her, but she tried to free her mind, not let herself be maudlin on such a glorious day as this.

When they returned for lunch Michelle displayed what she had collected and talked about how Hugh had found this shell or that. They listened to the ocean spray as they attacked the sandwiches, Paula enjoying the good time that Hugh was having with the children.

And the good time she was having with him as well. She couldn't keep her eyes off Hugh. His legs were strong and muscular, his stomach tight, and his chest patterned with curly dark hair that reached high up to his neck. His hair was swept backward by the wind and water and glistened in the sun. Hugh looked up from his sandwich, caught her looking at him, and smiled; Paula hoped his thoughts were on her, as hers were on him. A week ago she hadn't even known him.

A Frisbee landed on the picnic basket. Jeremy reached over, picked it up. A boy about his age stood beyond the perimeter of their blanket. "I'm sorry," he said, then asked, "Want to play?"

"Sure!" Jeremy jumped up eagerly. "Come on, Michelle."

"Watch her!" Paula called as the children ran off to the hard-packed sand at the water's edge. "Don't go in—" But her voice was lost to the call of a flock of seabirds.

"Don't worry about her," Hugh said. "Jeremy's very mature. He'll take good care of her."

"I think he's going to be an impossible teenager. He already thinks he knows more than I do."

"They all do. He'll do just fine."

"You're very good with them."

"I love kids," Hugh said.

"I can tell. I'll bet you were a very good father." Paula caught herself. "I'm sorry. I shouldn't talk about—"

Hugh held up his hand to stop her. "Don't worry about saying things around me, okay. I don't want you to feel you have to be on guard."

Paula nodded gratefully, then indicated her children, who were tossing the Frisbee back and forth to each other. She laughed shortly. "I think you've gotten closer to them in a few hours than Michael managed to in years."

"It seemed that Michael always had other things to do. They don't sense there is any threat to the time I'm spending with them." He twisted to reach into the picnic basket for the bottle of wine. Paula eyed the muscular curve of his upper body as he fished out the bottle, the half-moon birthmark beneath his right shoulder blade, the sensuousness of his physique.

Hugh unwrapped the bottle from the foil and poured the red wine into two plastic cups. "To us," he said softly, a lilt of tenderness in his voice that made Paula's skin prickle. Then he touched his glass to hers and raised it to his lips. They drank in silence for a moment, absorbing the sights and sounds of the seashore. The silence was comfortable, not at all awkward, as it might be between strangers. But neither of them felt like a stranger to the other.

"You know, it's crazy," Hugh said quietly, as he seemed to gaze off past Paula into the distance, almost as if afraid to look at her as he voiced his thoughts. "We've only known each other for less than a week, but I feel like I'm falling in love with you." Then his head cocked slightly and his eyes shifted and fastened on her. "Really, Paula."

"That is crazy." Paula smiled and attempted to joke, especially because she saw that Hugh wasn't joking at all.

Monday morning was tense as everything was readied for the meeting with Dwight Hempster, final flourishes put on storyboards, copy checked for the last time, but the afternoon glowed with relief when Arthur Witt and Glenn Adams came back to the office, having locked in the account.

"The ogre was just busting our chops," Witt said. "He went back to the other concept entirely. Said he was able to give it some thought over the weekend. He suggested a touch here, a change there, but it's pretty much exactly as it was before all the hysteria."

Paula saw the relaxed grin on Arthur's face. It had been a lot of extra work and wheel spinning, but they kept the account, at least for another season, or at least until the ogre decided to get ornery again.

Happily she called Hugh, who suggested a celebration drink. In fact he was coming right over to pick her up.

"But I can't," she protested, "the children—"

"Then we'll have to have the drink at your house," Hugh said, inviting himself to dinner.

Hugh stayed the evening. He helped clear the table, played gin with Jeremy, then watched as Paula put the children to bed. When all was quiet upstairs Hugh and Paula stretched out on the couch.

Two nights later they made love. For Paula nothing could have been more natural. She had known Hugh for less than two weeks but she had known almost from the beginning that she had wanted him to hold her, kiss her, love her. She thrilled to his touch, his tongue, his gentleness, and then finally his intensity as they rose in ecstasy together. She hadn't enjoyed herself so much in bed since her first months with Michael. Hugh had awakened her body again and she wanted more.

The following afternoon a magnificent pair of gold earrings was delivered to her office.

At dinner Hugh showed her the bound galleys of his newest book. He had changed the dedication to read, "To Paula."

As the summer passed they were not out of each other's sight. With the children in camp the weekends were theirs for picnicking on the grass in Tanglewood, seeing summer-stock theater in Williamstown and Stowe. Hugh bought Paula frivolous presents—stuffed animals he might have gotten for Michelle, but they were all hers, mementos of the times they spent together.

They went to New York for the premiere of a movie based on one of Hugh's books and a cocktail party at the Four Seasons. Paula's eyes jumped from person to person in the airy Pool Room and easily saw how well Hugh was thought of in the literary world, enjoying as he accepted the accolades of others, thrilling to be with him and part of the star-studded evening. They stayed overnight in a suite in the Sherry-Netherland high above Central Park, went for a ride in a hansom cab and a window-shopping walk down Fifth Avenue.

Labor Day weekend was spent in the inn in Woodstock, Vermont. Days were filled with crafts fairs, tennis lessons, and swimming in the country lakes. Nights were filled with each other.

They had finished making love Sunday night. Paula was nestled comfortably next to Hugh, her lips brushing his neck, her hand playing with the curly hair on his chest, twirling it around her fingers, the sensation of caressing velvet. A half-moon was rising beneath their open window, limning their bodies in fluorescent gold, an inquisitive eye, seeming to wink at them approvingly as a drifting cloud covered it and just as quickly blew past.

"Will you marry me, Paula?" Hugh asked. His tone was casual, as if proposing was the most natural thing in the world.

As was her answer.

"Let's have some people over," Paula said. "I want to show you off."

Hugh stuck out his tongue.

Paula laughed. "Why not?"

"Because I hate parties. I hated them when I was married to Judith, and I hate them now. Everyone wants to talk about me and my writing and believe me, Paula," he yelled to the rafters, *"I'm not that interesting!"*

"People think you are. How many best-selling authors does the average guy know?"

"They all ask the same questions. 'How do you get your ideas?' 'What do you do when you're not writing?' 'What do you *really* do?' . . . that's my favorite one."

"Sort of like the same questions I asked when we first met?"

"That was different." He smiled.

"How?" She mugged.

"Because I knew immediately that I loved you. And dumb questions from people you love are acceptable."

"Oh, are they?" Paula asked and kissed him lightly.

"Besides, what if Joan doesn't like me? That might give you second thoughts about us."

"You know that's not going to happen. She can't help but adore you, and I would never have any second thoughts."

"Well, I'm just not going to risk it. After we're married and you can't get away, then we'll have people over. There'll be plenty of time."

Hugh touched her cheek with the backs of his fingers, played them tenderly up and down her smooth skin, teased her mouth. Then with his other hand on the back of her neck he pulled her close to him. She giggled softly. Her lips parted, her eyes closed, and she was his. For plenty of time.

* * *

On the Saturday before the wedding Paula and the children were in Boston Common when Judith approached from the line of trees.

"Forget about Hugh," she warned. "He set the fire. He killed our children. If you marry him you'll all be in danger."

"No," Paula whispered hoarsely as she backed away from the other woman. She quickly gathered up her children and ushered them to the edge of the Common, where she hailed a cab for home.

She sent them upstairs to play in their rooms while she made supper. Hugh was coming over. But she couldn't concentrate on what she was doing, still hearing Judith's terrible words echoing inside of her. Hugh had told her about Judith, how after the fire her mind had snapped. But she wasn't prepared for what had just happened in the park. She cut her hand while slicing carrots and watched as the blood trickled down her finger and onto the counter.

Hugh's breath quickened as she told him. His jaw squared in anger and his fists closed.

"Oh, Paula, I'm so sorry!" he cried, and held her tightly in his arms. She was still quivering, still afraid.

"Why, Hugh?" she pleaded. "Why did she say those things?"

"Because she's sick!" he spat out. "She wants to frighten you away from me, break us up." The fear was still in her eyes, the confusion. She needed more from him. He spoke haltingly. "There are things that I never told you, Paula. Because they didn't seem important at the time. Because you didn't have to know. Because I didn't want to talk disparagingly about Judith and I didn't think she would ever—"

Paula's mouth was dry. "Please . . ."

"The night of the fire Judith accidentally left the gas on," Hugh said softly. "She was negligent, responsible for the explosion. But I never blamed her. That would have been heartless, cruel.

"After the funeral I tried to continue the marriage, but it was impossible. Judith was a bitter, lost woman. She knew what she had done but she couldn't face it. She began to withdraw into herself, then got progressively worse. She invented a 'watcher in the woods,' someone who had been there that night and had started the fire. The psychiatrists explained that this was to relieve her very stressful, overpowering feelings of guilt. She needed someone to blame.

"Then soon the watcher in the woods became *me,*" Hugh said. "She accused *me* of setting the fire. She tried to get the police involved, but they talked to the doctors and quickly dropped any investigation. I got Judith the best psychiatric help I could, but she resisted the therapy, clung to her delusions." Hugh shook his head sadly. "The divorce was inevitable.

"She's still ill," he continued. "She wrongly hates me and I can only imagine she doesn't want to see me happy and married again. That's why she did what she did today. To make you doubt me and frighten you away.

"But she is out of our lives, Paula," he stressed. "She can't hurt us or break us up."

"No," Paula agreed, wishing she could put the image of the tortured woman out of her mind.

Paula was a beautiful bride, and as she and Hugh skipped down the church steps, Paula's mother, Marilyn, and the children tossed handfuls of rice. They were going to New York for a three-day honeymoon. Then they'd use the rest of the week to move Paula and the children into Hugh's house in Wellesley. After Hugh finished his newest book at the end of the year, a lengthy vacation was planned.

Marilyn beamed as Paula ducked into the waiting limousine that would take them to Logan Airport. She was overjoyed for her daughter's happiness, yet something undefined was giving her pause, stopping her from being as happy as she, herself, wanted to be.

Although she had never voiced her concerns, she worried that perhaps Paula was rushing into a marriage with a man she had known only a short time.

But it was more than that, she knew, as the feeling prickled and teased just beyond touch.

It was because tragedy seemed to stalk Hugh Tolson.

Chapter 4

THE MCKITTRICK COMPANY WAS HUGH'S CENTURY-OLD publisher, located in the same Colonial building in downtown Boston as when they published their first books in the late 1870s on the values of rare coins. They grew from printing collectors' books and guidebooks into a prestigious publishing house of literature, belles lettres, history, and biographies. It was only recently that the publisher adopted a more commercial vision, and ten years ago a young editor took a chance on an unknown, unpublished English teacher who had written a pre-World War II spy thriller. Hugh's first novel soared to second position on *The New York Times* best-seller list and was kept from the number one slot only because a book by James Michener held firm anchor. Based on the success of the first, and subsequent novels, an excellent relationship developed between Hugh and his editor, Jason DeMille, who had worked on every one of Hugh's books and had flourished in the business with him. Now at the age of thirty-four Jason was executive director of the publishing house, helping to guide it into video and computer areas. Hugh wanted Jason to meet his new wife and on their first day back from New York he took Paula to the publisher's offices.

A slightly musty smell welcomed them into the circular reception area of the McKittrick Company. It was the smell of wood and time, the comfortable smell of an old and frequently used library. The receptionist smiled when she saw Hugh and immediately depressed the call button on her switchboard to alert Jason to Hugh's arrival. Glass display cases lined the walls, and Paula was pleased to see the prominent showcasing of Hugh's latest book at the apex of the room.

The smoky glass doors behind the reception desk swung open and Jason's secretary, Kate Forest, came through to escort Hugh and Paula inside. She was a tall, attractive girl of twenty-three, smartly dressed in a tailored suit. Her black hair was parted in the center and curled stylishly at her neck.

"Mr. Tolson!" Kate beamed, and extended her hand. Hugh took it and leaned to kiss her lightly on the cheek.

"Hello, Katie, my girl," he said in an Irish brogue. "I want you to meet my new wife, Paula."

As Paula smiled at her, surprise flickered across the younger woman's face then disappeared, replaced by a hardened stare. Kate's eyes were as dark as her hair, intense, and Paula had to waver from their glance. She immediately felt uncomfortable under the steely, critical gaze of the other woman.

Hugh held the door open for the two ladies, then linked arms with Paula as they walked down the corridor to Jason's corner office.

"Katie is the best assistant an editor could ever hope to have," Hugh said as soon as Jason DeMille came into earshot. "And if he doesn't treat you well, Katie, you just come to me."

"That's a promise, Mr. Tolson."

Paula knew that Kate had always gone out of her way for Hugh, personally delivering to him cover art, copy, galleys, and keeping him posted on reviews and publicity. It came with his success—the publishers wanted to keep their star author happy, and the staff was so instructed, but Kate often went beyond the call of the job.

"I might lose Kate pretty soon," Jason said expansively. "She's on the verge of a deserved promotion to editor. The next opening is hers."

"And I've got my eyes on a couple of spots," Kate said with a cool pointedness that telegraphed to Paula that she was an ambitious woman who got what she wanted. "Including Jason's," she added.

Everyone laughed as Jason led Hugh and Paula into his office, leaving Kate in the secretarial cubicle outside his door. As she watched the door close behind Paula, the smile suddenly left her face.

Jason opened a bottle of champagne and toasted Hugh and Paula.

"The champagne must be in your honor," Hugh said to Paula. "I'm lucky if I get club soda. And I have to beg for even that."

"With what your agent gets you," Jason answered, "you should be bringing me champagne. And caviar. And pheasant. And whatever else people in your tax bracket eat."

"Last night we ordered in pizza," Paula laughed.

"Ah, but it was what we were doing while eating the pizza that's the key here." Hugh winked.

Jason put his hands up in front of his face. "I don't even want to know."

Jason was a slight man with a dimpled chin and a just-too-wide mouth that flared even wider when he smiled. His belt and loafers were Gucci. His hands were long and slender and, except for a Rolex, free of jewelry.

"So I hope married life isn't going to interfere with your writing," Jason said with a mock disapproving look on his face.

"Quite the opposite," Hugh answered. "With three more mouths to feed all of a sudden, I feel driven again to produce my best work ever—and speedily get paid for it."

"You produce, we'll pay," Jason said.

Hugh turned to Paula. "He knows if he doesn't, my agent, Sol 'Sticky Fingers' Gewirtz, will be on the first shuttle from New York with an army of lawyers and the gossip columnist from *Publishers Weekly*."

Jason poured another round of champagne and prodded. "It's coming along well, I take it. I need it by the end of the year to bring it out next fall."

"No problem."

"We're building our whole list around it, but don't let that pressure you."

"Editors and producers," Hugh sighed. "They get paid to drive you crazy. Seriously, Jason," he added with a wink toward Paula, "with Paula's mother in for a copy, we're guaranteed at least a half-dozen sales."

"Make it a half million, and I'll never ask for anything again."

An hour later Hugh and Paula rose to leave. Jason took Paula's hands. "A pleasure, Paula. I'm glad that you and Hugh have found each other. Keep him writing, okay?"

"Slave driver," Hugh growled.

Kate stood up to escort them back to the reception area. She handed Hugh a book.

"Something we've just published. A history of the OSS. You might find it useful for some of your research."

Hugh took the book. "That's very sweet of you, Kate. Thank you."

Kate smiled and Paula caught the blush. There was a softness to the other woman's eyes now, a glistening as she walked down the corridor and spoke with Hugh. Kate looked joyous because Hugh liked what she had given him. She jiggled her shoulders coyly, bobbed her head lightly from side to side. She laughed when he did and leaned in to touch his arm. Paula saw in her manners and expression the same infatuation she had felt toward an English professor her sophomore year at BU. Kate was as transparent as glass and Hugh must have known how she felt about him. Paula couldn't help but feel a twinge of jealousy at Kate's obvious flirtation, then chided herself. Kate was fifteen years younger than Hugh, certainly no competition, no threat. Kate would undoubtedly get over her infatuation with Hugh as Paula had with her professor. And that was why she didn't let herself be bothered by Kate's narrowed, challenging glance at her as they said good-bye at the reception doors.

Kate's one-bedroom apartment was in a small converted three-story building in Quincy. The furniture was mostly secondhand, all that could be afforded on a secretary's salary. She was looking forward to the raise she would get when Jason awarded her her editor's stripes. Her only regret was that she would not be in as close contact with Hugh Tolson as she was now.

But becoming an editor was the furthest thing from Kate's mind tonight as she paced the floor angrily. Her briefcase was on the couch where she had slammed it when she came in from work. She hadn't eaten any dinner; her stomach was tensed and her neck knotted. Her world had collapsed. Today could very well have been the worst day of her life.

She could have died—or killed!—when she heard Hugh say he had married again.

But she had kept her face a mask, had not revealed her feelings. Outwardly she had been all charm. It had not been the moment to say or do anything. What was done was done. She had to take stock, figure things out . . .

What was there to figure out!

It was her own fault, *her—own—fault!* she almost screamed out loud, at the height of her frustration. She picked up a copy of Hugh's most recent paperback novel and hurled it across the room. It hit the wall with a loud thud and dropped to the floor, bending the cover and the first several pages.

All her waiting . . . her planning . . .

Hello, Katie, my girl. I want you to meet my new wife, Paula.

My new wife, Paula . . . She put her hands to her ears to block out the sound of Hugh's voice, and those terrible, terrible words, echoing inside of her.

And Paula's face, etched in her memory! Those greenish eyes, not half as attractive as her own dark ones—she could just scratch them out. And that smug, superior smile, that feigned innocence. As if she *knew!*

Kate's face was flushed and almost burning to the touch. Intense pressure narrowed her eyes. Her teeth were clenched, her jaw squared and tightened until it ached. Paula would love to see her like this. She had to calm herself. She inhaled and exhaled slowly to even her breath, relax her muscles. She opened her eyes wide and tried to quiet her pounding heart. All was not lost. Not at all. There would be a way. There was always a way, she knew.

When she felt calmed she knelt down and picked up Hugh's book from the floor, smoothed out the cover, and put it back on the shelf next to all of his other books. She touched them reverently. She had them all—hardcover and paperback, and an album of his reviews, personality pieces done on him, articles about the fire, all neatly pasted into a scrapbook. All lovingly gathered and carefully mounted.

Then drained, she sank to the couch and clutched a beaded throw pillow to her chest. Her expression was blank, empty; her eyes watered and tears fell. She loved Hugh and he had married someone else.

She had fallen in love with Hugh Tolson the first time she saw him in Jason's office. It was two years ago on a spring morning. She had been with Jason DeMille for three weeks, right from school practically, and had spoken with Hugh several times, already finding herself attracted to his voice.

He had brought her flowers when he came in, perched on her desk as he introduced himself, and chatted briefly with her. She sniffed his cologne, looked into his eyes and tingled. He had a thick mustache at the time which she envisioned tickling her as they kissed. He was talented, successful, and so good-looking.

She knew he was married, but flirted anyway. With winning, open smiles when he came into the office, with soft words over the phone. And he had flirted with her in return—staying on the phone talking to her longer than he had to, lingering at her desk, touching her lightly as they talked, sending her little gifts, flowers.

He had come to the office one day when Jason had been called out to an emergency meeting. The two of them had sat in Jason's office, her stomach churning with sexual anticipation at his closeness, and she had made a subtle pass.

He had smiled at her and said in his adorable brogue, *You're a lovely, desirable girl, Katie. But I guess I'm a little old-fashioned.* Then he had winked, a special wink just for her. His message was unmistakable: *I could fall for you in a second, if only I wasn't married. . . .*

And then all of a sudden he wasn't.

After the children's deaths and his divorce she went out of her way for him, making him baked goods, personally bringing him manuscripts, galleys, and covers, once even knitting him a scarf for Christmas. But she was cautious not to be too aggressive, although it was so difficult not to throw herself at him. She didn't want to come on too strongly and frighten him away. He was old-fashioned and that meant he wanted to make the moves.

One time it had almost happened. She had brought over a congratulatory bottle of champagne when Hugh's book became a Book-of-the-Month Club main selection. She said it was from Jason, then covered herself with her boss when Hugh called to thank him, saying she knew he meant to order it but was too busy, or something . . . she couldn't remember now exactly what she had said, but it was flattering to everyone. She had hoped when she brought the bottle of champagne that Hugh would ask her to stay for a drink and he did.

She had never felt happier than when she had sat in front of the blazing fire and sipped the wine with Hugh Tolson. All the times she had thought *What if Hugh wasn't married, didn't have children,* that was what she had dreamed of happening after—being alone with him, holding him, loving him. She ached to tell him how she felt, what she wanted, but it was too soon. He was still in mourning; his children had been dead for only several months, the divorce still was not official. She wouldn't rush him. She would resign herself to his pace. He would soon come to her, and would never know that it was really she who had laid the foundation for their relationship and called all the shots.

But she had been too cautious, moved too slowly, she thought bitterly, furious at the events of the day. He had married Paula, a woman who had come from nowhere and stolen Hugh while she was slowly wooing him! All the planning, the waiting, doing everything right. She never even knew he was dating her! She would have done something to stop it.

. . . *if only I wasn't married* . . .

And then he wasn't!

That's why the Cape Cod fire had been so—so *right,* so filled with potential.

But she had blown it.

She went over to the bookcase and pulled out a copy of Hugh's third novel, as much love story as it was espionage thriller. She loved the book, the romantic imagery that Hugh evoked, knowing that he was writing directly to her. She curled up on her window seat, opened the book to her favorite passages, the pages dog-eared and smudged from her constant reading. She had almost committed them to memory and they always gave her pleasure.

But there was no pleasure tonight. Tonight there was only fury because she had acted too slowly and now Hugh had remarried.

She knew she would have to do something.

And she knew she wouldn't blow it again.

Chapter 5

FRIDAY MORNING THE MOVING VAN TOOK MICHELLE'S AND Jeremy's furniture and all of their clothes and toys to Hugh's house, Paula's clothing, books, leftover canned goods, and personal items. Someone from Paula's office was buying the Boston town house and all of the remaining furniture, a neat and lucky sale.

Hugh's house was a three-story Victorian. The living areas were on the first floor, there were three bedrooms on the second, and the third was Hugh's garret office where he did his writing.

The den was large and comfortable. One wall was exposed brick with a fireplace in the center. Varnished pinewood shelves lined another wall with hundreds of books crammed into every available space. Another wall held a collection of antique typewriters in display cases—Underwoods and Royals dating back to the turn of the century. "From the Stone Age down here to the Computer Age up in my office," Hugh said. "We've certainly come a long way."

Two weeks prior to the wedding the children had selected their new bedrooms. Jeremy was first up the carpeted stairs and picked the larger of the two rooms that overlooked the front of the house, Michelle settling for the smaller one that faced the rear yard and was shaded in summer by the leaves of a large maple tree. Both children were happy, Jeremy with the size of his room, the nooks set under the eaves for his workbench and computer table, Michelle with the intimate, quiet nature of hers. And, indeed, Hugh's street in Wellesley was less noisy than Boston.

Paula remembered Hugh's hesitation about showing her the twins' bedrooms. The cleaning woman kept them dust free but he had not gone into them since the deaths and divorce. The doors had always been kept closed, the second-floor hallway receiving only light spilling out of the master bedroom. The air always seemed thicker in front of the children's rooms, tomblike, Paula had thought, until she finally saw them.

She almost didn't know what to expect when she first entered, feeling the nervousness in her stomach. It was like opening the door to a painful and forgotten past. And even though it wasn't *hers* she still felt Hugh's pain as her own. But nothing jumped out at her, nothing bit her; *death* was not in the rooms. They were two little children's rooms, as might be found in any house. A teddy bear and a Cabbage Patch doll were propped against Danielle's pillow, with a Cookie Monster staring at them from a bracketed shelf in the corner. Like the dolls were just waiting for their little mistress to come home. The same in John's room. There were Sesame Street hand puppets and a big stuffed St. Bernard wearing a plastic barrel, with wide dark eyes the size of campaign buttons. Silent. Waiting. Sentinels that had guarded for two years, and would continue for an eternity more if left undisturbed. There was nothing at all to indicate that these children weren't anywhere other than out for the day. Paula searched Hugh's face for reaction, but his eyes were dry and accepting. She closed her hand around his, in support, in love. Then together they cleaned the bedrooms out. Everything that had belonged to John and Danielle—furniture, clothes, and toys—was donated to a local church, neither Hugh nor Paula wanting anything left in the house to remind them of Hugh's former life. Emotionlessly, Hugh packed away the children's things in cardboard boxes. "I'm over it, Paula," he reassured her, and Paula prayed it would be as easy as that.

The honeymoon was declared officially over on Saturday morning when Paula's mother brought Jeremy and Michelle to their new house. They immediately went upstairs to inspect the results of the move and to unpack their things and put them away so that only they would be able to find them at any future point.

Paula and Marilyn had already discussed some redecoration of the living and dining rooms—new curtains over the bay windows, an oriental rug for under the table. And all agreed on a new bedroom set. Hugh had given her run-of-the-house as concerned redecoration—any room except his office.

They had also planned out what could be done with the grounds the following spring. The house was situated on more than an acre of wooded property set well back from the street. *Intimate* and *private* Paula said about it; *isolated* Marilyn said, *lonely*. From the master bedroom window her eyes searched the line of trees and hedges that fringed the house, hiding it from the road in the front, secluding the pool and patio in the rear. *Isolated,* she repeated to herself, *vulnerable.* But nothing to comment further on. Because Hugh's tragedies had not happened *here*. And she knew she tended to worry too much anyway.

Now Marilyn gave them a gift-wrapped box. "I've been saving my wedding gift to make it a housewarming gift as well." Hugh and Paula opened the fragile package together, and buried in reams of air-bubbled plastic was a Steuben glass figurine of two hands clasped together, fingers entwined. "May you always be as close and inseparable as these two hands," Marilyn prayed.

"It's beautiful, Mother," Paula breathed. "Thank you." She put it on top of the fireplace mantel in the den so they could see it from *their* spot as they had made the soft, plush couch in front of the hearth.

The rest of the day was spent unpacking whatever hadn't been unpacked the previous afternoon, and by dinnertime all five were exhausted. Even the pizza with extra cheese delivered at six couldn't fortify the children, and by eight both Jeremy and Michelle were upstairs in bed.

Marilyn exhaled loudly. "I'd call that a good day's work." She looked at Paula a little sadly. "I'm going to miss seeing you and the kids every day." She smiled at Hugh. "I'm glad that you'll be home working in the afternoons when they come home from school, but I'm going to miss picking them up. Although I guess they were outgrowing Grandma anyway."

Marilyn was a semiretired teacher who taught only as a substitute in the district and picked up the children at school and brought them to her house to watch until the end of Paula's workday. The system still worked with Michelle, but when Jeremy turned nine earlier in the year he had insisted on a key of his own, feeling too grown up to be taken care of. Now the school was only a few blocks from the house, a distance Michelle could easily walk, and Hugh would be home to look after them. Grandma, Marilyn thought, had just lost her job.

"Don't worry, Mom." Paula kissed her cheek. "We'll be together enough."

"Absolutely," Hugh agreed.

Marilyn shook a finger at Hugh. "You take care of them, do you hear me?" Then she took Paula's hands and held her at arm's length, smiling at her daughter. "Only happiness, okay?"

That prickly sensation teased her again and suddenly she felt afraid.

Was it because tragedy seemed to stalk Hugh Tolson?

But with a shake of her head she dismissed what she was feeling. *There would be no more tragedy in Hugh's life,* she silently swore. *She would not allow it.*

"Okay?" she repeated, as much for her benefit as for her daughter's.

Paula nodded and felt the tears in her eyes as well. "I promise, Mom."

They waved to Marilyn and waited until she pulled out of the driveway and drove around the corner before going back inside and locking the door, Paula feeling a pang of loss and odd finality as her mother was swallowed up by the night.

After Paula registered Michelle at the elementary school and Jeremy at the intermediate school, she drove to Boston. Her secretary greeted her with a week's worth of mail. "I separated the important from the unimportant," Amanda said, then grinned. Paula saw why. The "unimportant" folder had three interoffice memos in it, all on the firm's basketball team.

Arthur Witt came into her office and kissed her. "The blushing bride."

"Hardly." Paula smiled.

"You can blush for five more minutes, then back to work," he ordered. He made way for Joan, who hugged Paula and squealed welcome back, then growled, "You just cost me twenty dollars."

"Why?" Paula asked, confused. She thought about the gift the firm had given them on the Friday before the wedding. Joan couldn't be referring to that.

"I bet Arthur twenty you'd never come back. You and Hugh would just sail off into the sunset somewhere and we'd never see you again."

"I keep telling Joan she's too romantic." Arthur winked.

"You people just don't know how to live," Joan said. "You think *this* is life?"

"After Hugh finishes his book we'll do something exotic," Paula said. "He's on a deadline right now and that's why we postponed the honeymoon. So for the time being, it's sunset over Boston. So—what did I miss?"

"The usual chaos." Glenn Adams smiled and gave her a bear hug. "Welcome home." He was in his late thirties, with jet-black hair, thick bushy eyebrows that crossed his face without separation, a squared jaw, and high angular cheeks; he could have been a model in one of his own commercials. "I had an idea while you were away. I want to try consolidating three of Hempster's products in one ad. I think I have a good theme. After you go through your mail, would you come into my office?"

"Lunch today?" Joan asked from the doorway.

Paula looked at her desk and exhaled. "A fast one."

"See you later."

Paula never did get out to lunch, which was cottage cheese and salad alone at her desk. The work had piled up, two campaigns were late, and she was too busy to break away. Thankfully, Hugh called three times during the morning to tell her he missed her and loved her, and just hearing his voice made the day palatable.

The phone rang at three o'clock. Amanda wasn't at her desk and Paula grabbed it herself.

"I know." She smiled into the phone. "You miss me."

"Wrong, Paula," Dwight Hempster's voice said. "Last week I missed you. Now you're back and I want you."

The ogre was a big beefy man with a Colonel Sanders beard, a booming voice, and smallish, peering eyes set deep into his pudgy face that could pierce right through you. His mannerisms were demeaning—a curt nod of the head or a vague hand gesture when he wanted you to start or stop talking, a roam of his eyes around the room when he was bored. He was rude, irascible, ornery. An ogre. But he billed millions through Taplinger & Witt, and that made him important and someone to cater to.

"Paula, I want you to take out the ads you're working on for the power tools. Something's missing from the copy about the versatility of the product . . ."

Thank you for your wedding present, Dwight, which was nothing, and your good wishes, which would be easy and cheap, but to give them, which is only decent, might just ruin your ogre image because someone might glimpse a sliver of humanity and kindness and think of you as human, clearly, perhaps from your point of view a personality defect. None of which Paula said because that would have meant her job. What she did say was, "You may have a point there, Dwight, but I think the ad is getting a little crowded right now. I think we can take for granted that whoever buys . . ."

The other light on her phone was blinking and a fraction of a second later the bell started to sound.

". . . will know what they can do with . . ."

Again. The ring could not be turned off.

Paula pulled the receiver away from her mouth. "Amanda!" she yelled, hoping her secretary would get back to her desk and field the call.

The phone rang again.

"Dwight, hold for a second, will you?" she asked. She depressed the hold button and then the other line. "Yes?" she said brusquely into the receiver, annoyed at Amanda for being away from her desk.

"Paula?"

The woman's voice was vaguely familiar, but Paula couldn't immediately place it.

"Yes—I'm on the phone, can I call you back?"

"This is Judith."

The name chilled her and the image sprang to her mind: the woman standing against the backdrop of spiraling leaves on that fall morning two weeks before.

"I have to talk to you," Judith said. Her voice was low, conspiratorial, a hurried whisper, almost as if she was afraid someone might overhear. Paula glanced down at the phone. Her other line flashed, indicating the call that had been put on hold. She could imagine the ogre getting more and more annoyed as the time passed.

"Can I call you back?" she asked again, not wanting to listen to anything the other woman would say to her, yet somehow *knowing* what she was going to.

"Your life is in danger," Judith croaked. "And your children's. You have to listen to me, believe me—"

"No!" Paula yelled into the phone. Hearing the words was far more upsetting than just anticipating them. "I told you not to—"

"He killed—"

"Don't call me again!" Paula snapped and saw that she was trembling. She depressed the other button and disconnected Judith. She tried to steady her voice, appear calm and businesslike, but her heart was beating furiously, her cheeks flushed red. "I'm back," she said as she clicked on to Dwight Hempster, but the line was dead. The ogre had hung up. *Damn* she muttered, but was grateful for the extra moments to compose herself. She took a deep breath and exhaled slowly through open lips, then grew angry at herself for her reaction to the other woman. *Judith was sick and she shouldn't let the woman's illness upset her.* She hoped she had finally gotten through to Judith not to call again. She decided she would not tell Hugh. She could deal with this herself; Judith's call would only upset him.

A moment later she decided she was calm enough to continue working. She dialed Dwight Hempster's private line and weathered his sarcasm when he picked up.

"Are you free to talk to me now, Paula?"

"Yes, Dwight," she said. "I think you're right. The ad could take a little more copy."

He was dead wrong, but he was the client, and after the call from Judith all the argument had gone out of her.

Jeremy pushed his peas around his plate, sullen and close-mouthed about the day, grunting monosyllabicaly when asked direct questions. Paula tried to get him to open up about the school, his teachers, and the other children he had met, but Hugh called her off. "He needs a little time to adjust," he said to her when they were in the kitchen clearing the plates and soaking pots. "He'll make some new friends and everything will be terrific. So no worrying, Mommy, okay?" He playfully touched a soap bubble to her nose. Michelle had fared somewhat better, making friends with two girls in her class. For her the move was already a success.

After the children were upstairs Paula and Hugh curled up with coffee and a chocolate torte in *their spot* in the den. Paula's legs were draped over Hugh's, his fingers played tenderly at her neck, searching out the tight spots and massaging them out. She whimpered with pleasure and pain as he got deep into the muscles.

"Shall I stop?" he asked when she cried out.

"No . . . don't ever stop," she moaned. "Hurt me, it feels terrific."

He laughed as he put his palm against her back, rubbing her wings and hearing the cracking sounds as the muscles and tendons rubbed over the bone. Her tongue flopped out in pleasure. "I feel almost human again. What did I do when I used to come home and you weren't there? I guess I lived with tightness and kinks."

"No more," Hugh said to her softly.

She told him about the chaos of the day, Joan's bet, the ogre's sarcasm. Everything except Judith's phone call, which she felt so far removed from now it was almost as if it had never happened.

"What do you need that job for?" Hugh asked. "I make plenty of money. Remember that novel you said you wanted to continue working on—the one that brought us together? It's a perfect time to throw all your attention toward the book."

Paula shook her head. "Not now. Work is crazy but I still want to do it." She shrugged a little sheepishly. "Call it a need for self-esteem, to prove myself and all of that."

"You don't have to prove yourself to me, Paula," Hugh whispered.

Paula looked up into his eyes and smiled. "I know," she said. "And maybe one day I will quit and we can hunch over our word processors together." She raised her coffee cup. "It's my turn to propose a toast. To a writer's seminar where I met a writer who taught me more about life than I had ever dreamed of knowing. . . ."

"And to a woman," Hugh said, "who means more to me than

she can ever imagine. You know, it drove me crazy not to be able to be with you today. I doubt I wrote more than three pages. I couldn't wait until you came home to me." He looked deeply into her eyes, his own filled with love and need. "Swear that you'll always come home to me, Paula, that you'll always be with me."

His words and look made Paula tingle. "Always, Hugh," she swore.

She leaned her head dreamily back against the couch. Her hair splayed out like an oriental fan as she let her eyes follow a snakelike crack along the ceiling until it blurred out of sight.

"God, I love this room," she sighed. "I can't imagine a room any more comfortable than this." The dark-stained bookcases that lined the walls were protective, locking them in cocoonlike; the glass display cases with Hugh's typewriter collection were almost predatory, mounted heads on display, decidedly masculine. And the hearth, soon to be stocked with kindling and aflame with the passion she prayed they would always feel for each other. She couldn't remember ever having been happier than this moment, more at ease, more safe.

Hugh took her coffee cup from her, then silently led her from the couch. They shut off the downstairs lights, went up to their bedroom, where they graspingly fell into each other's arms, alive and immortal through each other, as close as the glass hands downstairs on the fireplace mantel, as far removed from fear and death as could be humanly imagined . . .

. . . and unaware that outside in the shadows of the tall hedges a woman watched their silhouettes behind the drawn shades.

Chapter 6

THREE DAYS LATER PAULA WAS EATING SALAD AND QUICHE at a small restaurant around the corner from her office, grabbing a quiet moment to read the advertising trades. Since coming back from the honeymoon she had caught up on all of her paperwork, soothed the ogre, worked out the copy for Glenn's three-in-one ad, and was in his office when Hempster called rejecting the entire concept.

But she was finding it difficult keeping her mind on the publications; rather, her thoughts were wandering to Hugh, her body still alive and tinged with their lovemaking of the previous night. It had been well past two when they could love no more and had lain curve to curve against each other, their breath still warm and anxious, and had made plans to travel the world, designing their fantasy trips, from a week on the Champs Élysées to a buying spree through the bazaars of the Casbah, to a lifetime on the beaches of Tahiti. They had barely slept last night and she should have been tired today, but she felt nothing less than exhilarated thinking of the future that stretched out before them.

Paula sighed happily as she finished her coffee. It was only four months that she had known Hugh, but such an intense period, it was almost as if there had never been life without him. Even every night this week when she came home from work he was constantly with her, not daring, it seemed, to let her out of his sight.

She thought for a moment how close she had almost come to not meeting Hugh, how she had almost sold her ticket at the lecture. Someone was watching over her that night, she concluded, and she shivered with the kind of total joy that comes only very rarely and to a select few.

"Paula . . ."

The voice pulled Paula from her daydreaming. She looked over the top of the *Advertising Age* she really hadn't been reading anyway, and her inner smile turned quickly downward, like a balloon that had been deflated. Judith was standing across the table from her.

"What do you want?" she asked flatly.

"Please listen to me," Judith said, a straining urgency in her voice. Her dress hung loosely on her almost skeletal frame; she had lost weight but hadn't bought new clothes, not caring about her appearance. Her face was clear of makeup, but not fresh like the ads promised, rather sallow, drained of flesh tone, a flour-and-water color except for dark raccoon shades of tiredness that rimmed her eyes. Her skin had the fine-lined texture of early aging. In total, she wore the haunted look of someone damned with insomnia.

Paula regained her control, fought to remain calm, although her stomach had already started to churn. She waved Judith away without looking directly at her. "I'm sorry, *no,*" she said. "I thought I made myself clear on the phone. I don't want to have anything to do with you." Her speech seemed husky, her words clipped. It was her reactive tone, something she had always tried to overcome, but that always surfaced when she was faced by sudden fear or confrontation. She knew she was too sensitive, betrayed by her choked voice and her face, which was undoubtedly now blushing a neon crimson. But she had never been able to control her emotions. Now she just wanted to get away. She signaled for the check and started to get up.

"Please don't run away from me," Judith pleaded in a shaky voice that could have been warning *Don't go out there, the ice is thin.* "I just want to talk to you for a moment. Please . . ." She reached out and touched Paula's arm. Alarmed, Paula pulled away quickly, as if something caustic had been spilled on her.

"Don't—" Paula inhaled sharply, then broke off and rifled

through her purse for a ten-dollar bill to pay for the lunch. She handed the money to the waitress without even glancing at the check.

"I know you don't believe me," Judith said. "I know you think I'm crazy, but I'm not. *I'm not,"* she repeated imploringly, and the desperation in her voice made Paula look closely at her, and she was struck suddenly with the vague familiarity. She had seen this face before, at another time, in another context. Then the picture clicked and she knew. The slight woman reminded Paula of Mia Farrow in *Rosemary's Baby,* with her short hair and sunken, hollow cheeks, her frail China-doll demeanor vulnerable to a good wind that could knock her through a plate-glass window. A woman twisted and manipulated to the limit. Frightened. Defenseless. Like there was no one she could trust. *The world* had betrayed her.

And suddenly Paula felt pity for this pathetic woman who had lost everything in that tragic fire . . . including parts of her mind. And she knew what she had to do—she had to listen to Judith now. The woman had feelings to vent and no one to go to. And besides, it was easier to listen to what Judith had to say than to have to endure her continual hounding. And perhaps, *perhaps,* she could even reason with her.

Paula sat back down at the table and motioned for Judith to sit opposite her. "Would you like a cup of coffee?" she asked.

"Please."

Paula signaled to the waitress and they waited silently until the coffee was poured. Then Paula leaned across the table, her fingers making patient steeples in front of her. She took a deep, readying breath.

"I know you believe what you're saying to me," she started to say slowly. "But it's not true. Hugh would never have done what you're accusing him of. . . ." Each word came carefully, deliberately, as if she were speaking to a child, a foreigner. Or an idiot.

"How can someone kill his own children?" She knew that Judith was sick, but still she couldn't keep the incredulity out of her voice. *"How can you believe that?"*

Judith jumped at the question. "Because I threatened to leave him. I told him I was going to the beach house that night to decide whether to continue the marriage or ask for a divorce."

"The fire was an accident—"

"You've been married only a week," Judith said, her voice ominous and filled with warning of terrors to come. "You don't know him yet. I didn't until it was too late and I don't want it to be too late for you. He's going to want to control you, *own* you." Her hand curled into a fist and her eyes rounded with bitter memory. "Because that's what happened to me. Whenever I wanted to do things for myself, have a life for myself, he wouldn't let me. He tried to close everyone out of my life except for him. And he was succeeding. Until I said no—enough! I had to get away."

She pounded her fist down on the table, an unconscious gesture, because the sound startled and interrupted her. She unclenched her fingers and reached for the cup. Her hand shook tremulously and Paula watched the effort Judith expended to control the spastic motions so she could sip the coffee, less perhaps because she now wanted to drink, more to show Paula she could do it. Paula remained silent, mesmerized by this slip of a woman.

"Don't you see," Judith said quietly as she put the cup down. Her hand shook again, rattling the saucer. "I couldn't live the way I was. I couldn't. So I went to Cape Cod to try to work out my future." She laughed derisively and closed her eyes. "My future. That's a laugh."

Quite different from *her* future on the Champs Élysées and a Tahitian beach, Paula thought. How lives can be irreparably altered by a moment's carelessness.

"Judith . . ." she said compassionately. This time *she* reached across the table and touched the other woman's wrist lightly, a gesture of sympathy, of understanding. Paula knew that what Judith was saying was more confession than accusation. She was explaining herself, justifying her actions the night of the fire, as the psychiatrist had said, defensively transfering her guilt.

"He tried to own me," Judith repeated as she stared into the cup of coffee, her voice reflective, and Paula wondered if she had disappeared into a private world of insanity. But then Judith raised her eyes, looked directly at Paula, and spat out a hoarse snarl of hatred and contempt. "And when he couldn't, he tried to kill me."

Paula shook her head pitifully at Judith, completely at a loss. "I can't . . ." she started to say. *I can't listen to you like you're making any kind of sense. A man doesn't go around setting fire to his house and killing his children.*

"He didn't set the fire, Judith," Paula said, exasperated by trying to get through to the wraithlike woman. "Deep down you have to know that. You've got to go for help—" Her tone was inflective, the words loud and suspended between them, open to the air, not what she had wanted. A diner in a pinstripe woolen suit passed their table and frowned at the raised voice. Paula glanced at him sharply and made him turn away with a mind-your-own-business frown of her own, then looked back at Judith, with eyes wide and brimming with Freud and therapy. "You've got to," she repeated in a clenched voice.

Judith shook her head like an autistic child refusing to listen. "How do I get through to you?" she begged with the same pity Paula had shown to her. "Your life is in danger. You must get away from him, far away where he can never find you. Because soon he won't let you get away, even if you want to. He'll kill you first!" And there was such a genuineness in her face that Paula knew that there would never be any dissuading her because Judith *believed.*

"I'm sorry, Judith," she said softly. "I've listened to you and I just can't listen anymore. I am appreciative of your thoughts because I know you mean well for me. But I just won't accept what you're saying, and please"—she stood and slipped on her sweater—*"please,* don't call me again, don't see me again. I'll take responsibility for my life and the lives of my children."

And with only a final, lingering glance at the other woman, Paula picked up her magazine and walked out of the restaurant. Her back was straight, her walk stiff and unnatural, like the time she had auditioned on camera for a role in a college television production; a self-conscious step, her arms swinging awkwardly, aware that she was walking, aware others were looking at her through the monitors in the control room, aware now that *Judith's eyes were following her out the door.* But she didn't turn back, as she had in the Boston Common, when Judith's glance had also bored through her. But now, she prayed, this was the last of it.

Judith twisted around in her chair after Paula had walked through the door. There was a slight, almost imperceptible cross-eyed quality to her gaze, a look of resignation. She understood Paula, suspected she would not get through to her, break the wall of love and trust she had for Hugh. Paula would never believe what she was saying about Hugh.

And that was too bad, Judith thought as her eyes narrowed and her look hardened. She took another sip of coffee, which was cold now to her lips, but she drank it anyway, her hand steady. And she was filled suddenly with a certain power that came from knowledge of the future, of what *she* would do to affect it.

What she had to do.

She would not allow Paula to take her place with him.

That, Judith swore.

Chapter 7

FOR JEREMY THE MATH CLASS WAS ENDLESS, THE CLOCK IN the front of the room seemingly stuck at 2:30. He rolled his eyes toward the boy next to him, one of the few with whom he shared several classes, including his homeroom period, someone he had begun to get friendly with. It was a bitch, though, having to meet a bunch of new guys, and with a great tug of longing he thought about the friends he had left behind in Boston. He was going to spend Saturday with them, and at least that was something to look forward to.

When the bell finally rang he quickly gathered his books and filed out of the classroom, hurrying down the hallway with the others to the lockers. He grabbed his jacket and slammed the math book inside with a good riddance and started out of the school. The day was cool and blustery with a hint of the coming winter. Jeremy was looking forward to skiing with Hugh in northern Vermont and each breath reminded him of the mountains he had been to the previous year—the crisp clean smell of the snow-swirled air, the diamond sparkle of the fresh fall beneath his ski tips, the near total silence of being all alone on a wooded trail. His mind was on perfecting his parallel technique as he turned out of the school gates and started for home, so he didn't notice the two boys who fell into step with him.

"So this is the new kid nobody's talking about," Jeremy

heard a snide voice say. "I heard he thinks he's tough. He don't look that tough to me. How about you?"

"Nah—not to me either," another voice answered.

Jeremy only quickly glanced at the boys who flanked him. Bill and Dennis were each a head taller than he was, and at least two years older. They had been pointed out to him by a classmate in the gym when they had elbowed a smaller boy away from a piece of equipment they had wanted to use. There were boys like that in every school. Assholes. Jeremy pulled into himself and quickened his step to try to ignore them.

The boys kept right up with him. "I don't think the kid's talking to us," Bill mockingly informed Dennis over Jeremy's head. "You know something—we don't even know his name." He tapped Jeremy's shoulder. "What's your name, sissy?"

Still keeping his pace, Jeremy squared his jaw and faced the bully. "My name's Jeremy and why don't you leave me alone. I don't want any trouble with you."

"Oooo, did you hear that?" Bill mimicked, feigning fear. "His name is Jer-e-my and he don't want any trouble with us. Well, we don't want to give Jer-e-my any trouble, do we, Dennis?"

"Oh, nooooo . . ." Dennis answered, a broad gum-chewing grin on his face. That was exactly what they wanted to give Jeremy and everyone damn well knew it.

Jeremy stiffened more, hoping that by ignoring the boys they would lose interest in him and drift away. He had done nothing to bother them.

All of a sudden Dennis pushed him, throwing Jeremy off balance and into Bill.

"Hey, quit pushing me, man!" Bill yelled and shoved Jeremy back against Dennis with the meat of his palm. And the game was on.

There were fewer students around now, most having drifted off in different directions, and those who were still around wanted nothing to do with the impending confrontation.

To the boys it was still a game, and Dennis grabbed on to Jeremy's arm with two closed hands and gave him a ferocious shove back toward Bill, whose palms were up and outright and caught Jeremy square in the chest with a stinging blow. Tears jumped into his eyes as he fought for composure and breath. He considered his options—running was the first, but he had never been extremely fast and it was doubtful that he could outrun Bill and Dennis, who were stronger and longer-legged. All possibilities flashed through his mind in the fraction of a second it took to spin back toward Dennis in a torturous human game of monkey-in-the-middle. He couldn't run, he *wouldn't* cry. To do nothing was suicidal because Bill was winding up to take a shot at him. To fight back was equally suicidal, but if he was going to go down, Jeremy decided, it would be swinging, like a man, not a frightened kid.

With a *banzai* screech he slammed his books into Bill's stomach, heard the surprised *oof.* Marks did not often fight back and Jeremy knew he had scored. He also knew that now it was a fight to the death. He jumped free and squared his fists, aware that his hands were pathetically small in comparison to Bill's and Dennis's. He stiffened his body and instinctively tightened his stomach, preparing to get the shit knocked out of him, knowing at that moment that he didn't know what was going to happen to him *specifically,* only that it was odds-on going to hurt.

Bill and Dennis advanced, circling Jeremy, wildcats and prey, feinting forward to try to drive him off balance, enjoying as he jumped away from one into the near clutch of the other. There were grins on the boys' faces; they were enjoying the game that wasn't really a game anymore. Jeremy's spunk had surprised and angered them and they were out for blood.

Then, as if on signal, they converged on him together in a melee of swinging arms. Jeremy went down under their fists, the wind knocked out of him, hunching into a ball on the sidewalk, trying to protect his head, taking the fists in his stomach.

That's when Hugh came running up.

He had been taking a walk toward the school when he saw Jeremy go down under the fists of the bigger boys. It wasn't coincidental he was there that afternoon. He had been following Jeremy home at a distance, concerned about his being new in the school.

He was on top of Dennis in a flash, hefting him bodily and tossing him out of the circle. Dennis stumbled to the sidewalk, picked himself up, considered going back and swinging, but saw the look of fury on the man's face and thought otherwise.

Hugh went after Bill next, gaining firm hold on his arm, wrenching it behind his back, twisting it, threatening to break it. From the sidewalk Jeremy watched through tear-streaked eyes as the bigger boy's face contorted as Hugh flicked his wrist, forcing the arm around even more, higher this time, closer to the boy's back. Another tug and Bill cried out involuntarily in pain.

"You don't like it, do you?" Hugh spat out.

Bill was too proud to answer and Hugh gave his arm another twist. *"Do you?"*

"No," Bill winced.

"What? I don't hear you."

"No!" Bill yelled louder, the word itself a cry of pain now.

"You touch him again, I'll break your arm. Do you hear me?"

"Yes!" Bill was panting; sweat glistened on his forehead.

"DO YOU?" Hugh thundered.

"YES!"

Hugh spun Bill out from his hold, toward a chain-link fence. Bill was able to put his hands out to break his crashing into the fence. Panting, he whirled around and glared at Hugh.

"You're crazy, man, you know that?" he hissed.

Hugh pointed a finger at the boy. "I swear it. I'll break your arm. Now get out of here."

"I'm going, I'm going," Bill said. "Don't sweat it." Once free from Hugh's grasp and aware that he could stay out of it by outrunning the older man if need be, he had recaptured some of his bravado. He casually, almost tauntingly, knelt down and picked up his notebook, a glance at Jeremy. "We were only playing, jerk-face—"

Hugh took a menacing step forward, his foot slapping against the pavement, and Bill jumped.

"We're going, man, we're going. . . ." Bill held up his hand conciliatorily, the challenge suddenly gone out of him. He and Dennis started down the sidewalk. "He's crazy," Bill said as he inhaled sharply, finally having regained his breath.

"Yeah," Dennis agreed, both needing to reassure themselves of that to protect their egos and dignity.

Hugh knelt down next to Jeremy, who had been silent throughout his stepfather's attack. He tried to sniff the tears back and wipe the cheeks beneath his eyes to dry them.

"You all right, guy?" Hugh asked as he helped Jeremy to his feet.

"Yeah." He glanced after the boys, who were rounding a corner and disappearing from view. "Motherfuckers," he spat out. "I tried to ignore them but they were itching for a fight."

"Well, we just gave them one, didn't we?" Hugh grinned.

"Yeah." Jeremy matched the grin. There was no shame at all in having your stepfather stand up for you.

"Some people can't just be ignored," Hugh said as he picked up Jeremy's books. "They'll understand only what they dish out." And Jeremy heard a note of anger in Hugh's voice that he sensed went beyond the situation. Hugh slung an arm around Jeremy's shoulder and they walked to a nearby ice-cream parlor. "I think you deserve a little something."

As they watched the sundaes being made, Hugh said softly, reflectively, "When I was your age I angered the leader of a local gang. After that everybody who wanted to join the gang would score points by knocking the hell out of me. Well, my father always came to my rescue and managed to scare off a lot of attacks and I was able to walk a little taller and breathe a little easier knowing he was around. That was good, but deep down I harbored the fear—what would happen to me if one day my father wasn't around to help me?"

Jeremy eyed Hugh silently, not knowing what to say. There was a distant look in his stepfather's eyes as he remembered his childhood. Almost feeling like he was intruding, Jeremy turned his attention to the sundae as the counterman squirted the whipped cream and plopped the cherries on top. In his mind he saw the boys' fists raining down on him, then Hugh hauling them off him, getting revenge on the boys from his childhood, Jeremy suspected, ones he was never able to beat up himself, the look of fury on his stepfather's face now identified. It had happened to *him* and he wasn't going to let it happen to anyone else.

"I'll always be around, Jeremy," Hugh said. "You don't have to worry like I did."

"Thanks." Jeremy remembered that Hugh's father had died when he was young and wondered what happened to him after he lost his father's protection. It must have been hell for him, Jeremy thought, thinking of what his own predicament would be if Bill and Dennis knew Hugh wouldn't be around anymore.

* * *

Hugh had martinis waiting when Paula came home from work. When she saw the glasses her tongue dropped out gratefully and she held her hands up limp-wristed, a panting-dog look.

"Forgive the cliché"—she smiled when she finished taking a long sip—"but I needed that." She exhaled. "Wow, did I need that."

"Who knows you, baby?" Hugh whispered and kissed her, lightly at first, his lips barely brushing hers, his tongue flicking at hers teasingly, then hungrily as his mouth covered hers with passion. When she drew away from him her eyes were still closed and her mouth still partially open and desirous.

"I needed that too," she sighed dreamily. She took a deep breath to remove the headiness of the kiss. "Almost as much as the martini."

"Almost as much, huh? Well, I've got something planned for later that's guaranteed to top any drink."

"Guaranteed?" she challenged. "That's putting yourself out on a limb."

Hugh trailed two fingers down her face. "I expect to put you out on it too."

"And I expect to be there . . . I'd *better* be there." She hooked her fingers around his belt and pulled him closer to her and they kissed again, Hugh's hands lightly massaging the back of her neck, playing through her hair.

"Where are the kids?" Paula asked.

"Upstairs doing homework. They each seemed to have gotten a lot of it. *Shitload* is the word Jeremy used. Michelle was a little more delicate, although not by much."

"I'll go up to them in a minute," Paula said, then hesitated, her eyes betraying her.

"What is it?" Hugh asked.

"There's something I have to talk to you about." She paused, but then receiving silent assurances from Hugh continued, "Judith came to see me today."

"Paula, no—"

"I was eating lunch. She must have been waiting for me and followed me to the restaurant. She repeated what she said before about . . ." Paula made a circular motion with her hand; the words didn't have to be said. "I tried to talk rationally to her, but I wasn't getting through."

"No. I don't want you to talk to her at all," Hugh said angrily. "Rationally or otherwise." She watched his eyes narrow and the tension build in his temples, the reaction she had expected.

"She's a sick woman," he said with clenched teeth, then slapped his fist against his leg, trying to figure out what to do. "If she ever bothers you again, calls you. Sees you. Writes to you. *Anything.* I want you to tell me immediately. I'll have my lawyer do something. Get a restraining order, have her arrested, put her away. She can't be allowed to frighten you this way."

"She really doesn't," Paula protested, realizing she was tacitly defending Judith. She didn't want to see Hugh upset or, oddly enough, Judith harmed. The woman was sick, pathetic, but she could deal with her.

Although, she wondered, how often *did* Judith watch her and follow her?

Maybe she should be concerned.

Paula went upstairs, kissed the children hello, then went into the bathroom to wash her face. When she came out she was wearing only her bra and panties. Hugh was lying on the bed, propped up against the bolsters, appreciatively eyeing her body, the line of her legs, slender, yet strong and firm, the full scoop of her breasts, the tease of pubic hair.

"Marie made a roast for tonight," he said. "Rare. Just the way you like it. She walked the cow by the oven once."

Paula was at the closet selecting a pair of jeans. She turned to face Hugh and frowned, confused for a moment. "I told you I'd be going out to dinner tonight, didn't I?" She couldn't remember if she had reminded Hugh that morning. "I'm getting together with Joan and the others." She pulled a rust-colored knitted sweater down from the shelf and held it up in front of her with the jeans. "How does this look?"

"Actually you did tell me you were going out," Hugh admitted. "And I was really hoping you would change your mind and stay." He rounded his face and looked like a disappointed child, and his sad, forlorn look made Paula laugh.

"It's our regular meeting tonight. I missed the last one because we were on our honeymoon. Remember?"

"Oh, vaguely . . ." Hugh replied. "By the way, the sweater looks terrific. I love that on you." He got up from the bed and stopped her from slipping the sweater over her head. He trailed a finger from her lips down the line of her neck, then slowly traced the outline of her breasts. Paula weakened and swayed beneath his touch.

"Don't do that or I'll never leave," she groaned, then promised, "I won't be home late. It's just dinner and a little gossip. I have to report on what a wonderful husband you are. I think they'd rather hear that you beat me, but I guess they'll have to settle for the truth."

She was disappointed he didn't smile. "You don't want me to go?" she asked.

"No, not at all." Hugh shrugged, then smiled sheepishly. "I'm just afraid that because all your friends are single or divorced, they might be a bad influence on you." He helped her on with her sweater, ran his hands down her sides, molded her ass with his palm, then snuck his hands back around her waist and hugged her.

She leaned her head against him. "That's not going to happen. Besides, I might even be a good influence on them. Show them all marriages don't have to be lousy."

Hugh pecked her on the forehead and held her with his eyes, deep, glistening brown, infinitely sensual. "I guess I just worry when you're out by yourself. I know it's silly and I know I shouldn't . . ." He stepped back from her and held his hands up, palms out. "Go ahead. I promise not to worry."

Paula shook her head, filled with the moment and her feelings for Hugh—her love for him, and her sympathies for all that had happened to the people dearest to him. "I don't have to go tonight," she said. "I'll phone Joan and tell her they can feel free to talk about me and make up any lies about you that they want."

"No, go out with your friends," Hugh protested. He hitched himself up in a macho I-can-take-anything stance. "I can survive one evening without you, pod-ner."

"Well, I'm not about to let you," Paula said as she started to pull her sweater back over her head.

"You're sure?" Hugh's grin was lopsided; she could see he was pleased yet embarrassed that she was staying home.

"Yes, I am sure. Who can pass up your rare roast beef?" She teased him through his pants and shivered as he responded to her touch.

"I love you so very much," he said, his voice soft and floating. "And to be perfectly honest, I'll admit to being somewhat selfish and say I don't want to share you with anybody else. Not tonight. Not ever."

Paula shook her head happily, dizzily, as she drank in her husband with her eyes. His arms were wrapped around her waist, his body pressed against hers, making her almost swoon with excitement. Everything she had ever wanted was standing right in front of her now. *Everything.*

Then she remembered something and wriggled out of his hold. "Let me catch Joan before she leaves." She went to the bedroom phone and made her excuses.

"Oh, by the way," she said when she hung up. "Joan invited us to dinner a week from Saturday. She's met a new guy and wants my approval. Also, she wants to meet you. Except for the flowers and the phone calls she says she doesn't really have any in-the-flesh proof that you exist."

Hugh reached for her again and she felt his erection inside his pants.

"Do I exist?" he asked.

"Yes." Paula grinned. "You exist. Now do us both a favor and put that thing away until I've fed the children."

They locked the bedroom door because he couldn't and she didn't ask him again.

It had been an exciting and hectic day for Kate Forest. It had finally happened. A senior editor had quit and Jason had promoted her into the editor's spot. She had her associate's stripes, new responsibility, and the possibility to prove herself by acquiring and editing her own books. Although Jason agreed to let her continue to assist him with Hugh's books. But the new job also came with headaches and she immediately inherited all of the former editor's. There was a manuscript that was late getting into production, a cover that came out of the art department with the color and lettering all wrong, and the art director had yet to acknowledge her authority to request changes. There was also a heated conversation with a very prominent literary agent about the mistreatment of his client's book by the former editor.

It was an exhausting day, yet a satisfying one, and she had survived the way Jason knew she would. At five-thirty he asked her out for a drink to celebrate her new status, and to tell her while the job didn't get better it got easier. Over wine and canapés they talked about the direction of the company, Kate's personal future, and her limitless possibilities.

Kate sipped the wine headily, enjoying her new position, her initiation into the club. It had been a very exciting day with nothing but promise for the days and years ahead.

But something was missing, Kate thought distantly, her sensations dulled by the wine. Somehow all that had happened to her was not enough. She didn't have that one person to share it with, and felt a clawing loneliness deep inside of her.

It was a little after seven when they finished their drinks. Jason kissed Kate good night and gave her final congratulations. She picked up Chinese food on the way home and ate it out of the containers as she took a manuscript out of her briefcase to work on.

But she couldn't concentrate. Her thoughts kept wandering and she ended up putting the pages down without knowing what she had read, a less than auspicious ending to her first day as an editor.

She took a hot shower to try to relax but it had the opposite effect, drawing attention to her body, her nakedness. As she dried herself the towel played across her and she knew what she wanted to do. She got into bed and slipped between the sheets with Hugh's novel. She would just read a few pages; that would make her feel better. A picture of herself and Hugh stood on the nightstand next to her bed. It had been taken at the McKittrick Company's Christmas party the previous year. Hugh almost hadn't come to the party but she had called him and begged him; the party would not have been the same without the company's most successful author. In the end he had come and the photographer had snapped the picture of Hugh thanking Kate for convincing him to attend, his arm draped around her shoulders, pulling her close to him, his cheek against hers in embrace, silly grins on each of their faces. He had signed the picture "Love, Hugh."

Love, Hugh.

Kate breathed in deeply as her eyes slipped dreamily, expectantly, closed. She thought about Hugh touching her and her hands brushed across her breasts and teased her nipples. She imagined the warmth and sensuous pressure of his lips as he kissed her eyes, her neck, her breasts, her soft downy hair, the pungent muskiness of his cologne as it overtook her; the feel of his lean and rugged hardness as he mounted her and pressed into her body. Her breath quickened and her head fell back on the pillow, her neck elongated. Her hand moved lower and faster, and she inhaled sharply as he entered her, and faster still as he thrust into her again and again, their bodies moving together rhythmically. Her imagination and excitement grew until it could expand no more and overwhelmed her in a peak of passion as she shuddered ecstatically and called out Hugh's name.

That was how it would always be if they could only be together . . . *if they could only be together,* she panted as her breath slowed and evened and her body cooled . . . if he wasn't married . . . if Paula was out of his life.

If.

A half hour later she picked up the manuscript again and tried to work. But still she couldn't concentrate.

Because something was missing.

And as pleasing and stimulating as her touch had been, it was, like the job and the day, not enough.

Hugh was not with her.

Her feeling of contentment and fulfillment quickly turned to anger, and a fierce determination to right a situation that was very wrong.

Judith lived in a small, one-bedroom rear apartment on the second floor of a three-story Victorian house which she had rented since the divorce.

After the deaths of the children Hugh had tried to revive the marriage, attempting to forget that Judith had been about to leave him. There was tragedy to overcome, only the two of them now, time to draw together. Because he still loved her.

But as the physical shock of the deaths wore off, Judith's dreams began, jarring her memory into moment-by-moment recall of the night of the fire, and the figure standing at the edge of the woods watching the house burn. Hugh—who had set the fire to kill her. She phoned the police repeatedly, but they dismissed her accusations as ludicrous. Hugh took her to a psychiatrist who was able to get her to believe that Hugh no longer wanted to kill her but was unable to make her accept that the fire had been an unavoidable tragic accident, with no one to blame. Although at least she was ambulatory, functioning. Sudden and intense loss and guilt could have driven her to catatonia. A grim plus, the doctor had said and regretted being unable to bring her out of mourning.

She moved out of the house and filed for divorce, which Hugh did not contest. As much as he had once loved Judith he could no longer live with her and her sickness. He gave her a sum adequate to live comfortably on for a lengthy period of time without having to work, which he didn't think her capable of. He offered to continue to pay her psychiatrist's bills but by the time the divorce was final she had stopped seeing the doctor. She wasn't sick, she insisted; she just didn't have the proof she needed to convict Hugh. She withdrew into herself, barely went out. She passed her time looking at television and thumbing through romance novels and magazines. She had taken the children's pictures with her and would look at them for hours at a time, remembering John and Danielle as they were, imagining how they would be today, entering school, starting camp, growing, learning. She never could concentrate for very long on anything else. Her mind kept wandering to her children and to the night of the fire.

Now to Hugh and Paula.

Since she had seen them together she had thought of little else. Just the two of them.

And Paula's children, the boy who was nine and the girl, six, the same age her children would have been.

The bell rang and she buzzed the visitor in. She opened the door and was surprised to see Hugh coming up the stairs in his jeans and leather jacket.

"What do you want?" she asked, her mouth curled in revulsion at the sight of him.

Hugh hadn't seen Judith in more than a year and was momentarily stunned by the gaunt, trembling figure that stood at the apartment door. He remembered how Judith had looked when they had first met, when he had married her, even *the day before the fire,* her eyes sharp, her cheeks full, her skin darkened with a healthy blush. She had always been so vibrant, full of life. A beauty he could not keep his hands off of. Now she was a woman in limbo—not living, not dead, someone who would pad through the rest of her life never finding peace, a lost soul, and he pitied her for the way she looked and what she had become.

"I want to talk to you, Judith," he said. "How are you feeling? Let me come in for a moment."

She looked at him defiantly and drew to her full height. "No. You go to hell."

Hugh considered her answer, looked into her eyes, which were flaming with hatred for him, and decided he could talk to her from the doorway, state his business, and leave.

"I don't want you ever seeing or contacting Paula again," he said flatly.

"You don't?" she spat out contemptuously. "Well, you can't stop me."

Hugh shook his head disbelievingly. He had once loved this woman who was now a stranger to him. "You'd do anything, say anything to try to frighten Paula away from me, wouldn't you? Try to split us up. Is it possible for you to hate me this much, Judith? Can you want to punish me this much?"

Judith's eyes narrowed and she answered spitefully, "I lost everything I ever loved in that fire you set. I don't have anything else to live for now. Except," she added almost challengingly, a hint of a vindictive grin across her face, "to get Paula and those children away from you."

Hugh shook his head and reached out toward Judith to touch her lightly, as if sense could somehow magically pass between them. She pulled away from his hand and he let it fall limply to his side. "Judith," he said softly, tenderly, straining for control as he faced this madwoman, when what he really wanted to do was grab her and *choke* reason into her. "Nothing will bring John and Danielle back. Certainly not your hating me. You have to accept that. We have to get on with our lives. And you have to go for more help. Please do it," he begged.

"You can't expect to get away with what you did," Judith said bitterly. "And you won't live with her and the children. I'll make certain of it. I will." She wiped her mouth with the back of her hand where saliva dotted her chin.

Hugh tried to keep his composure. Judith was sick and he didn't want to engage her in a screaming match he could never win. And he fought a wave of hatred for this woman he had once loved so deeply.

"If you don't leave us alone, I'll have no alternative but to contact the police," he said in a nonthreatening voice. "I'll press charges against you, believe me. You'll be arrested, perhaps even be put away somewhere. You can't harass people. You don't have the right to do this to us, destroy my life," he hissed. *"Our lives."*

"Like you destroyed mine?" Judith challenged. "Go on. Call the police. Maybe they'll reopen the investigation, find out what you did."

"Judith, *no,"* he said helplessly. He wasn't getting through to her, Hugh knew; *there would be no getting through to her.* His body weakened resignedly and he shook his head. Tears sprang to his eyes in an uncertain, shifting mix of frustration, anger, and pity.

"Judith, please understand that nobody means you any harm. All Paula and I want to do is live our lives."

"What about *me?"* she yelled at him. "What about *my* life?"

Hugh walked down the stairs, stopping at the double glass hallway doors. He turned and looked back up at her, standing on the landing, a tiny, hunched, infuriating figure.

"Judith, please," he begged hoarsely, "leave us alone."

Chapter 8

THE NOVEMBER RAIN SLASHED THE WINDOWPANES FOR THE third straight morning, and for the third straight morning it woke Paula before the alarm. She squinted against the gray glare of the day and turned off the clock radio. She sat up in bed and stretched. Hugh stirred beside her and she patted his back, soothing him back to sleep. A morning ritual, as he always slept later than she did, waking at nine and working from ten until five.

The children were eating breakfast when Paula came downstairs. Jeremy summed up the thoughts of all of them:

"This weather sucks. I wish it would just snow already."

"Yeah," Michelle echoed, her little chin rounding defiantly.

Paula smiled and admitted she had to agree with them. Then she asked, "So what's doing?" Another morning ritual instituted the previous week when it had occurred to Paula that she really had only these precious few moments over breakfast to spend alone with her children. When she came home from work the four of them ate a family dinner and afterward either all spent time together or else the children went up to their rooms to do homework. Before she married Hugh she and the children had a good deal more time with each other—over the preparation of dinner, during the meal, and the evening afterward. Now, ironically, Hugh had a lot more free time alone with

Jeremy and Michelle than she did and she fought off a twinge of jealousy; she wanted Hugh to be close with the children. Well, maybe she would take them somewhere over the weekend. That would give them a chance to catch up, because none of them were particularly communicative in the morning rush, the children barely grunting to her attemptedly cheerful "What's doing?" What could be doing at seven-thirty in the morning?

When she was all dressed and ready to leave for work, she tapped Hugh lightly to kiss him good-bye. He reached up for her and pulled her down next to him. "Stay home with me today. We'll build a fire, snuggle, and watch afternoon TV."

"Sounds dreamy . . . especially since I'll be able to get back into bed. But Hempster's coming in and I have to be there to salute him."

"Just so long as you come home to salute me."

"Count on it, general." She saluted.

She dropped the children off at their schools and joined the line of traffic that was crawling into Boston. The rain was still falling heavily, the sewers were overflowing, and there was roadway flooding. A delivery van skidded on the wet pavement, narrowly missing her car, and she was forced to drive several blocks out of her way because a fire truck was stationed in the middle of a key interchange. By the time she got to the garage where she parked, the lower tiers were filled, forcing her to drive all the way up the circular ramp to the roof level, where she lost her umbrella to a gust of wind. The garage elevator was broken and she had to walk back down the ramp to the street. In her high heels, she took it mostly in her calves.

When she got off the elevator and picked up her messages she saw that her lunch date had canceled.

"At least something good happened today," she sighed.

"That may be it," Glenn Adams said as he stepped into her office. "I just got a hint at what Hempster wants. A whole campaign aimed at women."

Paula made an are-you-kidding? face. "For his tools?"

"He did some demographic research. With the number of women living alone, especially in cities where they may not know anybody to help them with things, they are more likely than ever before to need—read 'buy'—a hammer, a screwdriver, a wrench. He's going after the young singles market. *Cosmo. Vogue.*"

"How about trying *Modern Maturity?*" Joan tried. "For the woman who sets her false teeth with Hempster Super Glue. I think it's a natural."

Glenn smiled patronizingly. "Really, darling Joan. I'll let you bring it up with Dwight today. Then when he throws you out you'll know why you buy the space and we write the ads."

Joan rounded her mouth poutingly. "I still think I came up with a good name and concept for that new fruit-flavored soft drink."

Paula laughed. "I love that one." She held up an imaginary pop bottle and pretended talking into the camera. "Drink Beri Beri. The soft drink for Vitamin B deficients."

"And now for the bad news, Paula," Glenn said.

"He wants the whole new campaign by tomorrow morning."

"No—don't be ridiculous."

"Thank goodness."

"Try the day after."

"You're kidding." Glenn's silence was her confirmation.

"The *whole* thing?" she asked incredulously.

"Just some preliminary plans so he can sort through them over the weekend. But this afternoon we have the casting downtown and I want you to be there with me, and then tomorrow we have the diet bread presentation."

"So when do you propose we do this work for Hempster?" Paula asked, then quickly answered her own question. "Tonight."

"He's bringing in the demographic material at noon. Look through the reports whenever you can steal some time and let's try to start kicking something around when we get back from the casting session at five. Then we can hone it tomorrow."

"Oh, Glenn, I don't want to work late," Paula groaned.

"Yeah," Joan said defiantly. "She's a newlywed. That carries some privilege."

"Only if she wants to be a full-time housewife." Glenn grinned. "All right, Paula?"

Paula saluted resignedly. "Aye aye, sir."

After the meeting with Hempster, Paula had to admit that the idea was a good one. The ogre had come well prepared with studies and test marketing his company had done in some of his retail outlets, in the inner cities as well as the suburban malls.

More women were browsing and buying. There was no doubt a market out there. What was needed now were the ads.

Paula phoned Hugh.

"I don't want you staying there till all hours. That's ridiculous, Paula."

"Hugh—it's just one night."

"Well, I don't like it. Your evenings are your time, *our* time. Hempster can give you more time to work out the concept."

"Tell you what—" Paula offered as a deal. "Next week is going to be light. What if I steal a day off then and we build that fire, snuggle, and watch every soap on TV? We'll even tape the ones we miss."

That mollified him and she heard the smile come over the phone. "You got a deal. What time do you think you'll be home?"

"No later than nine. We'll probably leave here about eight, eight-thirty. But if it's going to be later, I'll call."

"I love you, Paula," Hugh said.

"I love you, too," she said, and those words gave meaning to everything.

She phoned Hugh at seven to say they were going to be much later than she'd thought. She and Steve Fishman, the other member of the creative group, both had some good ideas and Glenn was excited. Paula enjoyed these sessions when the creative juices were turned on and successful campaigns were born. Although this wasn't going to be a multimillion-dollar ad campaign, they were still servicing their major client, and a commission of forty-five to fifty thousand wasn't anything to sneeze at either. It would certainly help all of them at Christmas bonus time.

At eleven Paula decided she would call it quits. Glenn and Steve were finishing up some final copy and would stay an extra hour. Paula was exhausted as the mental energy she expended dissipated her strength.

"See you all in the morning," she sighed.

"If you get a chance before going to bed," Glenn prompted, "see if you can take a look at your notes for the Magic Bread presentation."

Paula looked at her watch and smiled. *"Now* is before going to bed. I'll do it in the morning. They're not coming in till twelve."

"Really good work tonight, Paula," Glenn said. "I'll be certain to tell Arthur."

Paula managed a half wave and slipped out the door. She grabbed her coat, thought of calling Hugh to tell him she was finally on her way but it was late and she didn't want the ringing phone to wake the children. There was no traffic at this hour and she'd be home in less than thirty minutes.

She said good night to the building guard, who unlocked the lobby door and let her out.

"No umbrella, Miss Weller?" the white-haired guard asked.

"It went south this morning, Ben." Paula smiled.

"I have an extra one you can borrow."

"Thanks, but it doesn't look too bad out."

It wasn't, but it was still drizzling and the night was cool and raw, thick with a swirling gray fog that almost engulfed her like a ghostly mist. Rain fell in a fine sheet and, buffeted by the breeze, slanted into her face, filming her eyes. Paula could barely see ahead of her. She drew her coat tightly around her and started for the parking garage a block away.

The downtown street was deserted, nobody out walking on such a dreary night, and only a few cars buzzed past, their tires whining on the wet pavement, headlights slashing the turbid air, making it seem almost solid, impenetrable. Streetlamps struggled valiantly to shine through the fog, breaking the dark and shadowy pavement with circles of tentative light.

The blue fluorescent sign of the parking garage had been turned off. The lot closed at seven, but Paula was a monthly user and had a magnetic card to let her out. She slipped through the pedestrian door and entered the garage, grateful to be out of the night. She took a breath, free of rain and fog, and wiped the moisture from her face. The "Out of Order" sign was still posted on the elevator. *Terrific,* Paula thought, wondering how, as tired as she was, she was going to make it up the five garage levels to the roof where she had parked her car that morning.

She started up. The garage was nearly empty of cars now. Most of the people who used the garage were day workers, in by nine, out by six, and only a few cars were parked on the ramps as she walked up and around the first two tiers. A new thought hit her. She should just pull the car down to one of the prime spaces and take a cab home; that way she'd have a good spot for the next day. She laughed—in part because of what she had just thought, in greater part because all of a sudden being alone in the garage was making her nervous. This wasn't the first time she had been by herself in the garage at night, but tonight the combination of the rain, the eeriness of the fog, and an intuitive sense of *something being wrong* made her particularly edgy. She considered going back and getting Glenn or Steve to walk her up to her car, but she was already past the second level and there was as much behind her as ahead. And she didn't want to go back out in the rain. Besides, who would be hanging around this open-air garage on such a miserable night.

She looked above her. The line of bare light bulbs burned a muted orange inside their wire mesh globes. Some of them were burned out, others flickered uncertainly. Her footsteps echoed hollowly on the concrete. She kept her step purposeful, her eyes straight ahead so she wouldn't have to think about the dark patches of shadows where the bulbs didn't illuminate—squared corners of the garage, thick concrete support posts, shadows of vans and parked cars, *all possibly hiding lurking figures waiting to pounce.* The thought was a sobering one: She was alone—and vulnerable—in the half-darkness of the lonely parking garage. *Not what she wanted to be thinking now.* Rather, she wanted to be thinking that the night reminded her of *Brigadoon* and she started to hum the title song.

As she passed the third tier she swore to herself that the next time she had to work late she would move her car closer to the ground level or have someone walk with her. She clutched her purse tightly to her body. *For no reason, no reason at all.* The ramp opened onto the roof. Her car was around the bend. Just a few more steps. Except for the faint patter of rain against the roof, the silence in the garage was thick, tomblike. *Like being in a concrete mausoleum,* she thought uneasily, aware suddenly that she had been holding her breath.

Then she was on the roof level and exposed to the rain and fog again. In the minutes it had taken her to climb the garage it had begun to come down more heavily. She squinted and looked above her and her eyes watered immediately. She ran to her car and fumbled to put the key in the lock, finally stabilizing it with both hands and she was inside the car, the door pulled closed and locked behind her.

She breathed deeply, finally feeling safe and very silly for her imagined fears.

Lurking figures, she thought derisively.

She rubbed her eyes and shivered. Her hands were cold and she closed her fists to warm them.

Lurking figures. She should save those words and her emotions for her novel. She put the key in the ignition.

The car would not start.

The engine must be cold. She pumped the gas several times, turned the key again. The engine cranked but would not turn over. It whirred and groaned but it would not catch. She pumped the gas again, five times, six, the pedal squeaking, seven, eight. She turned the key again. Nothing. "Come on, come on," she coaxed, but still it would not engage.

"Damn!" she said out loud. "Why now!" She pounded her fist against the dashboard.

She tried the lights and they went on, illuminating the waist-high concrete wall. It wasn't the battery, but then she remembered that even with a dead battery headlights would still go on, not that much current was required. She was so tired now she could barely think straight. Rain sounded on the top of the car. She didn't even want to leave it now. "Damn!" she swore again. There was a cab service the office used frequently. She could call them and then deal with the car in the morning. "Stupid car!" she muttered and struck the steering wheel. Her eyes filled with tears of frustration. Now she had to go all the way back down to the first level where there was a pay phone.

She flipped off the lights, locked the car door, thinking she was as stupid as the car was. It wouldn't start so it couldn't be stolen. She'd call Triple A the next day.

Starting back down the ramp, she shivered from the rain. Her hair was matted down against her forehead. A strong breeze blew in through the metal gratings of the open-air garage, chilling her even more. She thought about what they had worked on that evening, accomplishing more than they had anticipated. If Hempster approved the concept, the campaign would feature a girl who lived in a crowded studio apartment, the way many single women did. She would be surrounded by everything she needed tools for—from hanging a plant from the ceiling to drilling a hole in the back of her cabinet so the stereo wires could connect to her speakers. Everyday chores that men took for granted but were mystifying to women. They had already worked out most of the ad copy; only fine-tuning was left.

The sound broke her thoughts. It was sudden. Singular.

She furrowed her eyebrows and shook it off. There hadn't been anything there. But her head was suddenly clear, free of thoughts of work. Her nostrils flared as she searched the air.

She heard it again. A thud, the sound of a shoe pressing against the concrete floor.

A footstep? she puzzled.

She swiveled around, suddenly alert. Was someone in the garage with her? It was open to the street; anybody could come in. But she had probably just heard the *echo* of a footstep—*her own*—reverberating through the cavernous garage.

Silence. A beat of expectation. Like the split second of anticipation before the clap of thunder complemented a slash of lightning. Or like waiting for the other shoe to drop.

It did. She heard the sound again.

It wasn't *really* recognizable as a footstep, she tried to tell herself. It could have been the clang of a pipe, the shifting of concrete, the movement of the metal grillwork in the wind, a sound from somewhere outside.

Again she heard it and now there was no denying it. It was a footstep.

Her skin felt prickly, as if tiny knives were jabbing her. She tried to tell herself there was nothing to get alarmed about. Someone had come into the garage after her and was walking to his car now. In a moment she would hear the slam of the door, the start of an engine. But the steps persisted and she knew why she was wrong. The footsteps were coming from somewhere above her. From the roof level or from the fourth tier. She was just now rounding the ramp leading down to the third level. There were several cars left on the roof, others on the ramps. Someone *could* have been in one of them and was just starting down now. But even if the driver had been a monthly user and had access to the garage after hours she would have heard the car; she had been in there long enough. And no one would have driven all the way up to the roof anyway. They would have parked on the first tier, near the entrance. No, someone being in their car now did not make any sense. No one should be above her now! *But someone was there.* And the person had not come in after her. The person had already been up there. Watching her. Waiting for her. For *someone* to come in. And she was it. Fear gripped the back of her neck with the realization and her stomach weakened. There was no more rationalization, no more explanation. She was in danger.

Instinctively she stiffened and quickened her pace. *Stupid to be out alone,* she chastised herself. But it was too late for that now. She turned around to see if anybody was above her but the bend of the garage ramp protectively hid any figure. Concrete support poles and the metal railings also blocked her view. The air suddenly seemed heavier, ominous. No one was in sight. But there was no mistaking the footsteps that sounded from above, growing louder, coming closer.

She had to run but knew it would be impossible in her heels. She slipped off her shoes and scooped them up by the straps and in her stockinged feet started to run downward. *Stupid, stupid, stupid car.* The frustrating words formed a litany in her head as her feet pounded against the cement floor. She almost skidded. The concrete was slick. Puddles of oil and grease stains dotted the floor. She slowed down. To fall now was to be overtaken. She considered hiding behind one of the parked cars, letting whoever was there run past, but if she was spotted she'd be trapped.

She couldn't sort it out. She kept running.

Without her shoes she barely made a sound, only the beat of her heart as it thumped loudly in her chest and the rasping press of her breath as it whistled through her open mouth.

The levels were endless. She grew disoriented and lost track of where she was. Then she saw a giant red "2" and was past the second level and running toward the first. Out of breath now. Panting. Adrenaline surged through her and she picked up her pace, going as fast as she dared. Level one and a half. She skidded on an oil spot, almost tripped, righted herself. Pain stabbed through her, then ebbed. She had almost turned an ankle, she thought. Another ramp, another turn, the *final turn* because now the entrance gate and tollbooths were in sight. Just a few more steps, a few more, she prodded herself. She glanced over her shoulder; he hadn't yet reached the first level. She was faster than he had been. She was going to make it. Safety was almost within reach. Almost. *You can rest later. Get out of here now.* She ran out through the doorway and into the street. She looked both ways down the deserted fog-bound street, praying for a passing patrol car. Nothing. Only a car going in the opposite direction. She raised her arms, the shoes waving maniacally in the air, and shouted for help. But the car raced past, its taillights lost to the mist, dimming like closing eyes.

Still barefoot, she started to run down the street, away from the garage, splashing in puddles, soaking her feet. Only when she was half a block away and her office building was in reach did she dare to turn around. She gasped and stepped backward as she saw a dim figure coming out of the garage, protected by the night and mist, flat, two-dimensional, featureless. She could not make out height or weight, or even sex, she thought; she would never be able to describe the person.

The figure paused, looked after her, *knew she had won,* then started to run up the street in the opposite direction and was quickly swallowed up by the fog.

She was finally safe. Although she still didn't feel it.

She ran the rest of the way back to her office and pounded on the revolving doors for the building guard to let her in. Her legs and raincoat were muddied. Her hair was flattened against her face. Rain trickled down her back. Her body was still chilled with fear.

"Ben, hurry!" she pleaded, and finally the old guard plodded to the door and unlocked it to let her in.

"Someone was chasing me," she gasped. "In the garage. My car wouldn't start and there was someone there."

The white-haired guard was instantly alert. "We'd better call the police."

"Thank you," Paula said weakly, and slumped into his reclining swivel chair.

Two officers arrived within minutes. Paula had finally caught her breath and dried herself with a handkerchief Ben had given her. She put her shoes back on.

"There was someone in the garage who was chasing me," she repeated. "I was parked on the roof level and my car wouldn't start and I was going down to the street to call a cab when I heard footsteps behind me. I was able to outrun whoever it was."

One of the policemen nodded. "I don't think we'll catch him.

He's probably long gone. Let's take a look at your car. Maybe we can help you with that."

"No," Paula said. "Let it keep till the morning. I'll just call a cab now and take care of it then."

"Would you like us to stay with you until the cab comes?"

Paula shook her head limply. "Thank you, but I'm all right. Just a little shaken up, that's all. I'll just wait here."

The cab arrived in ten minutes and took Paula home. She asked the driver to wait until she got into the house.

Hugh was at the door the second he heard her key in the lock.

"Where have you been? Do you know what time it is? I've been so worried. I've been walking back and forth for the last two hours." He saw her pale face and trembling body. "My God, Paula, what happened?" he asked, shocked.

"I was almost mugged," Paula blurted out, then told him about the garage.

"Why didn't you call me?" he asked, his voice raised, almost yelling, angry at her for being hurt. "I would have come down for you in a minute."

"I didn't want you to leave the children alone."

"We would have been back in less than an hour. They can stay by themselves. But forget all of that." He put his arms around her, rubbed the back of her neck, which was cold and wet from her evaporating perspiration. "As long as you're all right."

Swept up by the warmth of his touch, she nodded. "I am now."

"You must have been so frightened," he said, soothing her. "Why don't you get out of those wet things and take a hot shower?" He led her up the stairs and into the bathroom.

"It's all right," Hugh said, his voice still worried, yet calmative as he continued to stroke her. "The danger is over."

A half hour later Paula came out of the shower drying her hair. She managed a smile. "I'm feeling better now."

He had a cup of hot tea ready for her, which she sipped gratefully.

"I tried phoning you about ten," he said, "but nobody picked up. I thought you were on your way home."

"Once the switchboard closes at seven-thirty we can't take

incoming calls except on our private lines. I was in Glenn's office and probably didn't hear my phone. I'm sorry."

"No, *I'm* sorry you went through what you did. I knew I should have picked you up."

"It wasn't your fault, Hugh. I wouldn't have let you come for me."

"And I swear, Paula," he added earnestly, "that you'll never be in danger again. I won't allow it."

The next morning Hugh drove Paula to the office, then called Triple A to come and jump-start the car. When the mechanic tried the engine he shrugged and said, "Battery sounds fine." He opened the hood and immediately identified the problem. "Ignition wire shook loose."

He reattached it and started the car.

Chapter 9

SATURDAY MORNING HUGH AND THE CHILDREN GOT fiercely competitive over a game of Asteroids on Jeremy's Atari while Paula made pancakes for breakfast. She was flipping the first batch when her mother called.

"How about doing a little shopping today?" Marilyn asked. "I don't really need anything but it will give us a chance to get together. Do you realize we haven't seen each other alone since you two got back from your honeymoon?"

Paula did realize. She and her mother talked almost every day but in the three weeks since she had moved into Hugh's house they had not spent any time alone together. Marilyn had been over for lunch the previous Sunday, but both had missed the private girl talk they had so frequently enjoyed. Shopping was the perfect excuse. Paula would leave the children with Hugh and the computer games.

But Hugh wanted to go shopping with her.

"Don't be silly," Paula laughed. "I can't imagine you'd want to go shopping with me. I don't think there's a man anywhere who actually *wants* to go shopping with his wife. Besides, you're almost finished with your book. Why don't you work today?"

"Because"—he circled her with his arms—"I have been working all week, need to take today off, and I'd rather spend the time with you than with my keyboard and terminal." He brushed his lips to hers. "You taste like pancake syrup, you know?"

"I've been nibbling."

"I'd like to do a little nibbling too." Hugh passed his tongue over her lips again. "Let's go shopping," he prodded. "Maybe we can get you something nice. And something for the kids."

"You want to go shopping with the children too?" Paula asked with a smile of incredulity. "I think I've died and gone to heaven. I couldn't get Michael near a department store with any of us on a Saturday."

"I'm not Michael. And if I haven't said this too many times yet, I really *like* being with you, Paula. At home. In a department store. Anywhere."

"I know."

"Did you also know that when you're at work I think about you a lot?" He smiled and touched her forehead with the tip of his finger, trailed it down her nose and chin. "I keep that picture your mother took at the wedding on top of my computer when I'm working and I find myself staring at it. It's very distracting."

"You should be concentrating on your writing," Paula laughed.

"Come on. Let's all go out together. We'll get something for everybody and we won't come home until we do."

"I promised my mother—"

"Believe me, she'll be delighted. Just remind her how miserable you were with Michael and now you're married to a man who actually likes shopping. And buying."

Paula raised her shoulders in indecision. The offer was so tempting, but she didn't want to disappoint her mother. Then she saw Hugh's face darken.

"Besides," he added seriously, his voice low, "I'm still worried because of what happened at the garage."

"Oh, Hugh . . ." she protested.

"When I'm not with you, Paula, I'm afraid something's going to happen to you."

His eyes were so wide and filled with concern and love, Paula had to give in. "I guess I can see my mother during the week at lunchtime. We'll find a day when she's not teaching and get together. Hey—I haven't told you about Michelle. Her tastes are getting awfully expensive. That little kid could break you."

"If we're all together, Paula," he said, "then nothing can break us. *Nothing,*" he repeated. "You remember that."

Marilyn hid her disappointment. She had wanted to get together with Paula for the day but lunch the following week would be okay. She recalled all the times Paula had complained about how Michael was ignoring her and the children. Hugh was a polar opposite; he wanted to spend every free moment he had with his family. There was nothing wrong with that, Marilyn accepted, except that she was feeling a little left out. But she had had Paula and the children to herself for years and couldn't begrudge Hugh wanting a turn with them now.

And besides, she would at least see the children tonight. Hugh and Paula were going to dinner at Joan's house and she had been pressed into baby-sitting.

It was a successful shopping day for everyone. Paula and Michelle each got new dresses and ski parkas and Hugh and Jeremy walked the aisles of the sporting goods shops looking at bindings and boots, comparing the merits of short versus longer skis. Jeremy had outgrown his equipment from the previous year and was thrilled to be outfitted with brand-new everything.

They brought a pizza home with them which Paula gave to the children. She took a shower to get ready to go out and when she came out of the bathroom Hugh was stretched out in bed, his back propped against his pillow.

"Come on," Paula prompted. "Joan likes her guests to be on time." She grabbed Hugh's hand and tried to pull him off the bed. She was surprised at his resistance. She dropped his hand and his arm fell limply to the bed. "What is it, darling?" she asked, concerned.

Hugh shrugged listlessly. "I haven't really been feeling well all day."

"What's wrong?"

"A little stomach thing, maybe. Nothing serious." He forced a smile. "Not your pancakes, I promise, but I started to feel a bit off this morning. I guess I got up with something. I tried to ignore it and shake it—apparently unsuccessfully."

"You barely touched your lunch," Paula remembered.

"I guess it got the better of me. I'll be all right." He put both his palms on the bed and lifted himself up to a sitting position. "I'm tough."

Paula sat down next to him. "Do you have a fever?" She touched his forehead.

"I don't think so."

"No, you're cool."

"Just one of those stomach things, I guess." He touched a spot above his belt. "A churning right here."

"I'd better call Joan and cancel."

"No, I don't want you to do that," Hugh said. "I'll get through the evening. I'll fake being pleasant." He winked at her. "In other words I'll be my usual self."

"Your usual self does not have to fake," Paula scolded him playfully. "And I'm not going to have you go out if you're not feeling well. Especially to a dinner party."

"Do you mind?" Hugh asked.

"Well, I hate to do it at the last minute. Joan's undoubtedly all prepared. But it would be worse if you went over there and just picked at your food."

"Tell Joan we'll make it up to her, okay? And tell her now she'll have her new guy all to herself."

"I don't know if she wants to," Paula laughed.

As she dialed she looked over at Hugh, who was still stretched out on the bed, his hand holding his stomach, tucked partly into his pants. Obviously the pain extended down below his belt.

"It's all right," Joan said. "I can use tonight as a test. This is the first time I've invited Marvin over to dinner. If he doesn't jump me I'll have him back again. Although I guess my real problem is I haven't yet found a guy I've really wanted to jump me. Like you have, Paula," she said.

"See you Monday," Paula said into the phone. "Hang in there."

She plopped down next to Hugh and watched him wince as she jolted the bed. "Sorry."

He put his arm around her shoulders and pulled her close to him. "I can take it. I'm tough, remember."

"Can I make you some tea or soup?"

He shook his head. "Nothing. Oh—you'd better call your mother. I guess we won't be needing her tonight."

She pulled the phone onto her stomach and dialed. As she talked to Marilyn Hugh nuzzled her neck in just the spot that always made Paula purr. She stifled a giggle and hurried her mother off the phone. She put the phone back on the night table and hit Hugh playfully. "You know I can't stand when you do that."

"Which is just why I do it."

"You can't be up for *that* tonight," Paula said.

"We'll see what I'm up for," he joked. His hand snaked down the front of her robe and teased her nipple. She snuggled in closer to him.

"Now," he asked. "Isn't this more fun than going out to dinner?"

Paula nodded dreamily, lost to the delight of Hugh's touch. "Yes, it is." She couldn't help but think if she had had more evenings like this with Michael there would have been no question of her going to New York with him. She would certainly go with Hugh—anywhere.

Later that evening the children were downstairs watching television and Hugh and Paula were slouching on the bed enjoying a movie on HBO. The phone rang and Paula reached for it.

"Paula," the familiar voice said. "Would you get your copy for the women's campaign? I want to suggest a change of wording."

"Yes, Dwight," she sighed. "In a second." She put her hand over the mouthpiece of the phone. "It's Hempster."

Hugh sat up in bed. "What does he want?"

Paula put a finger to her mouth to keep him quiet. "It'll only be a minute," she whispered. Hugh got up and turned down the sound on the television.

She went to her attaché case and pulled out the file they had worked on during the week. They had met with Hempster on Thursday at noon. He had basically liked what had been presented but seemed uncertain about some of the ad copy. He had promised to think about it and get back to them after the weekend.

"I've got it, Dwight," she said, and propped the phone between her ear and shoulder as she made notations. "That's good," she murmured. "That'll work. . . . Okay, I'll tell Glenn and Steve and we'll recast it on Monday." She pulled the phone away from her ear and scowled. "You could have at least said good night!" She slammed the phone down and shoved the folder back into her briefcase and turned up the sound on the TV. "Nothing that couldn't have waited until Monday morning," she fumed, then mimicked. "But it was on his mind and he wanted to test it out on me. Saturday night! He thinks he owns us!" She settled comfortably in next to Hugh again, reclaiming her curve-to-curve position of a moment before. But her body was still wound up from the phone call.

"He can't treat you that way," Hugh groused. "He doesn't have the right. You've got too much talent for bullshit like that. You should just tell Hempster what to do with himself and get to work on something of your own. That novel of yours is still waiting for you and I'd love to see you leave your job and finish it."

Paula sloughed it off. "I've done only two chapters. And I haven't even looked at it in months."

"It's quite good, you know."

Paula was surprised. "I didn't know you read it."

"I snuck a peek."

"You weren't supposed to see it, Hugh. I never even told you where I put it."

"Actually I helped you unpack it. Remember that box with all the books? It was right in there."

Paula remembered. "I guess it was. But I was afraid you'd—"

"Hate it," Hugh finished.

"I was embarrassed. I didn't want you to tell me you liked it if you didn't and I knew if you didn't like it I would be crushed."

Hugh smiled. "I liked it. End of problem."

"You can't tell that much from two chapters. A chapter and three quarters really. I didn't even finish the second chapter."

"I could tell it was good," Hugh said.

"Really?" she pressed, enjoying the compliment. Whether it was completely genuine or he was just being encouraging to her, she liked hearing his words.

"Really," he said. "And I think you know by now that I'm a little crazy when it comes to writing—Jason's called me a perfectionist. I'm not going to lie to you, Paula. It's good and should be worked on."

"Maybe," Paula said wistfully. "It's a lot of work—as you know."

"But it's fun. When it's working, when a scene or even a phrase is right, *feels* right, there's almost nothing better."

"I know. I feel that way about my ads sometimes. The writing makes me proud and gives me such a sense of accomplishment."

"Think how much more you'll have with a novel."

"It's tempting, believe me."

"It would be so nice to have you here all day." Hugh winked. "We can pinch each other in the hallways while we're both working."

"We'd never get any work done," Paula laughed.

"There's more to life than just working. There's—pinching."

"Pinching is very good," Paula said.

"And don't forget tickling."

"Tickling is—not as good," Paula laughed as she rolled away from Hugh's mincing fingers. "Stop, please," she begged. "You know I can't stand being tickled." He followed her across the bed. "Stop, I can't . . ." she continued to giggle.

He stopped and leaned over her, the play suddenly over. His body rubbed against hers, their faces inches from each other's.

"It's really tempting," she said, then questioned. "But don't you think it might be a little confining?"

"Confining?" Hugh repeated. "Having you here all day, all to myself? Never! Having you close by would be the most wonderful thing in the world."

"Someday," Paula said.

"Think about it."

He was pressing into her. "Tomorrow," she sighed. "I'll think tomorrow."

Chapter 10

JUDITH SAT IN HER CAR, PARKED ACROSS THE STREET FROM the elementary school which Michelle attended. The November afternoon was raw and windy. A moody sun had stayed behind thick gray clouds for the day and the sky was the gloomy leaden color of winter. The trees in the school yard were barren.

Judith checked her watch impatiently and watched the time inch toward three o'clock and the end of school. This wasn't the first day she had sat here waiting for school to finish, then observing at a distance as Michelle walked home. But this would be the day that—

A fire engine roared by, its wailing siren disrupting her thoughts. On the second floor of the school children stared out the windows at the passing fire trucks as they put on their coats. Judith thought she saw Michelle behind one of the windows; she knew which one was her classroom.

A few minutes later Michelle came out of school dressed in a light blue down jacket. She was walking with two little girls, one with pigtails, the other with dark curly hair. Her new friends. Both girls lived a distance away and would be taking the bus. Thankfully, for what Judith wanted to do, Michelle had not yet made any friends on her block and would be walking the short distance home alone.

Michelle said good-bye to the girls and started down the

street. She would walk two blocks until turning off into the cul-de-sac where she lived. Judith started to follow her, looking back at the brick school building. Paper cutout decorations adorned some of the windows of the younger grades. This was the school that John and Danielle would have attended. She and Hugh had bought their house because of the proximity to the school. John and Danielle would be six, in first grade. And she would be waiting here *right now* at three o'clock to take her twins home from school, give them snacks, and hear about their day. Her heart pulled as she thought about her children, then fixed on Michelle. It wasn't right that Michelle and her brother should live while her children were dead.

Even though nothing could bring John and Danielle back, there really could be retribution for what Hugh had done. While she couldn't bring him to justice she could still punish him by taking his new family away from him.

If only Paula had listened to her, she thought, she wouldn't have to be here today.

It had been a good day for Michelle. She had gotten a 100 on a surprise current events test and had come in second in the class spelling bee. There had been only two of them left when the word *independence* had given her trouble, and she had missed the next to last vowel, making it a shoo-in for the other girl. They had shaken hands and the teacher had the class applaud both of them for having successfully spelled words on a sixth-grade level. The school spelling bee would be held next month and the teacher was recommending that both children compete against the fourth- and fifth-graders in the auditorium. The thought of that made Michelle swell with pride. She had already made a mark in the new school. She couldn't wait to get home and tell her mother and Hugh. This was even worth a call to New York to her real father.

The woman stepped out from behind a lamppost and fell into step with her. Startled, Michelle stiffened and tried to separate herself from the woman who kept up pace with her.

"Hello . . ." Judith said.

Surprised that the woman was speaking to her, Michelle looked up sharply, then turned away and kept walking. She wasn't supposed to speak to strangers, that's what her mother had always said.

"Your name's Michelle, isn't it?" the woman asked.

Michelle cocked her head and hesitated. The woman knew who she was, but why didn't she recognize the woman? She tried to place her. A teacher in the school? Someone from the neighborhood? No—she was certain she had never seen this person before.

"I'm not supposed to talk to strangers," the little girl said definitively. She was on safe ground that way. She tucked her chin into her jacket and clutched her books and notebook tightly in her folded arms.

"But I'm not a stranger. My name is Judith. Do you know the name?"

The older woman loomed above her, uncomfortably close. She was walking near the fence of the school yard. Two boys from Michelle's class were playing handball against one of the walls in the yard. Michelle thought about going to join them but she didn't know them very well. Instead she took a step away from Judith and hoped the woman would just leave her alone.

"I was married to your father."

Michelle now knew who the woman was. It was like when Kathy spoke about her new father's *ex*. Judith was her new father's ex. And that meant she wasn't a stranger. Michelle relaxed, although she couldn't help but wonder what this woman wanted with her.

"I had two children. Did you know that?" Then without waiting for Michelle to answer, Judith continued, "Come walk with me to my car. I want to tell you about my children." She reached out toward the little girl. "Here, give me your hand, Michelle." Uncertainly, Michelle shifted her books to her right arm and let Judith take her left hand. The woman's palm was cold and moist.

"Danielle was a beautiful child. Just like you. She had auburn hair which she liked to wear in a ponytail, and the bluest eyes you've ever seen. They always seemed to follow you around the room. 'My little *Mona Lisa*' I called her, although she never knew who the *Mona Lisa* was. Do you know?" Michelle shook her head. "A very enigmatic woman. Like my Danielle would have become. Because even as a child she was coy and flirtatious. A room would light up when Danielle would smile. And John was a handsome, handsome boy. I loved my children the way I'm sure your mother loves you and Jeremy. I still love them but I know I'll never see them again. They died, you know."

Michelle did know, but the suddenness of what Judith said caught her off guard. Then Michelle said, "I'm sorry," remembering that's what you were supposed to say when you heard that someone had died, although the words were a mumble, she wasn't entirely comfortable with them.

"Excuse me?" Judith asked, then the words filtered through. "Oh, yes. You're sorry."

"Are you coming home with me?" Michelle asked, hoping that that was what Judith was doing, uncertain what this woman wanted with her. "Do you want to see Hugh?"

"They died in a fire," Judith said, not responding to Michelle's question. "Did you know that your stepfather set the fire?"

Michelle looked questioningly. She sifted Judith's words, trying to make sense out of them. Then she crinkled her nose distastefully and shook her head back and forth.

"No—"

"He did," Judith said. "He killed the children."

"I don't believe you," Michelle said uneasily, remembering what she had been told. "The fire was an accident."

"It wasn't," Judith said flatly. "He set it. Then he ran into the woods and disappeared. Later he pretended he wasn't there at all. But I saw him. Come." She tugged gently on Michelle's hand. "We must continue to walk. You know, I like walking with a little girl. I haven't done this in some time. I could almost love you like my own, Michelle, but of course I really can't."

Michelle looked both ways up the street, suddenly nervous and unsettled, feeling out of control of her circumstances. She didn't want to believe Judith, didn't want to think anything bad of Hugh, who she really loved now. And despite what Judith had said, she needed *right then* to get away from this woman and home to Hugh. She felt a mounting sense of something being very wrong. She had never before felt unsafe with an adult, and there was something about Judith that was making her feel that way now. Two boys walked nearby but she was afraid to cry out for fear they would laugh at her. Even though the day was cool, perspiration layered her body. "I don't want to talk to you anymore," she said. "I have to go home now."

"I tried to warn your mother not to marry Hugh. But she didn't believe me. Then I told her to get away from him, but she wouldn't listen. Everyone thinks I'm crazy, but I know what I saw. You don't think I'm crazy, do you?"

Michelle didn't want to think anything just then. She had never heard an adult speak this way before and she was frightened. Tears welled in her eyes. "I want to go home now," she cried, and tried to pull away, but Judith held fast to her hand.

"I'm sorry, Michelle," Judith said. "But not quite yet. We have to talk. I have to tell you things. Let's go to my car now. It's just around the corner."

"No—I don't want to—"

Michelle tried to stop, stand her ground, but was dragged forward, stiff-armed by Judith. She tried to step away but the older woman tightened her hold on Michelle's hand, cramping it. Her fingers felt numb, tingly.

"Let go of me," she whimpered, and started to cry. "I'm scared."

"Yes, of course you are, Michelle. And John and Danielle were scared too. Very scared," Judith said bitterly. "Do you know what they experienced? How they died? No—you couldn't possibly. They died a horrible, horrible death."

"No," Michelle said and shook her head. Tears slipped down her face.

"Yes, I want you to hear this, Michelle. I want you to know what it was like for them. What *he* did. So you will understand why I have to . . . do this."

"No, I don't want to hear—"

"They died slowly, painfully—"

"No—"

"Helplessly," Judith said over her. "And they watched it coming. They knew they were going to die. Even little children know when death is about to happen. Even though they don't *understand,* they *know.* I can still see my babies, hear their screams. As if it were this very day. Oh, how they suffered, Michelle."

"Please, I don't want to listen," Michelle whimpered.

" 'Help us, Mommy,' they cried to me," Judith continued pointedly, her voice growing more and more excited as she remembered the night. " 'The fire! It's hot. So hot . . .' I heard them through the bedroom door but flames blocked my way and I couldn't get to them from inside the house. So I ran outside to try to reach them. They saw me from the window and screamed to me to save them. They pounded on the glass. 'Mommy! Mommy!' The fire raged around them, burning the walls, the ceiling. The house was being consumed. 'Help us, Mommy!' they screamed. But then they inhaled the smoke and couldn't scream anymore. The glass became too hot to touch. The heat seared their faces and burned them. They must have been in terrible pain. I saw their eyes in the brightness of the flames, how terrified my children were. And how helpless I was. I couldn't get to them, couldn't save them. *I couldn't.*"

Then she abruptly broke off, her voice suddenly soft, reflective, her eyes turned inwardly. "Yes, they were scared, too, Michelle. They cried too. Because they knew what was happening to them."

"Please," Michelle begged.

"It's not right, is it?" Judith asked. "He shouldn't be able to get away with what he did. But you see, nobody believed me. I called the police. I told them what I saw. But they didn't believe me and sent me to a doctor. A doctor," she laughed. "Isn't that a joke?"

Michelle shook her head weakly, unable to say anything. She didn't know what Judith was talking about. She really didn't know anything right now except that Judith was holding her hand tightly, almost crushing it, and she felt very scared.

"That's why I have to do something. I won't let him have a family around him again. Because of what he did."

They were coming abreast of Judith's car. Frightened, Michelle tried to pull away again. She didn't want to get inside the car.

"Yes, my children were scared, Michelle. But you shouldn't be afraid. This will only take a moment. We'll soon be finished and then he will know that he can't . . ."

Judith opened the passenger door and pushed Michelle into the car and slammed the door behind her. The little girl sat wide-eyed in the seat, but when Judith went around to the driver's side to get in Michelle seized the moment. She grabbed the door handle and pushed hard, lurching out of the low car, fumbling, almost dropping her books but steadying them.

"Michelle!" Judith called from her side of the car and started around the front toward the girl.

"Don't you touch me!" Michelle cried, and keeping her hands close to her body so Judith couldn't grab hold of them again, she started to move farther away from the older woman, taking half-backward, half-sideways steps, always keeping Judith in her sight and making certain she was far enough away so she couldn't be captured again. "I'm going home now," she yelled. "I don't want to go anywhere with you. I don't like you." When she was confident she was safely out of Judith's reach, she turned her back and ran away.

She burst through the front door as Hugh was coming down the stairs to get a cup of coffee. She ran to him and threw her arms around him, crying, struggling for breath.

"What is it, honey?" Hugh asked and stroked her head.

Hugh set the fire. He killed my children.

Michelle sucked in her tears and pulled away from him. At arm's length she looked at him and couldn't imagine that he could have done such a thing. But still *she didn't know. And it was also possible her mother didn't know either.* And her mother was still at work and wouldn't be home for hours.

"What, baby? Talk to me. What's frightened you so much?"

"Where's Jeremy?" she asked, breathing deeply, staring at Hugh through animal eyes. She was regaining her breath but still wasn't calm. Her heart was pounding rapidly.

"He isn't home yet. Did somebody hurt you? What happened?"

"Judith said you set the fire that killed your children."

Hugh's jaw went slack. He knew why she was so frightened. "When did she say that?"

"Just now. Did you?" There was challenge to the child's voice and an odd go-for-broke fearlessness that completely dried her tears. While something inside of her was saying maybe she should be afraid, she wasn't any longer. She wanted an answer. "Did you?"

"No, darling, of course not," Hugh said, openly, expansively, filling with tears himself for what Judith had just put her through. "Of course not. Tell me about Judith. When did you see her?"

"She was outside of school. She took me to her car but I got out. She said you did those things. Did you?" she demanded. "Did you do what she said?"

Hugh knelt down next to the little girl and made a move to dry her tears. Michelle shied away from his touch toward the door, but it was closed and she had nowhere to go. Hugh persisted and finally was able to flick the tears from her eyes and push the hair off her forehead. He held the child with his eyes and spoke soothingly to her.

"None of what Judith said is true, baby. It's all a terrible lie." He watched her face, the catlike confusion that was still in her eyes. "You have to understand why she said those things. Because she wants to hurt me. She feels sad because her children have died and she has no one. She was very bitter and jealous and now I have you and Jeremy and your mother and I'm happy, and she doesn't want me to be happy. That's why she said all those terrible, terrible things."

Michelle looked at Hugh questioningly, not completely understanding but beginning to feel better. She let his calming words wash over her and, wanting to believe them, she sniffed back her tears and slowly regained control. Hugh had not set the fire. There was no danger to herself or her family.

"Now why don't you give me a big hug and kiss," Hugh prompted, and sudden exhaustion made Michelle quick to fall into his arms. The afternoon was a blur behind her.

Hugh waited for Paula at the door and herded her into the kitchen to tell her what had happened before she heard it from the children. He had already called his lawyer and gotten a restraining order against Judith's making any contact whatsoever with the children. It would be temporary until a court appearance scheduled for the following week would make it permanent, but the lawyer promised to have the sheriff personally inform Judith of the order. If she disobeyed it she would be in contempt of court and subject to being put in jail.

"Oh, Hugh, she can't do this. She has to leave us alone," Paula cried, and rushed upstairs to Michelle's room, where the little girl was doing her arithmetic homework. Paula watched her from the open door, hunched over her notebook as she tried to solve a problem with a stubby pencil.

Michelle sensed her mother's presence and ran to her, happily flinging her arms around her.

"Come, sit with me, baby," Paula said, and led Michelle over to the bed. "Hugh told me what happened today and I just want to make certain that you're all right."

Michelle smiled. "I know Hugh wouldn't have set the fire. And he said that Judith wanted to hurt him and you."

"That's right. And we've told Judith never to bother you again, so you don't have to worry about her. If she ever tries to talk to you again, you run the other way and immediately tell Hugh or me, okay?"

"Okay, Mommy. But I'm not scared anymore." Then she brightened. "I came in second in the spelling bee . . ."

Paula barely heard Michelle talk about what had happened to her at school today, just grateful that the episode with Judith was behind her. And praying it would be the last.

After dinner she told Hugh that she wanted her mother to pick up Michelle after school and bring her home.

"I agree that she should be picked up," Hugh said. "But *I'll* do it. It's a distance for your mother to travel every day and I'm right here."

"But I don't want to disturb you," Paula said. "My mother doesn't mind. And besides, Michelle is used to having her grandmother pick her up after school."

"But it'll take your mother until at least three-thirty to get here after she finishes teaching and I don't want Michelle in the school building after hours. I can pick her up at three. It's only a few minutes out of my day and, believe me, I want to." His chin rounded with bitterness. "Judith is my problem, and I'm the one who should deal with it. And I swear to you," he said, as if reading her mind, "I will not forget to pick up Michelle."

"You don't think Judith will defy the court order, do you?" Paula asked nervously.

"You know, I almost hope she does," Hugh said. "If I can put her away, get her out of our lives, then our problem will be solved."

"Yes, it will be," Paula said softly.

"Just let me pick Michelle up at school. Jeremy can take care of himself, I'm sure. If she dares to go near him he'll know enough to stay away from her."

"All right. But if it becomes too much for you, tell me immediately and my mother will be happy to come over."

"It won't become too much, Paula," Hugh said. "We don't need her. You and I don't need *anyone* else."

"No . . ." Paula said, although still filled with concern. She glanced out the back window at the moonless night. The yard was as black as pitch. There were no houses to the rear of them, no illumination from the street or porch lights in front. *Too dark,* she considered as she thought about what her mother had said when she first saw the house. *It's isolated, vulnerable.* Even in the daylight there was a forest of trees that could conceal watchers, intruders.

Hugh touched her lightly and whispered in her ear, "I won't let her disrupt our lives, Paula. I promise you."

Chapter 11

JUDITH CAME ALONE TO THE COURT HEARING. HUGH'S ATtorney presented the relevant facts—the background, the deaths of the children, Judith's accusations, all of the psychiatric reports. Clearly when she accosted Michelle she was trying to frighten the child and must be restrained from doing so.

Paula stole glances at Judith as she sat silently throughout the procedure, sorry it had had to come to court. Judith was perched stiffly on the edge of the wooden chair, looking very small and very alone. But Paula absolutely had to protect her children first. When the judge called upon Judith she was slow to respond, then she stood and faced the bench. She spoke softly, her throat dry, her voice weak. "I just wanted to warn Paula," she said, slaking her tongue over her lips, "and when I couldn't get through to her, I thought . . . I thought . . . I would try to talk to her child. . . ." She swallowed and looked quickly at Paula, her eyes teary and brimming with pity. Then she turned back to the judge and, defeated, said, "I won't bother them again, your honor. I swear it."

The judge quickly made the temporary order permanent and Judith was barred from any contact whatsoever with Jeremy or Michelle.

On the way home in the car Paula rubbed her eyes and stared blankly out the window, exhausted from the day. "She should be ordered to go for help," she said. "It's such a waste of a life this way. She's just vegetating, slowly killing herself."

"I agree," Hugh said. "But clichéd as it may sound, it still is a free country." Then he asked, "Does she worry you at all?"

"I'll be honest. Yes. But as long as the children understand her problems, they'll be able to turn the other cheek—if they have to." They had all had a long talk that night, explaining Judith's sickness, and why she was so jealous of Hugh.

Paula exhaled loudly. "You know, I feel for her. I can't help it. She's driving us crazy, she wants to break us up, but—" She laughed shortly. "I completely understand why she can't get herself together. A friend of my mother's lost a teenage child. The woman aged dramatically overnight. I don't think she'll ever get over the death. Nor will Judith."

She felt Hugh looking at her and turned to him. There was a tightness in his jaw and in his grip on the steering wheel, a nervous look in his eyes.

"Does *Judith's insistence* about—you know—concern you?" he asked cautiously.

Paula's eyes narrowed and a flash of anger crossed her face. "Don't be ridiculous, Hugh. How can you even ask me that? Or think I could have married you or stay with you if I had the slightest doubt."

"I'm sorry. But she has really been on our backs. And from advertising you know the more you hear something—"

"No," she said loudly.

"What about your mother?"

"No, stupid." Paula forced a laugh, trying to lighten the conversation, understanding then that after what they had just been through he felt insecure and had had to ask the question. "She doesn't think you set the fire either." She touched his shoulder tenderly and watched him relax.

The McKittrick Company was having its hundred and tenth anniversary party. They were taking over Tavern on the Green in New York and flying down the staff of the Boston office, inviting salesmen from around the country, agents, editors, authors, and bookstore buyers. Jason called Hugh personally to extend the invitation, offering to put him and Paula up for several days in the Sherry-Netherland hotel on Fifth Avenue. An invitation that could not be turned down.

Paula was pleased at the prospect of getting the children out of Boston for a few days and asked her mother to come with them.

They spent two days walking and shopping New York, seeing a Broadway show and taking the children through FAO Schwarz, the toy store. The night of the party they let Jeremy and Michelle and Marilyn, who was pressed into baby-sitting service, order anything they wanted from room service as they dressed for the affair.

They took a cab up Central Park West and turned into the entrance to Tavern on the Green, which was all lit up against the New York night. Thousands of tiny lights dazzled on the surrounding trees.

They passed through the restaurant to the private rooms in the rear. The windows opened onto the park, where a light snow had started to fall, sparkling in the lights on the trees. The room was springlike with colorful floral arrangements. Waiters circulated with hot and cold hors d'oeuvres and glasses of champagne. A band played in the corner of the room and couples were dancing.

Hugh greeted Jason and the other McKittrick executives and introduced Paula to the head of the Book-of-the-Month Club and Sol Gewirtz, his agent, a short, dour-looking man who was grumbling that he wished he had a tenth of what McKittrick was shelling out for the party. "Don't worry," he growled to Hugh, as he held a drink in one hand and a plate in the other, "we'll rape Jason on the next deal."

"An agent's heart." Hugh grinned, and at that moment Jason joined them and said, mugging, "Where? Find me one."

Sol then pulled Jason into a huddle and Kate came forward. She was dressed in a black organza evening dress and a strand of pearls. She was excited about tonight and had thought of little else all day when she checked in with McKittrick's New York office. Her stomach had been fluttering since early morning.

"How is your novel coming along, Mr. Tolson?" she asked, batting her eyelashes. "I'm such a passionate fan of yours, I can't wait to read it."

"If I only had three million fans like you, Katie," Hugh grinned, pleased.

"If you need any help at all on typing, or editing, just let me know. . . ."

"You know I will."

A smile passed between them and Paula took his hand possessively. "Shall we dance, Hugh?"

"Sure. Would you excuse us, Kate? We'll see you a little later."

Hugh twirled Paula onto the dance floor beneath the rotating disco lights. Other couples danced past them, and as Hugh spun Paula around she caught a glimpse of Kate watching them. The younger woman turned away as her eyes met Paula's.

Later, when Paula went to the ladies' room, Kate asked Hugh to dance.

As soon as he put his arms around her, Kate practically melted. She had had several glasses of champagne and the combination of the wine, the soft lights over the dance floor, and the closeness to Hugh made her knees weaken. She almost slipped between his arms and he caught her and supported her as he twirled her around the floor.

"How are you feeling?" he whispered into her ear.

"Wonderful," she sighed. She was feeling lighter than air, more like a woman than at any other time in her life. She closed her eyes, rested her head against his shoulder, pressed her body next to his. She had to make him know how much she wanted him, how good she would be to him. "Wonderful," she repeated in a wistful voice as airy as she was. "And so are you." She hoped her touch and scent were arousing him.

But then the dance was over and Kate watched as Hugh weaved across the floor toward Paula and swept her up in his arms. And as they laughed they danced again.

Back in their hotel room, Paula stood at the window looking out at the view of Central Park and lights of Manhattan.

"Absolutely breathtaking, isn't it?"

Hugh came up next to her and met her glance warily in the glass. "You're not thinking you made a mistake by not coming to New York with Michael are you?"

Paula turned to him, surprised. "Not at all. That was the furthest thing from my mind. None of this would be the same if you weren't here."

"That's all I want to hear." Hugh kissed her neck, then

wrapped his arms around her waist and lifted her, hurtling her onto the bed, where he jumped on top of her, both of them giggling like children.

Neither was ready to sleep. They lay comfortably next to each other and Paula said thoughtfully, "I think Kate's in love with you."

Hugh sounded surprised. "She's only a child."

"She is not a child. She's an adult and I've been watching her and I think she's in love. I don't think she took her eyes off you all night."

Hugh shrugged. "Well, I've certainly given her no encouragement. One time she tried to come on to me, but I just turned it into a joke so she'd know I wasn't serious. I'm always friendly to her because she helps me so much, but that's all." He grinned. "Jealous?"

"A little."

"Well, don't be. I have no more interest in Kate than I have in—Sol Gewirtz."

Paula started to laugh at the image of the man whose mouth hadn't stopped all evening—either talking or chewing. "That makes me feel pretty safe." She thought of asking Hugh to say something to Kate, maybe deflect her. But why call attention to anything? She would eventually get the message and go out and find someone for herself.

"Tired?" Hugh asked.

"A little," she answered drowsily, dreamily.

"Happy?"

"You know it."

"Me too."

In the light that slanted into the room they smiled at each other. Then Hugh asked, "Too tired?"

Paula laughed. "God, yes!"

"Good. Me too. So I'll just lie here and tell you how much I love you, how much I worship you, how much you mean to me. . . . Have I left anything out?"

"You're doing fine."

"How I'll never let anyone take you away from me, Paula."

"More." She snuggled in closer to him.

"And how I'll never let you go either." He raised himself up and touched her lips with his. *"Never, Paula,"* he repeated. "I swear it."

In a downtown hotel Kate turned off the television. She had tried to watch a movie but couldn't keep her mind on the story. She was thinking about tonight. About what should have happened.

It had been the first time she and Hugh had danced, in fact the first time they had touched so intimately. She had been waiting for such a moment. She had been excited, and knew that from Hugh's pressure against her leg he had been too. That he wanted her was not the question; his body had told her that. But he had broken away from her abruptly afterward, with just a hurried thank you, not even an acknowledgment of what had passed between them, to go right back to Paula.

That's what the problem was, Kate knew, that's why her plan hadn't worked. Hugh couldn't appear interested in her when his wife was there watching him.

... *if only I wasn't married* ...

It was Paula who was keeping Hugh from her.

Paula was the problem, she thought angrily. Like Judith had been the problem.

Kate put a cigarette in her mouth and lit it. She watched as the flames spiraled down the length of the match, almost burning her fingers.

Well, she reassured herself, there were solutions to problems, weren't there?

Chapter 12

IT IS A KNOWN FACT THAT GOSSIP IN AN OFFICE CAN FLOW from office to office, floor to floor faster than the speed of sound. Therefore, what Paula heard when she arrived late came as a surprise to her, although the source—a clerk in the accounting department—didn't surprise her at all. Glenn Adams had accepted another job.

Joan had heard it already, from another source altogether, and came into Paula's office. Anything was better than working, especially prime gossip such as this.

"A New York firm. Otis and Keene. Creative director."

Paula whistled, impressed. Otis and Keene billed out fiftyfold what Taplinger & Witt did. "How does Arthur feel? Or shall I ask the mail boy coming around for some up-to-the-minute information?"

"No, I can answer that," Joan said. "A little put out because he thinks of us as a family, but he's happy for Glenn. It's a big step up for him. So I don't think Arthur's going to ask him to clear out his desk by noon and have the guard escort him out of the building."

Amanda buzzed. "Arthur wants to see you, Paula."

"Be right there. Lunch today, Joan?"

"You bet."

Paula was surprised to see that Glenn was sitting in Arthur's office and the two men were enjoying a joke, obviously off-color because they both silenced together as she came in. She could be one of the boys, she knew, but she would never be one of the boys.

She immediately offered Glenn her congratulations. "I just heard. I think it's terrific for you. When did all this happen?"

"Last week. Absolutely unsolicited. I would never pick up and leave you guys, but Jim Otis asked me to fly down and talk to them and one thing led to another and . . . well, he made me an offer I couldn't refuse." He smiled sheepishly. "So I guess I'm going to leave you guys at that."

"I'm asking him to give us three weeks severance pay," Arthur laughed. "I feel like I've been fired. Either that or kicked in the ass."

"And I've promised not to take anybody with me," Glenn said, referring to clients who often jumped agencies with their creative personnel, as well as to associates of an executive who might be wooed away with him to the new firm. "I love you all too much to do that."

"Which brings us to part two of this meeting," Arthur said, pausing dramatically. "When Glenn told me what was up, we talked about replacements for him as creative director. You headed both of our lists, Paula."

"Congratulations," Glenn said.

"I think we've got some breathing room for a bit now so you can get settled in," Arthur continued. "Everything will be slow because of the holidays, Hempster's under control, thank God, the new presentations are all coming along nicely, although now *you'll* have to make them, so plan on spending some time with Phil and Steve and the other groups." A broad grin broke out on Arthur's face as he enjoyed the stunned expression on Paula's. "Which part of this aren't you getting, Paula?"

Her mouth was hanging open she knew. Everything was happening too fast. She let it sink in. She was being offered the job of creative director.

Arthur winked at her. "We'll discuss salary later, but in anticipation of coming to a mutually acceptable figure, I assume your answer is yes. Please say yes, Paula," he twinkled.

"I don't think I'm capable of saying anything right now!" she exclaimed happily, overwhelmed by the moment. "I guess yes.

Let me talk to Hugh, but why not? Sure." Creative director at thirty-three. Not bad at all.

"Think about it overnight and let me have your answer in the morning. And it better be positive."

"I don't start in New York until after the first, so I'll be around for at least another week," Glenn said. "I'll be able to pass everything over to you cleanly, and it'll give you a little time to hire someone to fill your old slot."

"O—kay," Paula said in a dizzy, playful tone, indicating she still hadn't absorbed it all.

She skipped out of the office and Arthur's secretary beamed at her. "Best of luck to you, Paula."

"Thanks, Helen," she said, wondering how many others already knew. The offices had to be bugged, she swore.

She immediately went back to her office, shut the door, and dialed Hugh.

"Glenn Adams is leaving as C.D. and Arthur just offered me the job."

She waited for his words of congratulations and was surprised when there was only silence over the phone.

"Did you hear me, Hugh?" she asked.

He cleared his throat. "Yes. That's wonderful news indeed. Did you take it?"

"Not officially. There are still details to be worked out." She wondered about the distance in his tone. "Why? Is there anything the matter?"

"Oh, no, of course not."

"What's wrong, Hugh?"

"Nothing. I'm very happy for you."

"Why don't I feel that then?"

"I don't know what you're talking about, Paula. It's a wonderful promotion, a fantastic opportunity. It proves your worth and I know how much it means to you."

The words were there, but she still didn't hear it in his voice. So much of the excitement in getting the job was being able to share it with him and she was surprised and disappointed with his reaction.

"We'll talk about it tonight, okay?"

"Let's go out to dinner and celebrate," Hugh suggested.

"No, let's stay home tonight. We'll talk."

"That's fine too. Whatever you want. I love you, Paula." And Paula thought she caught a note of fear creep into his voice.

"I love you, too, Hugh."

She tried to enjoy lunch. She and Joan traded advertising gossip and picked apart others in the industry. Joan toasted Paula's promotion as a great day for the sisterhood. But she saw that Paula's heart wasn't really in it.

"What's wrong?" she asked. "Why aren't you flying?"

"I don't know," Paula answered. "I hope nothing."

"Are you nervous about the job?"

Paula shook her head. "No." Then she offered a smile. "It'll work out."

"How could it not? You've got a great support team here. Me! I guarantee not to undermine you."

The afternoon dragged. Paula wanted to leave early, but felt that today wasn't the day to do it. She finished up a storyboard she had started for a local television station's news department that was trying to boost its ratings. She wasn't satisfied with her work; her mind was on other things—how happy she should be now, and why she wasn't.

Hugh kissed her when she came in and he smiled weakly at her.

"How was your afternoon?" he asked.

"Pretty lousy," she admitted.

"Mine too. Say hi to the kids and let's go into the den. I've mixed some martinis."

Hugh was waiting for her. He had built a fire.

"I'm happy for you, Paula," he said. "Really."

"What is it, Hugh?" she asked. "What aren't you saying to me?"

"Nothing," he said broadly.

"Hugh, talk to me." She was frightened suddenly.

"I'm happy for you," he repeated. "It's really wonderful news. You deserve it."

"But . . . ?"

"No buts," he hedged, then smiled awkwardly. "But here." He pulled two stubs out of his pocket. "Tickets to the new Marsha Norman play in Boston. They're for tomorrow night. I was holding them to surprise you." Her eyes lit up. He knew she had wanted to see it. "You're going to laugh, but I count on your being home every day at the same time—that helps me to be so spontaneous."

"But what, Hugh?" she pressed again, glossing over his joke. "What do you want to say to me?"

He gathered his thoughts and exhaled. "Look, maybe I'm wrong to say anything at all—"

"No, I want you to—"

"—and believe me, I apologize for being such a wet blanket this morning and spoiling your excitement." He took her hands and held her at arm's length. "I'm so proud of you, honey. Becoming creative director is an absolutely terrific accomplishment and you really deserve the promotion . . . but I guess what I'm a little afraid of is what's going to happen to us when you take the job. There's going to be a lot of pressure on you—because of the job itself and because you're a woman, and I'm sure there are going to be time commitments up the kazoo—dinners you'll have to attend with Arthur, new clients to entertain, emergency meetings, evening hours and weekends. You've told me how hard Glenn works, and knowing you you'll probably work twice as hard. You'll always be running around. You'll exhaust yourself. You'll start living on antacids . . . and we'll end up rarely seeing each other."

Paula watched him closely, hearing what had been in his voice at lunchtime. "There's a lot involved," she admitted quietly.

"Maybe I'm not as liberated as I'd like to think I am," Hugh continued. "Maybe I'm more traditional and would prefer my wife didn't work, especially because we don't need the money. But I respect your wanting to work, and because of that, you *should* work. I guess what I'm trying to say in my own bumbling way is that I'm afraid of your working too hard, taking on too much . . ." He shrugged. "Maybe even eventually becoming like Michael."

"Never," Paula said softly, dropping his hands. "Michael denies himself a life. I would never do that."

"Until you get caught up in the pressures of the business, the excitement of it too." He looked away from her, into the fire. "Because of what happened to you and Michael, I'm afraid it could also happen to us, Paula. In reverse." He turned back to her, his eyes pained and eager. "I so look forward to your coming home every night. I'm cooped up in the house all day working, and I can't tell you the excitement that runs through me as the afternoon passes, the anticipation. Even if I'm caught up in my writing, I can't help but watch the clock, looking forward to your coming home to me. To us. Look, I'm being very honest with you about my feelings, and maybe I'm being a selfish shit, but if I am I'm being selfish for both of us. What we have is so special, and I wouldn't want to risk losing it."

"No," Paula said distantly, surprised by what Hugh had just thrown at her. Then she finished the thought. "I wouldn't want to either." She had never thought herself so driven to succeed in the job that she could ever see sacrificing her life for it.

But being creative director was not just a job. It was *the job,* a position she had always distantly dreamed about. To be an advertising copywriter was to strive to be creative director. And to be a *young, female* C.D. would put her on top of the world. She would be a good one. But at what cost? That was the question now. Creative directors lived in a constant whirlwind as they assumed complete responsibility for every campaign the company took on. It was where the buck began and stopped and began again. Glenn had driven that point home when he had dragged a gag ball and chain into her office and symbolically turned it over to her. She had laughed and tied the chain to her leg. But she wasn't laughing anymore.

Suddenly things had become a lot more complicated.

She looked off into the fire as it lapped at the top of the hearth. She blurred her eyes and let the flames form figures, imagining them as dancing spinning couples in embrace, intertwined, the movement of one affecting the other. Like she and Hugh were a couple, any decision made by one affected the other. Especially one as important as this.

"You want me to turn down the job, don't you?" she asked softly.

"I want you to do what you want," he said earnestly. "I know how important this can be for you, how much it proves your talent. I just wanted you to be aware of the possible problems so we can know what we're up against."

"I could try to be both," she said hopefully. "Creative director and the wife that I am now." But even as she said the words she knew she wouldn't be giving the job her full attention if she was always concerned about time and what Hugh was feeling. There would be too much juggling involved and something would have to end up suffering. She couldn't shortchange Arthur or the company, not after they gave her her chance. Nor could she shortchange Hugh and their life together.

"You know, if I was Michael, or *any man* who didn't want to chuck it all and live off the land, the decision wouldn't be so difficult. There would be no decision. I would grab it in a minute. I guess women have softer genes than you guys or something."

There were no other lights in the room and the firelight danced across her face, caressing it in sleepy patterns of light and shadows. She looked away from Hugh. This was such an unexpected opportunity.

"Damn! Why do they have to make things so hard?" She shook a fist at the air and feigned exploding. "Why couldn't this day have been like any other? Take back your offer, Arthur Witt! Don't make me have to decide." But she shook her head and smiled sadly. There was really no decision. Not when her marriage was so new and so precious.

"For the job to be what I'd want it to," she said slowly, thoughtfully, working it out for herself as much as for him, "I would need to spend too much time away from you and the children, Hugh, and—that's just not something I'm willing to trade off right now. We're a family and that has to come first." She turned it over once more, then stated definitively, "It'll be hard to do, believe me, and I'm sure Arthur will think I'm crazy, but I'm going to tell him no."

"Only if you can do it without regrets," Hugh said nervously. "If for one moment you will regret this decision or resent me or our marriage in any way, I would say don't turn it down, take it and let's chance what happens."

"No, there will be no regrets," Paula promised. "Just talking it out like we are, knowing how you feel, and knowing as well that you're right, I wouldn't even want to chance the future. The hassles that come with the job are unavoidable. And it wouldn't be fair to Arthur to take the job only to give it up shortly. I'm happy in what I do now. I get a good deal of satisfaction. And at least we all know they think I'm good. I'm sure Arthur will understand."

"After all, you can tell Arthur we're still newlyweds," Hugh offered. "Maybe you can take the job later, after we've gotten a little older, a little more crotchety. . . ." He smiled. "When some of the romance is gone."

"The romance will never be gone," Paula said as she searched his eyes. "Don't even think that. And we'll always be newlyweds. I promise you."

"I pray," Hugh whispered. He held out his arms to her and she let him fold them around her.

It had all come down to what she wanted most, she thought, and she knew that it was *this*. This, and something else she had been thinking about.

"I want to have a child with you, Hugh," she said. "Soon."

"Yes," he agreed. "I had been thinking exactly the same thing."

He kissed her deeply, passionately, and when they pulled apart he said, "And like I offered this morning, let's go out to dinner tonight and celebrate. Anyway. The four of us. Our family."

"That sounds good to me," Paula said. Because it really did.

And there would be no regrets.

Except perhaps one, she thought distantly. With his support it might have worked. They could have at least given it a try.

Chapter 13

THE FIRST LASTING SNOW CAME AS SCHOOL WAS BREAKING for the Christmas holidays. In the backyard Hugh and the children built an entire family and then went sledding on a local hill. They all went together to buy a Christmas tree and spent the Saturday before Christmas stringing decorations. Paula was grateful for the holiday diversions. It freed her from having to think about the C.D. job and the new creative director Arthur had hired away from another agency, a sharp enough man—Nathan Blume—although Paula felt he couldn't hold a candle to her talent. She had thought she had her emotions under control but had gotten into a fight with Nathan about a new campaign they were starting for a local fast-foods outfit, the new man wanting to go with comedy and Paula insisting it would work better with a radio jingle. They took the argument up to Arthur, who offered to consider both ideas, then held Paula longer in his office to tell her he was supporting Nathan.

"But I know I'm right," Paula complained. "Studies show that music—"

"I know what the studies show," Arthur yelled at her for the first time since she had worked for him, "but Nathan is still C.D. and I'm going to let him run the show the way he wants. That's why I hired him. And in any event there are ways of handling things that don't involve fights that stretch down the hall. Besides"—he softened his voice and looked at her almost fatherly—"this isn't about the campaign, is it? You turned down the job, Paula. Nobody twisted your arm not to take it."

"No," Paula said contritely.

"Do you need a little time off? Would that help you at all?"

"No." Paula shook her head and inhaled deeply to calm herself. "And I'm rather ashamed right now for acting like I did. I'll go apologize to Nathan."

"Thanks, Paula," Arthur said. "Remember, we're all still a team here." And, as they both concluded, she was only thirty-three, her working life was far from over, and soon she would find time enough to take on the job. Paula just hoped that the new C.D. wouldn't be so well entrenched by then that there wouldn't be an opening for her.

She didn't tell Hugh about the fight with Nathan, knowing he would see through it immediately as well and be upset by it. And as she helped Hugh and the children hang the star on top of the Christmas tree, taking candid snapshots with the Polaroid, she truly had no regrets about her decision. Especially when they all stood together in the living room, threw the switch, and watched as the tree lit up in a burst of color and brilliance. Because *this* was what gave the most meaning to her life—not a radio jingle, not the job of creative director. And the next year there might even be another child.

Marilyn came over with presents on Christmas Eve and they all sang carols. Michael called to wish them happy holidays and to make certain they had received his gifts, which Paula assured him were under the tree. They built a fire, toasted marshmallows, and roasted chestnuts. They had a midnight snowball fight and enjoyed the slightly salty taste of the flurries that had started to fall.

Marilyn slept over on Christmas Eve, and the next morning dawned white and brilliant with a light dusting of snow. They ripped open presents and littered the living-room floor with ribbons and wrapping paper. After assigning Jeremy and Michelle to the clean-up brigade, Marilyn took the children to church. Then Paula sent Hugh upstairs to his office to work while she prepared a holiday dinner of turkey, stuffing, yams, and cranberries.

She was in the kitchen when the doorbell rang.

She grabbed a towel to dry her hands on the way to the door.

"Who is it?" she called, and when there was no answer opened the door anyway, a Merry Christmas smile on her face . . . which fell when she saw Judith standing at the entranceway.

"You're not supposed to be . . . ?" Paula said, startled. Her instinct was to close the door, but as she was confronted by the other woman she stood rooted. Her eyes squinted against the sparkle of the sun's reflection on the snow.

"Please don't be angry with me," Judith said. "I don't want you to hate me. I want to apologize for all the problems I've caused you and the children. Here—I brought these for them." She held two colorfully wrapped packages out in front of her.

"I don't think it's a good idea, Judith . . ." Paula mumbled, softening. "I know how Hugh thinks and this would upset him. He's upstairs now and I don't want him to know that you're here."

"Please, we don't have to tell him."

Judith shoved the gifts at Paula, who had no choice but to take them. Then they stood for a moment looking at each other. Paula couldn't help but feel uncomfortable at the awkwardness of the situation. This used to be Judith's house; she wasn't accustomed to ringing the bell, standing outside on the doorstep. But it was *her* house now—Judith hadn't wanted to keep it after the divorce—and Paula knew it wouldn't be right to invite the other woman in.

"Paula, I'm so worried about you," Judith blurted out. She pounded her fist against her palm in frustration. "How do I convince you to take me seriously!" Then she lowered her voice to a whisper for fear Hugh might hear her. "I can't help it. I know what's going to happen, because it happened to me. Every day you stay with him he will get worse and worse, more and more possessive of you until it's too late. Then he'll never let you go. Even if you want to. He'll kill you first."

"Judith, please," Paula said softly, averting her eyes. "I know what you think Hugh did, and I'm so terribly sorry it's eating you up alive." She was no longer angry or upset, nor did she anymore want to play therapist. She was just tired of it all. "Please, Judith, go home. Forget about Hugh, about us, and find a life for yourself." She started to close the door. "I'm sorry, but it's cold and I have a turkey cooking and have to go in. Thank you for the presents. I'll make certain the children get them."

"You don't have to tell them who they're from," Judith said nervously. "I know I'm not supposed to have any contact with them, so you don't have to tell them. Just say a friend, okay? A friend who cares about them."

"I will," Paula said, feeling bad that she was shutting the other woman out of what had been her house. And *she* had never been this rude to anyone before. "Merry Christmas, Judith," she said softly, "and believe me I wish you well. I do. . . ."

Paula closed the door and leaned against it. Then she went to the window, pulled back the curtain, and peered out. Judith was slowly walking down the path to her car. Her shoulders were slumped and from the back she looked like an old woman.

Then Judith turned and looked back over her shoulder and the two women stared at each other. Paula was the first to break the contact by letting the drapes flutter closed, although she couldn't help but be affected by the haunted look in Judith's eyes, and tears dotted her own.

Hugh came racing down the stairs. "I just saw her from my window. What did she want?"

Paula sniffed back her tears, not wanting to show Hugh she was in any way touched by the woman's visit. Angrily he opened the door, ready to run out after her, but her car was already pulling away.

"You didn't let her in, did you?"

"No. She came to give these to the children. And to . . ." She hesitated.

"And to tell you about me again, right? To warn you I killed our children. And that you were in danger?" he sneered.

Paula nodded.

Hugh looked in three directions at once. "I have to do something. I'll call my attorney. I can't let her—"

Paula touched his arm. "Let's just leave it alone. I closed her out this time. I doubt she'll be back again."

Hugh took the gifts from Paula's hands. "I don't want the children to have these. I'm going to put them into the trash."

"Yes."

When Hugh came back inside Paula was back in the kitchen checking on the turkey. Hugh came up from behind and put his arms around her. "She's not getting to you, is she?" he asked.

Paula turned around, still in his clasp. "No, of course not."

"But you still can't help but feel sorry for her, right?"

"I'm sorry." She shrugged. "I know how you feel, and I guess I should have called you down immediately to ask her to leave, but I just couldn't."

"I understand." Hugh touched her nose with his and smiled warmly. "And I guess that's one of the reasons why I'm so mad about you. You're so full of compassion and love. I'm finished working for today. Let me help you here. What can I do?"

"Would you set the table?"

"Sure. Would you help?"

She smiled. "Sure."

The holidays passed quickly. Hugh took as much time away from his writing as he could to play with the children. Michelle found some girls on the next cul-de-sac and Jeremy met new friends on the sleigh-riding hill, which held its snow until a thaw on New Year's Eve day left more brown patches than white. Bill and Dennis wandered onto the hill, considered giving Jeremy a rough time of it, but then decided his old man was crazy enough to come after them, maybe even with a shotgun or something. Jeremy's friends cheered for him when the bigger boys left. His stature in the neighborhood had definitely increased.

Joan was having a few people over for New Year's Eve. Paula wanted to accept the invitation, but Hugh begged her not to. He had other plans for them. The children were spending the night with Marilyn, and Hugh had already arranged for a catered dinner to be delivered in. They built a fire, kicked off their shoes, and ate in the den, then snuggled in front of the blazing hearth together.

"I hate going out on New Year's Eve," Hugh said. "Isn't this better?"

"Um hmm," Paula sighed as she blurred her eyes and watched the rising flames. The party would have been fun, but this was certainly an acceptable substitute. A very acceptable substitute.

They played oldies music on the stereo—fifties for Hugh and sixties for Paula, then watched the celebration on television as the New Year was rung in. Hugh popped a champagne cork and they drank to their happiness, their lives together, their future.

Then on the den carpet in front of the fire, they tried to make a baby.

"Good news and bad news," Hugh said. It was a week later and Paula had just come home from work. "The good news is that Sol called today. CBS is considering exercising its option on my last novel for a four-hour miniseries."

"That's terrific!" Paula whooped. "What's bad about that?"

"They want me in Los Angeles to consult with the producer over some changes. Only when the script is in final order will it be recommended for production. I have to be there, like yesterday, for about two or three days of meetings."

"That's all right," Paula said and mimicked Hugh from months before when she had wanted to go out with the girls. "I can survive without you for a couple of nights, pod-ner. Especially for something like this!"

"I would love to take you and the kids along for a little vacation, but I can't. There just isn't time. I'll be tied up in meetings all day, and I'm behind on the book. Jason is being understanding but I know he isn't happy. He's given me an extension until the middle of February and, believe me, I'll need every second."

"Another time then," Paula said. "I don't think we should take the children out of school anyway."

"You'll be all right here all by yourself?"

"Of course. I'm a big girl."

"This is a big house."

"I was divorced and living alone for two years. It's only going to be a few days. I'll be all right. When do you have to leave?"

He made a face. "I'm booked on a six A.M. flight tomorrow. When CBS calls . . ."

"Well, I'm sure the rewrites will go terrifically, and we'll have us a miniseries!"

The cab came for Hugh at 4:30 the next morning and Paula kissed him good-bye. "I'll call you tonight," he said. "I'll be at the Beverly Hills, but probably just for a few hours of sleep every night."

"I won't bother you," Paula promised.

"If you need me, of course," Hugh said. "But I'll call you."

Then he was gone, the taillights of the cab lost to the late-night darkness. Paula shivered and went back into the house. This was the first time she had been separated from Hugh since the wedding, virtually the first time they would be alone for as much as three days since they started seeing each other in early summer of last year.

She invited her mother to come over to eat and play Scrabble.

While they fixed dinner Marilyn said, "I'm glad you turned down the C.D. job. Had you taken that position I don't think I would have ever gotten to see you, you would have been so busy."

Paula couldn't help but feel a twinge of guilt, thinking her mother was referring to the past as much as to the future. Except for the holidays she hadn't seen her mother all that much since she had gotten married, and Marilyn hadn't visited with the children as much as Paula knew she wanted to. Marilyn had been working a full substitute schedule so they hadn't been able to meet for lunch, and Paula's evenings were spent with Hugh and weekends with the family. From seeing them all every day down to once a month, or even less than that, was cold-turkey withdrawal. Marilyn hadn't complained, but Paula suspected her mother was wounded.

That wasn't all Paula had been feeling guilty about. She hadn't been together with the girls either. She saw Joan every day and spoke twice weekly with Marge and the others, but hadn't gone to the monthly dinners. Something had always come up, this and that, and Hugh usually wanted her to spend time with him to help him unwind after a day of writing. She would make an effort to start getting out more.

She hadn't realized how her world had seemingly shrunk. She rarely saw her friends and she and Hugh never socialized with anyone on weekends. Hugh had no friends either, just Jason, but that was more business. He had given up his and Judith's friends at the time of the divorce, to break all contact with his past, he had told her, and now he was content to spend his time with her alone. She would try to widen their circle of friends, get Hugh to meet hers. They were all clamoring to meet him, but he had been busy on the book she explained, apologized, it was due and running late. But she wondered how it looked to them, hoping they didn't think Hugh was snubbing them.

Hugh called a few minutes later. They had just broken for dinner.

"How's it going?" Paula asked.

"It's exhausting, but really well. Keep your fingers crossed; this may just work. We may be able to get away with just tomorrow but I won't know that until we've finished." The smile came over the phone. "I miss you," he said. "I'm working all day but I'm lonely out here without you."

"Yes, the same here." She cuddled the phone.

"The kids too. Is it too late to speak to them?"

"They just went to bed. I can get them—"

"No. Don't wake them up. I'll try to call earlier tomorrow. I love you, Paula."

"I love you too, Hugh." She smiled as he kissed her long-distance.

As they cleaned up the Scrabble board Paula kissed her mother on the cheek impulsively. "I'm glad you came over. This has really been a very pleasant evening, Mom."

"Yes, it has been," Marilyn agreed and suddenly was able to articulate to herself why. This was the first time she, Paula, and the children had been alone without Hugh since Paula had married him, and there *had been* something different about the evening at that. Something subtle. Something she didn't suspect Paula had picked up on. There had been less tension, she felt, and wasn't that an odd thought? Although now when she addressed herself to it, it seemed to her that when Hugh was there it was almost like he was resentful of her presence, jealous of her time with Paula and the children, limited as it was. That was the reason the evening had been so pleasant, Marilyn thought. Hugh's eyes hadn't been trained on her as he telegraphed his feelings that she was somehow taking something away from him.

Chapter 14

THE NEXT EVENING PAULA COULDN'T DECIDE IF IT FELT like she was on vacation or divorced again. It was strange to sit down to dinner with just Jeremy and Michelle, and it was almost as if she were a stranger suddenly in her own home. The children sensed the difference too. The house seemed empty without Hugh, larger even, and Paula wondered if she should have asked her mother to join them this night as well. Although inside she knew she had planned it this way. Like her mother, *she* rarely had time alone with the children. There was something anticipatory about being with them tonight . . . and something missing as well. Because they had truly become a family.

Dinner was a Chinese meal eaten with chopsticks right out of the cartons. She didn't know if she had been looking for anything special to happen tonight alone with the children, like they had been holding things just to tell her about privately, but wasn't really disappointed when the meal passed uneventfully, with neither child disclosing very much. They started a jigsaw puzzle together in the den after dinner, then Jeremy went upstairs to work on his math homework. Then television until bedtime. All in all, uneventful.

Paula double-checked the front and rear door locks, turned off the lights on the first floor, and went upstairs. She lounged in bed thumbing through the advertising trades that she had brought home to read tonight. The television was half on in the background, and she came to the same conclusion she sensed the children had arrived at. She missed Hugh. In the months they had been married his presence had always been a certainty, a comfort. Maybe he was a little possessive of her, as Judith had said, but she kind of liked it. She smiled. She liked it a lot.

She was dozing when the phone woke her.

"Great news!" Hugh exclaimed without even bothering to say hello. "We're all done, it looks good, and I'm going to catch the Red-eye tonight. I'm leaving for the airport right now and will be home sometime tomorrow morning."

"That's great! When will you know about CBS?"

"That's anybody's guess. It's being recommended but the option runs until September so they can pick it up now or wait."

"I'm sure they'll pick it up."

"What are you doing?" he asked.

"Absolutely nothing at all. Just lying here and missing you."

"Well, I intend to do exactly the same thing on the plane trip home. We're going out to eat tomorrow night. Make it Michelle's choice." Paula heard a sound in the background. "They're here for the luggage, Paula, I have to go. Love you—"

"Me, too, Hugh." But he had already hung up.

She stretched. Just hearing him, the excitement in his voice about the miniseries, about coming home, had picked her up. And reminded her that it was bedtime. She went into the bathroom and rinsed her face, then changed into her nightgown. She smiled. She had unconsciously reverted to the habit she'd fallen into when she was divorced because lying next to Hugh she always slept in the nude. She went in to check on the children and found them both sleeping comfortably. She adjusted the blanket under Michelle's neck and the child stirred. *Her choice,* Paula laughed. With Michelle choosing, dinner for four could run them over a hundred dollars. She was already worldly and sophisticated at the tender age of six and a half. That came, in part, she imagined, because of the divorce, when she had gone out of her way to take the children out nicely, show them they were still loved. And in part now because Hugh spoiled the hell out of both of them. She leaned over and kissed Michelle on the forehead, then tiptoed out of the room. She flipped the nightlight on in the children's bathroom, which spilled out into the hall, then went into her bedroom. Tonight, like last night, she left the door open a crack, like when just the three of them were living together. That way she could hear if anything was amiss.

At three-fifteen that morning something was.

She knew what time it was because the distant sound brought her out of sleep and with still unfocused eyes she looked at the clock.

The next sounds were also deceptive, softened by her half-conscious state; they could have been there or she could have been imagining them. But they persisted and very quickly Paula came full awake. And despite the warmth of the covers, her skin was chilled. *What was she hearing?* She stiffened her body so not even the sheets would make a rustling noise as she strained to listen.

The sounds were coming from inside the house. Downstairs. Muffled at first, unrecognizable, teasing, then she focused in on them and there was no mistaking the faint pad of footsteps. She sat straight up in bed. *There was someone in the house!* No! She choked back the thought. It wasn't possible. It was only one of the children walking around. Jeremy or Michelle couldn't sleep; they had gone downstairs. But in their months in the house they never had, and besides, when she replayed the first sound, the one that had awakened her, she remembered hearing a high-pitched squealing. The whining cry of a door hinge. But she had checked the doors. She panicked, still straining to hear the sounds downstairs. Although she hadn't checked the basement door. And by default now, that was the way of entry.

Just take what you want, she silently prayed, *and go.* But she knew the intruder would soon come upstairs. That was where people kept their valuables. She prayed as well that the children would remain asleep. Her heart beat loudly, high in her chest.

He was in the den. She could tell by the muffled press of footsteps against the wooden floor. The den was underneath her bedroom. If the intruder's sounds were muted, hers would be as well. She could call the police. But her door was open; she couldn't risk her voice carrying. Very carefully she climbed out of bed and tiptoed to the door to shut it—

Something crashed downstairs and she jumped! He had knocked over a glass vase. She froze, sucked in her breath. Apparently the intruder was doing the same because now there were no sounds from downstairs. Then the footsteps started again. Paula exhaled, too, and ever so gently pushed the door closed, twisting the knob so the latch was held open. Then just as gently she turned the knob so the metal-against-metal sound was minimized. She ran back to her bed and picked up the phone to call the police.

A lump formed in her chest. The phone was dead. She depressed the cutoff switch several times, hoping for a connection, but nothing happened. Several times more, more furiously, still nothing. *The intruder had cut the phone lines!* They were trapped in the house.

And now her door was closed and she could hear nothing.

Then she did. Shuffling footsteps right outside her door.

Her eyes burst wide in terror. She hadn't heard him come up but now he was there!

The bedroom was awash in night shadows from the light of the full moon that snuck in beneath the partially drawn shades. Paula's eyes had adjusted to the dim light and she could see the items on her dresser, shaded outlines of perfume bottles and framed pictures, and the ghost-light brightness of the brass handles on Hugh's armoire as they caught the moonglow.

She could also see the turning knob of the bedroom door, a faint curve of reflected light.

And hear the jiggling metal sound as she watched it slowly turn, slowly . . . good God! The intruder was here!

Pretend you're asleep, that's what the police always advised. Chances are he won't bother you. He doesn't want to be seen as much as you don't. Paula slumped down in her bed. The doorknob was loose from the outside. Hugh had meant to fix it but had been too busy working on his book. She heard the play of the metal as it slipped uselessly between the intruder's fingers.

Then the latch caught and the door was opening. Paula stiffened and tried to even her breathing. Her eyes were only open a slit. She was ready to slam them closed.

"Mommy?"

What?

Paula opened her eyes. It was only her daughter. Michelle was coming into her bedroom.

"I heard something, Mommy."

"Come here, dear," Paula whispered hurriedly and beckoned Michelle closer. She put a finger over the little girl's mouth and whispered in her ear, "Quiet now, there's a burglar in the house. Get into bed with me." She opened the covers and the child quietly slipped between the sheets.

"I'm scared—"

"Shh," Paula cautioned. "Whoever is here, he won't bother us. . . ."

She prayed, because the footsteps downstairs continued. They were fearless, she thought, because he had cut the phone wires; the intruder was in control. He could take his time, toy with them, terrify them. Jeremy was a heavy sleeper, hopefully he would hear nothing.

In a continuous, almost unconscious motion, she rubbed her hand over Michelle's head. The little girl was quivering. Her eyes were wide and focused on the door, her ears perked as she took in the sounds—footsteps, creaks, then long moments of silence. Paula swallowed tightly. The silences were almost the worst—then she didn't know where he was; they were vulnerable from every direction. But she had to remain strong, for Michelle.

That was when she noticed that Michelle had left the bedroom door open. She started to ease the covers back, to close it again, but stopped. It was suddenly too late to do anything.

Because the footsteps were now on the stairs. The intruder had started up. Michelle stiffened and Paula pushed her under the covers, and snuggled in next to her, her body protectively covering her, her hands over the child's ears. Michelle was barely breathing, as if afraid the very sound would give away their position.

The house was as silent as a tomb. Set at the end of a quiet cul-de-sac, there were rarely any sounds at all. Ideal for his concentration, Hugh said. Coming from the heart of Boston, it had taken Paula a little time to acclimate herself to the peace and quiet. Occasionally there were night noises—crickets, the rustle of leaves and the brush of branches against the windows, the click of a boiler, the settling of the house in painful groans and moans. Now the silence was absolute and amplified the only sound she was hearing—the intruder's footsteps as he walked slowly up the steps. Higher. Closer. Their own breaths seemed extraordinarily loud and Paula tried to muffle her daughter's and control her own. Higher. Closer. Straining creaks on the floorboards revealed the burglar's every position. Outside her window the dark shadows of bare tree branches waved ominously in the night breeze, silhouettes of tentacled arms behind the glass. Monster arms. Higher still. Closer still. Their hearts thumped in marching cadence. Michelle broke.

"Mommy—" The child's voice was strained, the word high in her throat. Fear had overtaken her common sense to remain quiet.

Paula clamped a hand over her daughter's mouth, but instinctively knew that they had been heard.

Dear God, let him leave us in peace, she prayed silently.

She wouldn't know if it was her prayer or Michelle's speaking that betrayed they were awake, but suddenly the footsteps stopped. Dead. Which for a moment was no comfort because whoever it was was still on the staircase.

Then the sounds started again. A stairboard compressed under the intruder's weight. Paula's first instinct was terror—he was coming!—but then suddenly relief flooded through her. Because the intruder was walking *down* the stairs. Away from them! He had heard them, knew that someone was awake and didn't want to risk being seen.

Paula held her breath again. As if to let it out would be to invite the burglar up the stairs.

She heard him reach the bottom, then the jiggling of the chain and the opening click of the front door. That was how he was leaving. Then the close of the door and he was gone.

She let her breath out slowly in a long, whistling exhalation. "Oh, baby, baby," she sighed, and stroked Michelle's face with her palm.

"Is he gone, Mommy?" the little girl asked.

"I think he is, darling," Paula whispered. "But be quiet yet, okay." She felt they were safe, but she still didn't know it for sure. Because he might have flipped the latch on the front door, leaving it unlocked. Maybe he would wait for them to settle back to sleep, then come in again, by the front door this time. "I have to go downstairs," she whispered.

"No—"

"I'll be right back. I have to lock the door."

"I want to come with you."

"No. You stay here."

Paula got out of bed and pulled on her robe, which was draped over a chair. Even in the quarter-light of the room she could distinctly see the fear that still remained in her daughter's eyes.

"I'll be right back," she repeated.

The night-light led her out into the hallway. She hesitated at the top of the stairs, her fingers nervously working the post. She breathed in the silence of the house, then tiptoed down the staircase, repeating the steps the intruder had taken only moments before. She didn't want to put a light on, and her eyes were accustomed to the darkness. Oddly enough, she thought she smelled perfume. The scent was remotely familiar but nothing to think about now. The chain was hanging limply and she lunged for it. Her fingers were damp with sweat and she fumbled with the latch. The metal felt flimsy in her hands. She half expected the door to burst open suddenly, a maniacal grin on the burglar's pockmarked or stocking-masked face, an ax in his hand. He had baited her, trapped her. That's the way it was in the movies. But she slipped the latch back into its groove and locked the door. The bolt sliding into place made her feel somewhat better.

They were safe.

No, they weren't.

He was still in the house.

The new thought hit her. He *had* baited her, *had* trapped her. He was still in the house and hiding. He would just wait until they were all asleep again. She whirled around, her back to the door. She peered into the living room. The corners were dark, the familiar objects shrouded in shadows, looming suddenly larger, suddenly unfamiliar.

She smelled the perfume again, a very delicate floral scent. Teasingly familiar, yet still she couldn't place it.

If he was still in the house, he was downstairs. He hadn't gone up.

Perfume. Could it have been a woman?

She had to search the house.

Nervously she looked up the stairs. Jeremy and Michelle were still up there. If she left the safety of the entranceway and if the burglar was still in the house, he could sneak past, up the stairs to her children. Too many *ifs*. She had to know. She had to look.

She took a deep breath and flipped on the light in the entranceway. The harsh glare almost blinded her and she blinked several times to adjust to the brightness. She walked into the living room. Could he be crouching behind the furniture waiting to spring up at her? She shivered involuntarily. The thermostat had been turned down, and the house was cold. She drew her robe more tightly around her and cautiously entered the den, where the burglar had been before.

The house was large, too large, she thought.

Broken glass was scattered across the floor. The intruder had knocked a vase off an end table. She was barefoot and carefully picked her way around the glass. The room was empty. She started to feel a little better, but she still had the other half of the first floor to check. The staircase bisected the house and a central hallway ran from the entranceway to the kitchen in the rear, which also connected to the den. She turned on the kitchen light. . . .

She heard the footsteps. Coming through the dining room into the kitchen.

He was still there! she shrieked silently.

Behind her!

Fear prickled her skin; tiny needles against her flesh.

She spun around to confront him only to find Jeremy standing in the doorway rubbing his eyes. "What's going on?"

"Oh, dear God, Jeremy!" she exhaled. "You just scared me half to death." At least, though, she knew the intruder was no longer in the house. She tested the back door again; the lock was still engaged. Although they still remained vulnerable from the cellar.

"What are you doing?" Jeremy asked. "What's going on?"

"Nothing. There was a burglar in the house but now he's gone. Go back upstairs."

"What are you doing?"

"I have to go down into the basement and check the lock."

"Did you call the police?"

"No. He cut the phone lines. The phone is dead."

Jeremy's eyes widened. Paula couldn't tell if it was fear or admiration.

"Did he take anything?"

"I don't know," she answered a little too sharply, her nerves frazzled by the events. "Please just go back upstairs. Michelle is in my bedroom. I don't want her left alone. Wait up there with her."

"Can I help . . . ?"

"Please just go, Jeremy."

As he ran up the stairs she stood quietly for a second, trying to decide what to do. The phone was dead, useless. She considered running next door to a neighbor to phone the police. She hardly knew the people on the block, but this was an emergency. But she didn't want to go outside. The intruder could still be around the house. He probably wasn't, he didn't want to be seen. But still she wasn't prepared to go outside in the midnight blackness. Although he was probably long gone, they were probably all right in the house till morning. A lot of *probablys*. She needed certainty. They had to be safe. She just had to close off his means of entry. She opened the door that led to the basement and flipped on the light.

The basement was paneled and tiled, a finished playroom. There was a pool table down there and Hugh was teaching Jeremy the game, and a Ping-Pong table, which they all used. A wet bar. A washer-dryer. A large storage room whose door was latched shut. And a door that led to the outside, to the patio and pool, something they hadn't used because they hadn't sat outside during the fall months. The pool had been closed and covered after Hugh's divorce and the plan was to open it again the following spring.

Quickly she crossed the basement. The door *was* unlocked. She threw the latch. The house was secure. She turned off all the lights on the first floor, then went upstairs to the children, who were sitting on her bed. She put a lamp on in the room. If he was outside the house watching, he would see they were still awake. She could amost think clearly again. The perfume was still puzzling.

"How we doing?" she asked.

"Is he gone?" Michelle asked.

"All gone." Paula mustered a smile. "Do you want to go back to sleep now?"

"Can I sleep here?" the little girl asked.

"Of course you can. Do you want to too?" she asked Jeremy.

"Nah," he scoffed. "I'm going back to my room."

He came back fifteen minutes later. A tree branch had whipped against his window and he decided there was safety in numbers.

Paula and her children drifted off to sleep with the light on and woke with the alarm to a bright and glorious morning, with no indication at all that anything out of the ordinary had occurred the night before.

"Come on, let's get ready for school," Paula said as she gently woke them.

Jeremy's eyes questioned if they still had to go to school after what had happened last night.

"Yes, you do," Paula said, grateful for the morning and the normalcy that getting dressed, eating breakfast, and going to school would bring. She would drop them off, then come home and call the police from next door.

Not surprisingly, nobody was hungry.

"Nothing was taken," she told the policeman who answered her call. The only indication that anybody had even been in the house was the broken vase. The policeman found the cut phone lines and called the phone company to come and fix them.

"All in all you were very lucky," he said. "You were home alone with your children?"

"My husband was in California. He'll be home soon, though."

"I think you'll be okay. Think about getting an alarm system that hooks up to the police station."

"I'll talk to my husband about it."

When Hugh came home he was surprised to see her there. She had been nervously pacing the house, looking out through the curtains every few minutes. When she saw the cab pull up she opened the door and rushed out to him.

"Is anyone sick?" he asked, alarmed. "What's wrong?"

"There was a burglar here last night. He cut the phone lines."

"Are you all right?"

"Yes."

"The children?"

"Yes, we're all okay."

Hugh rounded his chin angrily, helplessly, guiltily. "I knew I shouldn't have left you here alone."

"Hugh, you couldn't have known—"

"Where are the children now? In school?"

"Yes, I took them, and I'll pick them up later. The police suggested an alarm system hooked up to the station house."

"Yes, I'll have one installed. . . ." He was looking around. "Was anything taken?"

"No. Michelle made a sound and that scared him away."

"How did he get in?" Hugh asked suspiciously, and to Paula his eyes suggested a certain knowledge, as if he had already answered his own question.

"Through the basement door—" She broke off as Hugh slumped into a chair. "Why? What's wrong?"

"It wasn't a burglar," Hugh said softly.

"What are you talking about? I'm not making any of this up."

"It was Judith."

"Judith?"

Had the perfume she'd smelled the night before been Judith's?

"She still has a key to the cellar door. I never changed that lock. I didn't think it was necessary—"

"What would Judith be doing in the house?"

"Paula, I don't know. To take something? To scare you? To kill you?" He reached for the phone. "I have to call the police. Damn it! The line is still dead—"

"I don't understand—"

"She hates me. She resents you for marrying me. She doesn't want you living here. She's mad. I don't know what she's capable of." He grabbed his coat. "I'm going next door to call the police. I'll never leave you alone again, Paula. I'm sorry."

He left Paula at the doorway, staring, disbelieving.

Then the emotions and tensions of the night flew out of her and she collapsed in tears.

Judith adamantly denied being in the house and was taken to the precinct for a statement. She, in turn, accused Hugh of breaking in himself, setting her up so Paula would be afraid of her and not Hugh. She demanded he produce plane and hotel receipts from his trip to California, which to her surprise he did. The police refused to contact the producers he said he was with. But still the assistant district attorney wouldn't press charges against her; it would just be thrown out, he explained to Hugh. There was no hard evidence of Judith's breaking and entering.

"So what you're saying is that she really has to hurt somebody before anything can be done?" Hugh didn't wait for the D.A.'s answer.

They instituted safeguards for the children—Hugh would pick them both up after school and watch them if they wanted to play outside—and Paula promised Hugh she would be cautious going to and from work. They would have the house wired for an alarm system.

And, Hugh told Paula, despite her sympathetic feelings toward Judith, if she made even the slightest contact with any of them at all, in person or by phone, he would have her declared in violation of the restraining order and jailed.

He informed Judith of this in front of Paula and the district attorney.

Judith listened silently, then lifted her eyes to Paula. They were round, Paula saw, and filled with sadness. Although this time she turned away from Judith. This time there was too much uncertainty.

Chapter 15

PAULA DIDN'T WANT THEM TO LIVE THEIR LIVES IN FEAR, but still she had to be respectful and wary of Judith's anger and presence.

She didn't want to appear overly cautious around the children and unduly alarm them, but she had Hugh call her in the afternoon after he had brought both children home from school. Happily the weather was rainy and raw so there was no temptation for them to play outside.

Whenever she woke in the middle of the night she would slip on her robe and tiptoe into the children's rooms to make certain they were safe. It reminded her of the time when they were very young and she and Michael would take turns sneaking looks into their cribs to check that they were still breathing. Jeremy's and Michelle's teachers and principals were quietly apprised of the situation with Judith, and extra care would be taken at the schools as well. Marilyn offered to take them for a while, but Hugh didn't want it; the children belonged with their parents. He arranged for the local police department to make extra swings down their street throughout the afternoon and night.

Paula found herself particularly jumpy. At the office she was working alone in the conference room on a presentation when Nathan Blume quietly came in. He tapped her on the shoulder, scared the daylights out of her, and she practically leapt into the air. She felt so vulnerable to the other woman, helpless, and like Hugh regretted that nothing could be done short of extra caution. And the passage of time.

For the first time she considered the possibility that the night she was almost mugged in the parking garage Judith had perhaps loosened the ignition wire and lay waiting for her.

She advised the receptionist on her floor and the building guards of the circumstances. If Judith ever tried to get past them, the police would be called immediately. Paula even half hoped Judith would try. Because then at least she would be jailed. . . .

It was no way to live their lives, but for the time being they had to. There were three possibilities, Paula considered. First, Judith was sufficiently frightened by the threat of prison that she was staying away from them. Second, it hadn't been Judith in the house, the woman's protests of her innocence truthful. But the last possibility, the worst, was that nothing had changed at all and *Judith was just lying in wait.*

A week passed quietly, uneventfully. It was exhausting to remain constantly alert and Paula found herself finally relaxing. Although if she were looking for a descriptive image of the situation, it would be that she and Hugh still took turns sleeping with one eye open.

Arthur Witt came into Paula's office. "How about taking a little trip?" he asked. "Just for a couple of days. Coca-Cola's thinking of test marketing a new drink in New England and they want to meet with representatives of several local agencies. Nathan's still new so he doesn't have the feel of the office the way you do or know all the successful campaigns we've run, so I was thinking, if you don't mind taking a short trip down to Atlanta to their corporate headquarters with me, I think it would go a long way in helping us get the account."

"I don't see any reason why not. Let me talk to Hugh and I'll let you know tomorrow."

"I'm sorry, Paula, but that's absolutely out of the question," Hugh said.

She didn't like his words or tone. "What do you mean 'out of the question'? Why is it 'out of the question'?" She was bristling, her lower lip curling, but she didn't even try to stem her sudden anger.

"Because I'm not going to let you go, that's all."

"Hugh—" she protested. Tears were forming, which she tried to stifle and remain strong. Her voice was thickening. She didn't know if she was more angry or hurt. "I don't think I like this conversation very much. It's not for you to let me or not let me go. You had to go to Los Angeles so you went. There was no question, no discussion, nor would there be. Now I've been asked to take a little business trip with my boss, which I didn't say yes to right away. Although it would be good for the firm so I should have. But I offered to give you the courtesy of discussing it with you first. Maybe there is a particular reason I shouldn't go right now. You're finishing your novel and you don't want me to leave you alone with the kids. Whatever. But your saying 'I'm not going to let you go' is not 'discussing' it in my book."

"I'm sorry, Paula," he said contritely. "Perhaps I was a little short with you." He went to put his arms around her but she pulled away from him. "All right," he said. "Yes, it's because I'm almost done with my novel."

"That's just not good enough now, Hugh," she said tightly. "I deserve more."

Hugh exhaled and looked at her. There was a streak of defiance on her face. "Yes, you do," he said. "Let me explain."

"I think you'd better."

He pursed his lips thoughtfully and sat down on the edge of the bed. "It's difficult to put into words."

"Hugh, what's the matter?" she demanded, less angry suddenly, concerned, confused by his tone. *"What* is difficult to put into words. What are you talking about?"

"I'm afraid, Paula," he whispered, and coming on the heels of the argument, the words hung in the air, chilled her, dissipated what was left of her anger. She looked at him closely. There *was* fear etched in his face. She sat down next to him, touched his arm

"Afraid of what, Hugh?"

"Of . . . of . . ." He didn't want to say it. She saw the struggle on his face. Then he garbled the words. "Of something happening to you."

Surprise. "But what's going to . . . ?"

He held up his hand to stop her. "I'll tell you what could happen." He swallowed and stared straight out in front of him. There was an almost perceptible change to his face, a darkening, an eerie distance to his gaze, as if his eyes were suddenly seeing terrible things that no one else could.

"When I was a child and my father left me to go on a business trip," he said slowly, thickly, "he was killed. Then when Judith took the children away to the Cape Cod house, John and Danielle were killed." He swallowed again and tears of memory suddenly formed in his eyes. When he spoke his voice sounded choked and pained. "Every time people leave me, something happens to them."

"You can't believe that," Paula protested and immediately regretted her words. Very obviously he did. "But nothing's going to happen." She summoned a comforting smile.

"You don't know that, Paula," he said sharply, and banged the bed with his fist. "You just don't know. I'm sorry, but you mean too damn much to me to risk anything happening for the sake of a trip to Atlanta for some account."

He got up and walked to the window. Paula stood next to him, rubbed his arm lovingly. In the scrimmed blackness of the darkened window their faces were long and pained.

"I'm sorry I snapped at you, Hugh," she apologized. "I didn't know what was troubling you. I—I just took offense at what you said before. And how you said it. I guess I didn't like being told what I could or could not do."

"No, *I'm* sorry, Paula," he said. "I know now I should have approached it differently, explained up front how I felt, but I guess I flashed immediate alarm. Like there was a red flag all of a sudden waving in front of me. Paula is going on a trip. She's going to leave me. She's going to . . ." He waved away the concluding thought. "I was foolish for seeming to order you around and I apologize."

"Okay," she said softly.

"But I'm asking you, Paula, don't go. Even if I sound a little crazy for thinking something terrible might happen again, please humor me. Because of all that happened. Call me a little superstitious—"

"A little." Paula smiled. "But I love you so damn much too. But you know, Hugh, trips are going to come up for me. Before we were married I did some traveling for the firm as well."

"Don't go this time," he begged. "Maybe next time I'll be able to go with you. But my time is so tight now I can't. Can't you just tell Arthur that because of this whole Judith thing you don't want to leave the kids alone? I'm sure he'll understand."

"I'm sure he will too," Paula agreed. "But other trips are going to come along," she pressed, wanting some resolution that would seal the future.

"We'll face them then, Paula. But please, don't go now without me."

Irrational fear remained deep in his eyes. But she didn't know how it felt to suffer loss like he did. How it could make someone think and react. Both times there had been such a direct cause and effect.

"All right, Hugh," she said, then added quietly, "This time." They could deal with other trips at other times.

"How was your day, otherwise?" he asked.

"Otherwise," Paula repeated the word. "Uneventful."

"Good," they said together and smiled. A new ritual between them. It meant another day had passed without incident.

"Save Saturday," Joan said over the phone. "Ruth's giving a party." Ruth Taplinger, Jeff's wife, the other partner in the advertising agency, was a gracious hostess who, in the office vernacular, gave great party.

"Any occasion?" Paula asked.

"For Nathan Blume. To welcome him to the T & W family. Hey—and I'll finally get to see how gorgeous Hugh is in person. Book-jacket photos are not the real thing, believe me."

"Yuck." Hugh grimaced after Ruth had called.

"What?" Paula smiled uneasily.

"I hate parties!" He beat his chest with his fist and the children laughed.

"I guarantee you'll have a good time," she soothed. "My friends have all read your books and are dying to meet you. The party might be for Nathan, but you'll be the center of attention."

"And that's what I can't stand," he protested. "Paula, other people may love that sort of thing, but I hate it. I'm just not a partygoer."

"But I really have to go to this one," Paula said. "It's a political thing. My boss is giving it. Everyone will be there."

Her voice was ever so slightly higher pitched; she was trying to be cheery and convincing. But why did she have to be? she thought. Why couldn't just her needing to go or wanting to go be enough?

Hugh smiled and took her in his arms. "And we'll go, Paula. Because I love you and know you have to be there."

Paula's back was to the room and no one noticed the sudden distant look that crossed her face as she touched cheeks with Hugh. Something had just occurred to her. The marriage was wonderful, there was no denying that. Hugh loved her deeply and she him, but lately it seemed that so many things with him had turned into negotiations.

The Taplingers lived on Beacon Hill. There was a light rain falling and the highway was a little slick. They were in the center lane when a car shot past them on the left, then swerved into their lane, then into the right to try to get around another car. "Would you look at that clown," Hugh said disgustedly. Not ten seconds later they heard the squeal of brakes, and tensed. The metal-against-metal sound was fierce, a crunching report as one car bashed against another. The traffic automatically slowed to a halt, a sea of red brake lights.

Two cars were in the right lane and shoulder, one wedged against the guard rail, the driver's door crushed in by the other car. Headlights fanned out almost wastefully into the darkness, illuminating the falling rain. Cars were pulling to the side of the road to help. "Let me see if I can do anything," Hugh said, and swung onto the shoulder. "You wait here." Traffic in both directions had slowed to a crawl. Many people were going over to lend assistance, others were just inching by, gawking at the spectacle. Hugh stepped over broken glass to get closer. But suddenly he stopped short as he absorbed the scene.

The car against the guard rail had taken it badly. The entire driver's side of the engine was pushed in and enough of the door so it was wedged shut. Entry into the car by the passenger side was blocked by the railing of an overpass. There was a family in the car, a man and woman in the front seat, two children in the back, all of them screaming. They had been badly jolted, although no one seemed critically hurt. Had the other car hit farther back there would have been deaths. None of the people knew how to free the trapped family, but police sirens were heard in the distance; help would be arriving.

Paula saw Hugh standing motionlessly on the fringe of the accident. Concerned, she grabbed an umbrella and got out of the car and went to him.

"What is it, Hugh?" she asked, then frowned as she looked at his face. Even in the flat light of the car headlights she was able to see his disorientation. "Hugh . . . ?" But he didn't respond to her voice or touch. Instead he shook his head fragilely and whispered uncertainly, "Daddy . . . ?" And Paula shocked to the word.

There was a cacophony of noise around her—shouts and cries and approaching sirens—and Paula almost had to question if she had correctly heard what Hugh had said. A police car arrived and two officers assessed the situation, then ordered those inside to protect their heads under coats or blankets, anything available. They smashed the window and the crowd jumped back at the explosion of broken glass. Everyone was mesmerized by the scene but Hugh's expression remained blank, his face drained of color, his eyes distant and seemingly staring inwardly. Oblivious to the rescue and the falling rain which beaded on his forehead and matted down his hair.

"Hugh?" she questioned again, then when he didn't respond she shook his arm roughly. "Hugh!"

He came free. "What . . . ?"

"Let's go back to the car," she prodded. "The police have the situation under control." An ambulance drove up on the shoulder of the road. The policemen were lifting the people out through the broken window. "We have to get out of the way."

"Yes . . ." He was still dazed.

She held his arm as they walked. "Are you all right, Hugh?" She was frightened. *What had just happened? What was he thinking? What did he see?*

"Yes," he said, but there was still weakness in his voice, uncertainty.

"I'd better drive," she said. Then as they got into the car she asked, "What happened to you out there?"

Hugh leaned back against the passenger neck rest, inhaled and exhaled slowly and deeply. His eyes were open and he looked up at the padded roof of the car. Then he put his head into his hands and rubbed his eyes. When he looked at her again they were bloodshot. "I was really out of it, wasn't I?"

"Really," Paula agreed.

He shook his upper body fitfully, as if trying to erase what he had just experienced. "I don't know why it happened," he said almost disbelievingly," but when I got close to the crash, and saw the confusion, the blood, heard the sirens . . . I was thrown back to the car accident that killed my father. Wow! What a powerful recall. That night was just like what happened now. I had been thrown free of the car, *was outside of the car*, looking inside."

He was still seeing, remembering, Paula saw.

"The only difference was that these people tonight are alive, while my father and aunt were killed."

"Do you want to go back home?" Paula asked because she didn't know what else to say.

He shook his head, cleared it. "No. We have a party to go to."

"You're sure?"

He smiled. "I'm all right, Paula. I can even drive now."

"No way. You take it easy." She started the car, then after cautiously pulling out into traffic asked, "Do you want to talk about it?"

He shook his head. "No. I want to forget about it. It happened, it's over. But thanks. I guess we just have to stay away from car accidents," he tried to joke. But Paula saw that his smile was humorless; his face still showed surprise and strain. He reached over and turned on the radio. Classical music came over the speakers, and Paula was grateful for the diversion. As she drove slowly into Boston she replayed in her mind what she had witnessed at the accident site. And heard. Hugh *had* said "Daddy," she was certain of it now, an involuntary response to what he was remembering, she was sure, and strange, as the car accident that killed his father happened over thirty years ago.

Ruth and Jeff Taplinger welcomed them. Most of the guests were already there—personnel from Taplinger & Witt— copywriters, media specialists, artists, and accountants. "Sorry, we're late," Paula apologized. "But there was an accident and we stopped to see if we could help."

"Was anybody hurt?" Jeff asked.

"No, but it could have been a lot worse. A family was trapped in its car. The police were trying to free them when we left."

"Thank God you weren't involved at all," Ruth said.

Joan was making her way through the crowd. "You made it." She looked at Hugh and nodded approvingly.

"This is Hugh," Paula introduced proudly. "My friend Joan—I might have mentioned she's been eager to meet you."

"Once or twice." Hugh grinned.

"And Arthur," Paula continued. "And Jeff and Ruth. And Nathan—come over here—and Glenn!" she shrieked, happy to see the former creative director weaving his way toward them. "I didn't know you'd be here." They hugged each other.

"I couldn't let them have a party without me," Glenn said. "You'd talk about me all night."

"We'd only be saying what a fool you were to have left us," Arthur laughed. Then he shook Hugh's hand. "Pleased to meet you, Hugh. You're a lucky guy to get this one."

"Come in, come in," Ruth prompted. "The bar's right over there. The buffet table there. And we should have some hors d'oeuvres somewhere in circulation. I'll speak to you later, okay?"

Hugh curled his hand protectively in Paula's and went to the bar where a tuxedoed bartender was serving drinks. "Aren't they all nice?" Paula whispered. The buffet table was filled with cold foods—salmon, shrimp, and platters of cheeses, crackers, and fruit. The room was a loud hum of conversation, broken only by the clinking sound of plates and silver, and the light rock music playing in the background. The odors of the food mixed with fragrances from a number of different perfumes. Joan was beside them.

"It only took us a couple of months to get together, and I'm delighted it's finally happened."

"I've been looking forward to meeting you too," Hugh said. "All of Paula's friends. I've been a little remiss lately because my schedule has been somewhat demanding."

"I know. Hey—congratulations on the CBS thing. I'm keeping my fingers crossed for you. Let's hope."

"Thank you."

"And Paula tells me you're almost finished with your new book. I'm sure that must always be exciting."

Arthur Witt interrupted them and grabbed Paula by the arm. "May I borrow you for a little while? Joan, would you keep Hugh entertained?"

"Sure."

Hugh watched as Arthur led Paula through the party to a distant corner of the room where Nathan and Glenn were gathered. The older man's arm was draped around Paula's shoulders.

"How do you get your ideas?" Joan asked.

"Pretty much from thin air. I just lean back in my chair, close my eyes, let my mind drift, and—"

"A best-seller is born," Joan filled in.

"Well, hardly. That requires a little more work. And a few more headaches. But a germ comes. A starting-off point. Would you excuse me a second, Joan . . ." And without waiting for her answer he started to thread his way across the room to where Paula was.

Arthur still had his arm slung over Paula's shoulders, leaning into her almost flirtatiously as his forearm rubbed against her breast. They were laughing at a story Glenn was telling about a campaign he had been called in to fix. It was an absolute disaster of a campaign, an absolute disaster of a product, "but ours is not to reason why, ours is just to . . . sell, or die." He pantomimed putting a gun to his head and pulling the trigger. Steve Fishman and Don O'Shea, two other copywriters with the firm, had also joined the group and nodded to Hugh as he came over.

"I'll take that shoulder." Hugh smiled at Arthur. "I own it now, remember." He lifted Arthur's arm from around Paula and replaced it with his own. The men laughed.

"There goes our affair, Paula." Arthur grinned. "I knew it was too good to last."

"Speaking of clunker campaigns"—Steve traded a glance with Paula—"I'll say we've certainly had our share. Although I think Paula's had the worst of all time—"

"Oh, don't bring that up," she laughed, knowing where he was going.

"Nathan doesn't know about that, does he?"

"Nooo—I never told him. And let's keep it that way. He still thinks I'm good at what I do."

"It was an ad for some dishwashing detergent," Steve explained. "And for a reason only God and Paula know to this day, she did the entire copy in iambic pentameter."

"Talk about dying a thousand deaths," Paula groaned. "I thought it would be snappy. It wasn't snappy."

"It was dreadful."

"You didn't have to say it. God, I never thought I'd live that one down."

"Well, you haven't yet, my dear," Steve lisped. He held up his hands to the crowd. "Attention, everybody. May I have your attention—it's showtime."

"Don't," Paula said laughingly. "You're not going to do it? Please, not in front of Nathan. He thinks he can count on me."

"Well, he certainly can. If ever he needs anybody to write anything in iambic pentameter, you're the one." He cleared his throat.

"I think she asked you not to," Hugh interrupted. He spoke quietly, but his voice carried a certain authority. The party ground to a halt and the smiles faded. "Obviously it's embarrassing to her and she'd rather it be left alone."

"It's all right, Hugh." Paula smiled tentatively and touched his arm. "I don't mind."

"Well, I do," Hugh said coolly. "I don't want to see anything you've written made fun of." He spoke to the others. "I see how hard she works and the good ads she comes up with. If there's an occasional weak presentation, I think it can be safely overlooked. And if you're trying to score points off Paula," he said pointedly to Steve, "I'm not going to stand by and let you do it."

A general feeling of awkwardness settled over the room.

"I really meant it all complimentarily," Steve said soberly and shifted uncomfortably from foot to foot. "She comes up with so few losing campaigns it's almost an event when she does."

"Let it go, Steve," Arthur said quietly.

"Sure." He nodded, then reached for Hugh's hand. "Nice meeting you, Hugh. I meant nothing by what I said. I'm sorry."

Conversation slowly started up again. The group in the corner dispersed, Arthur and Glenn going to the bar, Jeff and Nathan stepping aside to conduct some business.

"I don't know what that was all about, Hugh," Paula said when they were alone, "but it certainly wasn't necessary."

"I didn't want them to embarrass you."

"I wasn't embarrassed. It was all in good fun."

"I'm sorry, but I just didn't see it that way. You're the most talented one in that whole group and they're just looking for ways to knock you down. I know the type, and he wasn't doing it for fun."

"Hugh, you're wrong," she said. "But let's just forget it."

"You're probably wasting your time with these people," he argued. "You should be home working on something more serious than some of those ridiculous products you have to sell. You haven't done any work on your novel and it's so good."

"Let's talk about it later, Hugh," she whispered hoarsely. "But just you remember that they're my friends and co-workers. Important people in my life. Okay?" Although she didn't suspect they'd be number one on anybody's guest list for a while. She stopped a waitress for a small cheese puff, but she wasn't hungry. She circulated with Hugh for the rest of the night, but the enjoyment had gone out of the party.

"All right, I was wrong. I owe you an apology," Hugh said contritely as they readied for bed. Paula was buttoning up her nightgown. For the first time in their marriage she wasn't going to sleep in the nude. They had barely talked on the trip home. Hugh had tried to make light conversation about the people at the party but Paula had only answered monosyllabically. "I just didn't realize. I made an honest mistake and didn't see it as a joke," he admitted.

"I don't see how you could have missed it," she said. "Look —I'm sorry you were shaken up by the car accident, perhaps we should have gone home, but you really didn't want to go to that party, did you? And was this your way of getting back at me for dragging you there. Well, it wasn't a bad party, Hugh. It happened to have been a very nice party and it was just too bad that you couldn't enjoy it."

"I'm sorry if I embarrassed you, Paula, but that guy was making fun of you, maliciously I thought, and it upset me."

Paula didn't want to argue with him. She was tired and wanted to think his intentions were good. She didn't want to be mad at him. Although for the moment she felt strangely removed from him, and as she looked at his face, sad and remorseful, she couldn't help but wonder if he was being completely honest with her, if there had been any other motive for what he had done. But it was over and not worth pressing.

"Okay," she said neutrally. "Let's forget about tonight. I'll deal with the guys at work. They'll understand you're a writer and protective of my creativity." She started to unbutton her nightgown. "Come on. Let's go to sleep."

"I love you, Paula," he said. "You have to know that." There was insecurity in his voice bordering on fear.

"Yes, I love you, too, Hugh." But she was disappointed in him, in his behavior tonight. She was so proud to be married to him and couldn't wait for him to meet her friends and make an impression . . . which he certainly had, she thought ruefully.

He flipped off the light and they kissed good night. Soon Hugh's even breathing told Paula he was asleep. She tried to relax and drift off, too, but something was preying on her mind. Something that had yet to take form. And then it did. Things had been quietly adding up, she realized almost subconsciously.

He tried to close everyone out of my life except for him.

Judith's words jerked her away from the edge of sleep.

Jeremy had a math problem that was puzzling him and he mounted the steps to Hugh's third-floor office. Hugh was working on the last chapter of his book; he would be finished in a week and that boded well for a skiing trip for all of them.

He knocked on Hugh's door, but when nobody answered he pushed it open a crack, then wider, and slipped through.

What he saw surprised and frightened him. He stood in the doorway unmoving, watching, waiting for sense of what he was seeing.

Hugh was sitting at his desk. His back was to the door as he faced his computer terminal and one of the windows that looked out over the patio, the pool, and woods that stretched to the next cul-de-sac behind them. There were blurred words on the screen; Hugh was working. But he wasn't. Not right then. His fingers weren't on the keyboard. Rather, he was moving his arms in front of his face, spastically, uncontrollably from side to side, as if trying to fend off an unseen attacker. And moaning. "No . . ." he was saying, his voice high-pitched, plaintive, almost childlike, Jeremy thought. "Don't leave . . ."

Jeremy called to him, softly at first. Hugh seemed to be in some kind of trance which Jeremy was afraid to break. Like he knew it was dangerous to wake a sleepwalker. Hugh continued to moan. "No . . ."

Then as Jeremy grew more and more uneasy by what he was seeing, he called out louder. "Dad . . ." And then again. A sharpness to the word.

Hugh's arms froze in midair as he reacted to the voice. But still he didn't turn. He looked at his hands questioningly, his palms open and facing him. There seemed to be a confusion to his posture. Then he dropped his hands to his lap.

"Dad?" Jeremy questioned again.

Hugh turned in his swivel chair. The dazed look was pronounced, unmistakable, almost as if he wasn't certain where he was. His eyes were narrowed, his forehead ridged. He was still looking at his hands. Jeremy remained rooted in the doorway.

Then Hugh seemingly snapped out of whatever he was in and grinned. "Jeremy, my boy, what can I do for you?"

"I was having trouble with some math and I was hoping you could help me." His own voice sounded strained, constricted.

"Sure. Come on over here." Hugh waved him to his desk, then swiveled back to the computer and depressed keys that saved on the disc what he had recently written. Jeremy stood at Hugh's side, glancing from the whirring, spinning diskette to Hugh's face, looking for recognition of what had happened. But Hugh seemed to have no recollection at all of his spastic movements.

As they went through the math problem together Jeremy had a thought. Hugh had been working out a sequence of action in his head, got so involved with his characters and story that he didn't hear him when he had called. And, not wanting to disturb Hugh at his work, he hadn't even called all that loudly, had he?

That had to be it, Jeremy thought. Hugh was visualizing a scene. Playacting it out. That was all.

The boy had no other explanation.

Chapter 16

HUGH CAME DOWNSTAIRS TRIUMPHANTLY HOLDING A REAM of paper.

"Is that what I think it is?" Paula asked.

"All done and ready for delivery."

"Terrific!" she yelled happily. "When do I get to read it?"

"I'll make a Xerox tomorrow, although I would almost rather wait until Jason edits it. I think I'm a little self-conscious having you look at it in draft form."

"Oh stop," she scoffed. "It has to be wonderful."

He blushed. "I won't say it isn't."

"When are you going to take it in?"

"Tomorrow morning, which means tomorrow afternoon I am completely free and we can start talking about our ski trip. How about next week? The kids are off because of Washington's birthday; let's take advantage and go up to Vermont. Can you grab some days?"

The timing wasn't ideal for Paula. She had a presentation due the following week which she was still working on. But—she considered—there were things she had wanted to say to Hugh since the party that she had put off because of his pressure to finish the manuscript. Things that had been troubling her. Things that were important.

"I have to do some rearranging, but I'll be able to make it," she said. When they were away in Vermont with no distractions, she could broach them.

The children, of course, had no problem. Jeremy walked around in his new ski boots all night.

Kate came out to the reception area to greet Hugh. She knew he was coming in and had made up her face and worn her best suit.

Jason eagerly took the box from Hugh's hands and massaged it lovingly. "My bonus," he sighed, his eyes heavenward.

"We'll be away in Vermont for a week if you need to tell me how wonderful it is," Hugh joked. He offered a piece of paper to Kate. "Here's where we'll be staying. It's a condo up at the mountain." He swung an arm around Kate's shoulders and whispered in her ear, "Call me after you've read it and let me know what you think."

"I will." Kate beamed and clutched the address and phone number in her fist.

Kate took the novel home. Anticipation had welled in her since seeing Hugh that morning, and just holding the manuscript now made her feel closer to him.

She remembered with delight the last time she had seen him and the feel of his arms around her as they danced at the party and he caressed her back and shoulders, made love to her on their feet. She closed her eyes and pictured Hugh, his hair, dark and straight across his forehead, his jaw, angled and strong. But mostly his eyes, deep and haunting brown. She could lose herself in those eyes. Her body responded longingly to her thoughts, her emotions enflamed with desire and love. She and Hugh were dancing, their bodies pressed together as they twirled to the beat beneath the spinning, pulsing lights, lost to each other, becoming one.

Then her line of vision widened and she saw Paula looking at her from the edge of the dance floor, a stern, possessive glance on her face, and Kate's fantasy snapped.

Her eyes opened and her body chilled as she thought of Paula and Hugh together now at their vacation house.

Then about what had happened at the other vacation house.

* * *

Bright sun and new fallen snow. A skier's dream. Six fresh inches had fallen overnight, the storm had blown off the coast, and morning dawned dazzlingly clear, the sky high and blue and only a teasing fluff of white clouds drifting lazily by. The temperature was in the low thirties, the most glorious of skiing days.

Breakfast gave way to excitement as the four of them piled into the Mercedes and headed for the mountain, counting mittens and scarves. They had arrived at the condo the previous night and the children barely slept at all, staring out the window, praying for more and more fresh snowfall. Michelle had never skied before and was looking forward to her initiation.

"I haven't done this in years," Paula said nervously, although her own excitement grew as the ski area loomed into view, the trails ribbons of white against the green and brown backdrop of the mountainside. "I hope I remember what to do."

"It's like riding a bicycle," Hugh said, then grinned and added, "I hope you didn't tend to fall off bicycles."

The children laughed and Hugh followed the directing arm of the parking attendant as he ushered them into one of the lots, which were quickly filling up.

They purchased their lift tickets and enrolled the children in the morning class of the ski school. Paula was tempted to take refresher lessons, too, but Jeremy was going into an advanced class, and pride (which goeth before a ski fall, she thought ruefully), prevented her from signing up for the rank beginner's class with Michelle and, she estimated, about a dozen other six-, seven-, and eight-year-olds.

"Besides, you are mine," Hugh said, and started to prod her with his ski pole toward the chair lift. She quickly made arrangements to meet the children in the lodge where the instructors would leave them after their lessons and followed Hugh to the bottom of the lift, struggling to keep her balance, which she promptly lost and flopped unceremoniously in the snow.

"I hope this does not portend things to come." She grinned.

"With me as your teacher? Never!" Hugh said and eased her onto the lift, which she managed to board with only a modicum of difficulty and flailing arms. An embarrassment level of only about two and a half, she estimated.

She waved to Jeremy and Michelle as they rode over the forming ski school classes, then turned her attention to the brilliance of the day. Snow capped the trees, piled thickly on the branches, creating giant snow statues, creaturelike, with wide, extended arms. The chair lift edged up the side of the slope and Paula could almost reach out with her ski pole and scatter the flakes of snow delicately balanced on boughs. In many places others before her had done so and the green-white contrast was sharp; the individual needles, bespeckled with white, glistened in the sun.

She was enjoying the ride. The nature. The freshness.

Hugh.

The morning flew by and could not have been more fun. Hugh draped his arm around her as they rode the chair lift, picked the easy way down the slopes for her, picked her up when she fell. He was a skillful and patient teacher, and while Michael would have given up on her and gone off by himself to ski off his aggressions, Hugh stayed and worked with her, and it wasn't long before her technique returned and her motions became less tentative and more fluid. On her last run before lunch she thought she might even look good. (Although when Hugh suggested having her next run videotaped, she quickly demurred.)

And, she thought happily, no negotiations were required. This beautiful, beautiful day was indicative of her marriage to Hugh. And while what happened at the party—and other things—still remained distantly in her thoughts, she chose not to say anything to Hugh now. Their life together was just too special. And she might have been wrong altogether, misreading signals and meanings that weren't there.

They skied the afternoon with the children, went back to the condo, where they swam in the indoor pool and baked in the sauna. Paula forgot how tiring skiing could actually be as she rediscovered muscles she hadn't heard from in years. The children were also wiped out, and no one had any desire to go out for a big dinner. They ordered in a pizza and sat in the dining room hefting slices. Although as tired as they were, tomorrow was another day, barely hours away, and they made plans for skiing first thing in the morning, Jeremy already mapping out the slopes he planned to conquer. A fire blazed behind them in the hearth and the sweet Vermont smell of burning wood filled the room. No, Paula thought, things were really just too good to say anything at all. What happened at the Taplingers' party disappeared from her memory in a puff of pine smoke and she smiled contentedly.

After dinner Hugh piled more logs on the fire and built it up to a roar. There were no other lights in the room and the fire leapt out at them. They sat stretched out in full view, Paula and Hugh lounging on the couch, legs propped up on a coffee table, after-dinner drinks at their side, the children lying on the rug in front, chins in their palms. Sparks crackled and hissed and soot swirled as the logs disintegrated and collapsed in upon themselves. Slender fingers of flames danced high in the hearth, hypnotically.

Hugh stirred. Paula stole a glance at him. His eyes were dull, unfocused, lost to the fire. Then she watched his face change. His look was somber, then suddenly troubled, fearful—his eyes narrow; there was pain behind his knitted brow. His jaw muscles stiffened, struggled, opened—

"Daddy!" he cried suddenly, his voice hoarse and gripped by anguish. "Don't die, Daddy. I didn't mean to do it. I didn't—"

He broke off. The moment hung suspended on a slender strand of webbing. Even the fire seemed to silence. Hugh heard his words at the same time the others did—for the first time, Paula thought. His expression changed from blankness to one of confusion, his eyes rounded and frightened by his outburst as much as the others.

Paula touched his leg. Catlike nervousness flickered through his eyes; uncertainty was woven through the brown as he looked from Paula to the children. Jeremy and Michelle were twisted around on the floor, eyeing him strangely.

"Are you all right, Hugh?" Paula asked.

He shook his head to free it, then exhaled sharply, like blowing smoke rings, then smiled tentatively, and Paula watched the search for understanding as it crossed his face in waves.

"I was staring at the fire," he said carefully, as if trying to sort it out for himself as well. "Watching the patterns of the flames. I guess I must have fallen asleep."

His eyes were open, Paula thought.

"I was dreaming about the car accident again." He tightened his lips, bothered. "Ever since we saw that damn crash on the turnpike I can't stop thinking about the accident that killed my father." He laughed shortly, embarrassed, and managed a smile for the children's benefit. "And I guess we all know now that I talk in my sleep."

Then something else crossed his face. A dark shadow. Confusion. Paula saw it and it frightened her.

"What is it, Hugh?" she asked.

He glanced at the children and Paula picked up the cue. She slapped her hands together. "Hey, kids, upstairs, okay? It's late, you're tired, and Daddy isn't feeling well right now. So go get ready for bed and I'll be up in a minute."

Both children were reluctant to leave. This was *interesting*. But Paula nudged, a no-nonsense tone. "Come on." Slowly they rose, kissed Hugh and Paula. They paused at the bottom of the stairs but a flick of Paula's thumb sent them scurrying up. When they were out of earshot she asked again, "What else, Hugh?"

"I don't honestly know." He shrugged. "I don't know if there is anything else. You know, I haven't thought about that accident in years and now I can't get it out of my mind. I was there again, Paula. It was so vivid." He frowned. "What did I say just now?" he asked her.

Paula remembered. She still heard the words inside of her, and despite the warmth of the fire her body chilled. "You said, 'Don't die, Daddy. I didn't mean to do it.' What, Hugh? What didn't you mean to do?"

His forehead tensed as he struggled for memory. "I don't know. I can't remember. I can remember being on the ground after I was thrown out of the car, seeing the policemen, the ambulance, watching the people taking my father and aunt out of our car. Checking for pulse. For breath. Putting them into the ambulance. But I can't remember anything else about that night. What happened before those moments. I can't remember the accident at all. The police questioned me afterward; they wanted to know what had caused my father to go off the road. Was there another car? Was it a hit-and-run situation? But I didn't know then either." He shrugged helplessly, then turned away from Paula, toward the fire, his balled fist to his mouth, a faraway look in his eye. "I would have thought that thirty years would have wiped the whole episode out of my mind, and I guess I wouldn't have even thought about it at all if it wasn't for that other accident. Although it's funny. I can remember some things so clearly but I can't remember anything else about that night. *I don't know what I didn't mean to do,"* he said expansively, his voice touched by fear.

"It isn't important, Hugh," Paula said softly. "It was a very traumatic time for you. Your father and aunt were killed, you were all alone. I can understand your not remembering. And it doesn't matter what caused the accident. It was all so long ago."

"Yes," he said distantly, and in the red-orange glow of the fire Paula still saw the strain of recall on his face, flushed by the warmth of the fire and his inner struggle. If he could just will the night back into his mind, his expression said. Then he gave it up.

"You're right," he said. "What happened then doesn't matter at all."

Late that night Paula woke up coughing.

Choking smoke filled her nostrils and throat and strained her lungs.

Her eyes burst open and she was instantly alert.

Smoke was filling the room. Thick. Acrid. Noxious.

The house was on fire!

"Hugh?" she cried. She reached out for him but he wasn't there.

She saw the flames now, too, and felt the searing heat. The room was ablaze around her, daylight bright. Fire rolled in waves across the ceiling and toward the outside wall.

"Hugh!" she screamed, and gagged as smoke entered her open mouth.

Mommy! Michelle's voice. Faint. Barely coming through the walls, above the rush of the flames. Jeremy's cry too. *Help me, Mommy.* The children were trapped by the fire.

She needed air. She rolled out of bed. Low to the ground, she stumbled to the window and cautiously raised herself up. The wooden sill was hot, the glass burning to the touch. She steeled herself and opened it. The cold air rushed in and seemingly angered the fire, fueling it more. White billowing clouds of smoke poured out into the night.

Mommy!

She had to get to her children.

She was turning away from the window when through a break in the smoke she saw the figure. Someone was outside the house. Standing at the edge of the woods lit up against the night, seemingly aglow in the light of the fire. It was a woman. Watching her. Watching the fire.

"Help!" Paula screamed, then froze as in a burst of firelight she saw who the woman was. But why was she there? she grappled, although for only a second. She needed her now.

"Help us!" Paula cried, but then the woman turned and disappeared into the line of trees.

Mommy!

Her children!

She raced to the door. The knob was burning hot and she couldn't touch it. She knew fire raged in the hallway. She couldn't get out of the room.

Mommy, help us! The fire! There's fire here!

The smoke was almost overpowering her. The ceiling was darkening as the wood burned. The house would soon be consumed. She knew she wouldn't be able to get to the children. They would have to save themselves. They would all have to jump. *Hugh—where was he? Was he safe? And why was that woman there?* They were only on the second floor. There was soft snow outside and the house was built into a slope. They would have to risk it.

"You have to open the windows and jump!" she yelled to them. "Do you hear me?" A surge of smoke entered her lungs, gripped her chest. She started to cough. Hoarse. Racking. She had inhaled too much. She didn't hear the children's reply. She prayed she had gotten through to them, went to the window, said a prayer for all of them, and jumped.

She tumbled fearfully out of sleep before she hit the ground. Her chest was heaving like she had run a mile. Her throat was dry and parched, her breath cold, gasping. But her eyes opened in relief and she inhaled. *It was only a dream. It was over.*

It wasn't.

The smell of smoke wafted into her nostrils. It wasn't filling the room yet; she could see and breathe clearly. But still it was there.

It wasn't a dream. She panicked. *The house* was *on fire!* That's what had caused her dream. She had really smelled smoke and her subconscious had seized it, twisted it, made her dream of Judith.

"Hugh!" she cried, but he wasn't there.

She leapt out of bed, grabbed her robe, and had it on before she reached the door. "Jeremy! Michelle! Get up. Fire!"

Where was Hugh?

It was just on the rounded edges of consciousness that the thought pricked at her, saw her out of the bedroom. *Judith's accusations.* She twisted the knobs of the children's doors, banged on the wall, made a clattering sound. "Get up! Get up!" Fragmented thoughts struggled to take hold well beneath her conscious actions. *Hugh had set the fire. Like he had last time. He was outside the condo now watching it burn. Hugh was—*

—racing up the stairs to the second floor. "What's the matter, Paula? What is it?"

She wasn't surprised to see him. She knew she could not have believed it. "I smelled smoke," she gasped. "Is there a fire?"

But still she had thought it.

The children were in the hallway. "What's going on?" Jeremy asked.

"Nothing," Hugh said. "Your mother smelled smoke because I built another fire in the hearth, that's all."

That's all.

"What time is it?" Paula asked, still unsettled. She had smelled smoke. *She still did.* But she recognized the oakwood odor now.

Although what she had actually thought . . . ! God!

"A little after four. I couldn't sleep, had a new idea for a book, and decided to work on it. I went downstairs, got cold, so I built another fire. I had closed the flue to keep out the draft, forgot to reopen it when I started the fire, and some smoke got into the room. I didn't mean to scare you. I'm sorry."

"No, *I'm* sorry, Hugh," Paula said. "I feel like a fool." More than a fool. She felt infinitely ashamed. She searched his eyes. Could he read her mind? Did he suspect what she'd been thinking? She looked past him, down the steps to the living area. A fire blazed in the brick hearth, smoke spiraled up the chimney. The woodsy smell filled the room, the house.

The dream had unnerved her.

"Okay, back to sleep now, kids. We have to get up in a few hours to make that first run."

"We could get a head start now," Jeremy suggested.

"No head starts," Paula said. She swatted him on the back. "Scoot."

When they were out of earshot she went downstairs and flopped on the couch. She shivered and pulled a blanket around her, then took a deep breath. "We've both had our share of dreams tonight, haven't we?" She looked up at Hugh. His eyes were open and concerned and her own silently begged his forgiveness for what she had for one second thought.

Chapter 17

AFTER A VACATION EVERYTHING ELSE IS LETDOWN. THEY came home from the week of skiing. The children returned to school, Paula to work, Hugh hermited himself up in his office to work on his new outline. Jason loved the book he had just delivered and it was already in production. It would be out in October with a whopping first printing of two hundred thousand copies. And already Sol Gewirtz was sending the manuscript to the Hollywood studios.

It was a lazy Sunday afternoon. The children were at friends' houses. Hugh was upstairs trying to work. Every idea he came up with seemed to fizzle before he could commit it to paper. Paula was downstairs reading Hugh's book when Marilyn called. Did she want to come over just to gab? Paula had been reading since morning and was feeling itchy. Sure.

She knocked on Hugh's office door. He was staring at his computer terminal and she could see the hunch to his back and his scowl when he turned.

"Hugh—my mother just called and I'm going to go over there for a few hours. I'll be home in time for dinner. And there's the movie we all wanted to see on HBO tonight."

"Your mother?" he questioned. "Okay. I'll come along with you."

"No, you don't have to bother. It'll just be girl talk."

He flipped off the machine and reached for the dust cover. "I'm not getting anywhere today anyway. I'll come with you."

"Hugh, no," Paula said. "I'd like to spend the afternoon alone with my mother."

"So I'll just come along. I don't mind listening to girl talk. Besides, I haven't seen your mother in some time."

He wasn't getting it. "We just want to talk."

"So?"

"So I want to go by myself," she said stiffly.

He shrugged. "I don't understand why you don't want me to come with you."

Paula felt herself bristle slightly. "I don't 'not want you to come with me,' Hugh. I don't want you to get that idea."

"Well, it certainly looks that way to me," he said defensively.

They were on opposite sides of the room, the distance between them an uncrossable expanse.

"I'm sorry it does, Hugh, but it shouldn't. I haven't seen my mother for several weeks and we've got some gossip to catch up on."

"About me?"

"Hugh!" she exclaimed exasperatedly. "What is it with you?"

"There's nothing with me. I just don't understand why you don't want to spend today with me." He sounded hurt.

"Hugh, this just isn't getting us anywhere. I'm going to my mother's house by myself." Her throat was constricting, her voice thickening as annoyance welled up inside of her. The things she hadn't said to him in Vermont burned her tongue. Perhaps she had made a mistake in keeping silent—it had been, in part, a lack of communication that had ended her marriage to Michael. "Don't confine me, Hugh, okay?" she said tightly. "We don't have to do everything together."

"Confine you? What are you talking about, Paula? All I want to do is go out with you. If that's confining . . . ? Do you love me, Paula?"

"Of course I love you, Hugh. What does that have to do with anything?"

"If you really loved me you'd want to be with me. *I* don't want to do anything without *you,* Paula."

Paula looked at him incredulously, searching for the humor behind his words, but saw he was serious. "Hugh, I want to spend an hour with my mother. This is not a question of my not loving you." She shrugged, at a complete loss. "I honestly don't believe we're having this discussion." She didn't want to say more. She turned, started for the door. "I'll be back in time for dinner, okay?" And was out.

She came home three hours later. Hugh rushed to the door at the sound of the key.

"Where were you, Paula? I tried calling you at your mother's, but nobody answered. I wanted to apologize to you. I didn't mean to question your love for me or argue with you." He spoke hurriedly, needing to get all his words out before she clipped them off. "I was so worried about you. I didn't know where you were. I even thought that maybe you *were* at your mother's house but didn't want to speak to me. Or"—he forced a laugh—"that you had left me because we argued."

"We went out to a museum," she said flatly. She slipped off her coat and Hugh took it from her.

"I—I'm really very sorry about before," he stammered. "I don't know what came over me. I guess I was really uptight about not having an idea for my new book and didn't want to spend the day alone making myself even more crazy." He laughed nervously. "There's plenty of time to do that tomorrow and all next week." His entire body seemed poised, stiff. Like he was frightened, Paula thought curiously.

He held out his hand to her. "Friends again?"

She nodded slowly—"Yes. Friends."—and watched his face visibly relax.

He tried to take her in his arms but she stepped back.

"But I won't be smothered, Hugh. I won't. You are so many things to me that Michael wasn't, what I've been wanting for a lifetime now, but I have a life outside of the two of us and you have to accept that. Keeping me from that outside life will not ensure our happiness. Rather," she said carefully, "it will destroy it."

"I love you so much, Paula," he said tenderly. "And I won't do anything to hurt what we have going. I know I have to be more understanding of your needs."

"Good." She smiled. "Then that's the deal."

They touched each other's fingertips tentatively, then slipped into the other's arms, immediately stirring inside Paula all of the feelings and emotions she associated with his touch.

She didn't want to hurt what they had going either.

But she still couldn't help but feel that something was just out of grasp.

The idea came to Paula while she was making supper. Twice she went to the phone, picked it up. The third time she dialed Information. The fourth time she let the call ring through, although part of her prayed it would not be answered. She knew she was opening up a can of worms. But she wanted to find out more.

She was putting the phone down when she heard it picked up.

"Hello."

She hesitated. "Judith, this is Paula."

There was a long pause, then suspicion in the other woman's voice. "What do you want? Is this a trap to have me arrested?"

"No." Paula set her at ease. "But I would like to see you."

"Why?"

"To talk about Hugh. I . . ." she hesitated. "I want to ask you some questions about him." Now *her* voice was hurried, Paula thought, conspiring. *She* didn't want Hugh to hear her.

"It's happening to you, isn't it?" Judith asked.

Paula felt her throat tighten. She didn't want to answer the question. She already regretted making the call.

But then Judith said, "You can come. When?"

She felt like hanging up, telling Judith to forget it. But instead she said, "I have a meeting all day tomorrow. What about Tuesday at lunchtime?"

"Yes. Do you know the address?"

"Yes." Paula hung up the phone.

There were two more clicks on the line. One when Judith hung up and the other when Hugh hung up the bedroom extension.

Judith asked who it was over the intercom. Hugh pretended it was broken and said nothing. She buzzed him upstairs anyway.

At the doorway she asked who it was again and he answered in a falsetto, "Paula."

When she opened the door he burst into her apartment slamming the door shut behind him, latching it. His face was a chiseled mask, with a cool, piercing stare that Judith had never seen before. An intense, steely calmness. Judith felt an instinctive alarm in her stomach. "What are you doing here? What do you want?" she demanded

"All I *wanted* was for you to leave us alone," Hugh mimicked, with cold, threatening anger. "That was all. But you wouldn't. You kept coming back to her again and again. Until you finally got to her." He took a step closer to Judith. A couch bisected the room, facing the fireplace, its back to the door. Judith moved away from him, putting the couch between them, alert, frightened by his approach.

"The fire was a tragic accident," he continued, his jaw set. "I tried over and over to convince you that *I didn't set it*. But you kept telling her I did, *lying* to her. And you'll keep telling her more lies until she finally believes you. You'll ruin everything for me. You'll drive Paula away from me with your lies."

He held a handkerchief in his fist, and for the first time since his entrance, Judith smelled the ether that was already permeating the room. He meant to knock her out, she began to panic. "I—I won't talk to her, Hugh. I won't let her in. I won't bother you again," she stammered hurriedly and held up her hands to keep him away from her. "No more lies." She smiled weakly, tried to establish a rapport with him. "I know you didn't set the fire." But she tried not to take her eyes from his. They were locked on each other's, cobra and mongoose.

"I can't trust you. You never leave us alone." His voice had changed, his pitch had risen. From calmness to almost whimpering fear. "I can't let you drive Paula away from me. I can't!"

The feeling of cold dread flushed Judith's entire body. "I swear, Hugh, I'll stay away from her. I'll leave you all alone. I won't even let Paula in tomorrow."

She continued to back away from him as he advanced, always keeping the couch between them. Her glance went quickly to the fireplace. Ether was flammable. If only there was a fire she could ignite his hands. But the fireplace was cold and she was nowhere near the kitchen. The poker could be a weapon if she had to defend herself. But it was too heavy. She probably couldn't lift it before he'd be on top of her. She considered screaming, but she lived in a rear apartment, the windows were closed, and all of her neighbors worked during the day. Nobody would hear.

"I swear, Hugh—"

"I can't trust you. You'll get in touch with her. You'll keep coming back again and again. You'll find a way to see her." His voice was quavering, almost desperate. "I have to make certain you never see her again."

He was mad, Judith thought, and she understood he was here to kill her. Like he had killed John and Danielle. There would be no talking, no begging, no reasoning her way free.

Adrenaline pumped. Her eyes quickly scanned the room. There was a framed picture of John and Danielle on an end table. She grabbed it, held it threateningly in her hand. "You get back now—"

He moved closer. She aimed the picture at his head and with a grunt heaved it with all her strength. He ducked away and the picture crashed to the wall behind him, gouging the plasterboard, the glass matting shattering into a thousand pieces. There was a statuette on the fireplace mantel. She lunged for it, closed her hands around the metal, but before she could raise it to throw, Hugh leaped across the couch at her, grabbed her arm, forced her wrist downward, and wrested the statue from her grasp.

With one hand he tried to pin her hands behind her back, with the other he tried to cover her nose and mouth with the ethered handkerchief. She struggled against him, kicking her legs, flailing her arms to free them, trying to connect. But he dodged her thrusts and was able to get the handkerchief under her nose. He forced her head painfully backward, her neck at full flexion; she was afraid her vertebrae might even snap. She held her breath; to inhale the ether was to succumb and die.

He shifted his body weight for a fraction of a second to better position himself. It was enough. She bit down on his hand. He howled in pain and jerked away. She pushed him. He toppled against the couch. She seized the moment. She had inhaled some of the ether and was a little light-headed, but still clear enough to know that she had to get out of there. She had gained only seconds and had to make them enough.

"I'm going to kill you, you interfering bitch!" he raged behind her.

She grabbed for the doorknob, whiplashed her neck to look behind her. *He was on his feet. Coming.* She was screaming now, a cry of animal terror from deep in her throat. Too late she remembered he had latched the chain. She fumbled it, freed it, and yanked open the door. He was there and lunged for her, got a fingerhold on her sweater but she lurched away from him, stumbled through the doorway. He threw himself at her, to tackle her. He knocked her to the threshold. Still screaming, she tried to scamper away, her fingernails clawing at the hallway carpet, hooking over the top step, trying to hold on. She kicked out at him, catching him in the chin with her heel. He snapped back and let go for an instant and she broke away. But off-balance she couldn't regain her footing and fell headfirst down the stairs, somersaulting to the bottom.

And he was there.

Paula couldn't concentrate at work. She felt guilty for calling Judith and arranging the visit. And unfaithful to Hugh. Twice Tuesday morning she almost phoned Judith to call it off, yet she resisted. If talking to Judith might help her better understand Hugh, she would do it. Although, she thought, how she could be doing this on any rational level was beyond her—going to listen to a madwoman give her insight into her husband.

At lunchtime she told Amanda she didn't know when she'd be back.

She drove to Cambridge, parked the car a block from Judith's apartment, not far from Harvard Yard, and slowly walked around the block trying to get her courage up. Her stomach fluttered nervously. *This was wrong,* her conscience pricked.

She walked up the pathway to Judith's building, found the other woman's name on the directory, and rang the buzzer. When no one answered she rang it again. A third time, and it was evident that no one was home.

Paula swallowed, suddenly feeling relieved, as if she had been granted a reprieve. She didn't have to be unfaithful to Hugh, skulk behind his back.

With one final glance at the nameplate, J. Tolson, Paula turned and left the lobby. She considered that Judith might just be out for a moment, soon to return, but she chose not even to take that chance. She would take her reprieve. She looked up at the building and squinted against the sun that reflected off the window glass. Then she turned and started back toward her car.

* * *

When Paula came home at the end of the day, Hugh was waiting for her in the living room. He had made martinis, picked up two glasses, and gave her one. "Let's drink to us," he said.

"Yes," Paula eagerly agreed, grateful for his love and attention. It was not lost on her that this was a reversal of the previous Sunday when she had returned from her drive—everyone was indeed insecure, she thought. She still felt guilty for what she had almost done today, and knew Hugh would have been furious had he found out, and justifiably so. Her actions would have been a material breach of their marital trust.

When they finished and Hugh poured another drink for them, he said, "You know, I've been thinking. Perhaps I should go see someone. A psychiatrist. A psychologist. Maybe try to understand all that thinking I've been doing about my father's death. And maybe about why"—he lowered his voice and looked away from her—"I've been so possessive of you."

Chapter 18

DR. GERALD GROLIER LEANED ACROSS A ROUND COFFEE TAble, tipped a cigarette pack in Hugh's direction. Hugh shook his head no, and Grolier put one in his mouth and lit it. Grolier was forty years old and slender until very recently when his stomach had started to expand. He was balding, with light brown hair grown long and thick on the back of his head, curling at the neckline. He was dressed casually in corduroys and an open sport shirt.

"I've read all of your novels, Hugh," he said. "I'm really a very big fan."

Hugh grinned. "Thanks. Somehow I never tire of hearing people tell me that. Writers are really very lonely people, cooped up all day at their typewriters, or in my case word processor, and anything that feeds the ego is greatly appreciated."

"So what brings you here," Grolier led. He leaned back in a swivel chair and crossed his legs openly.

"You're very direct," Hugh admired with a nervous halfsmile. "No dancing back and forth."

"If we dance we just spend your money. I like the direct approach anyway and have found most people respond well to it. So why don't you take a deep breath and plunge right in."

Dr. Grolier waited expectantly and Hugh let his eyes roam

the room thoughtfully. It was comfortable and informal, softly lit by lamplight. Curtains closed out the day so there wouldn't be any glare or distraction from outside. The walls were dark wood paneling. Behind the psychologist's desk were diplomas from Columbia and the University of Michigan, where he took his Ph.D. Framed watercolors lined the walls, Impressionist nature scenes.

"I'm here because I've been feeling uneasy about my wife lately. Worried." Hugh rounded his mouth, gathering his thoughts. "I'll tell you what I'm afraid of. The possibility that Paula might leave me. She's so wonderful. I love her so much and she loves me. But the people around her are filling her head with ideas."

"What kind of ideas?"

"To walk out on me."

"Why do you say that? If you love each other so much, why would she leave you?"

"She wouldn't on her own, but I can't watch her all the time, I can't prevent her from listening to people. Her friends are mostly unmarried or divorced, and you know what they say about misery loving company. She tells them how happy we are and I can just see their minds spinning. 'Why should she be happy and we not?' 'What can we do to make her like us?' 'We'll get her to hate Hugh and leave him.' So they make up things about me."

"Has she actually told you that they've said this?"

"No. But I know they have. And if you hear something often enough—especially lies—it begins to stay with you. It's only a matter of time until she listens to them. I also know her mother doesn't like me. Whenever we're together—which I try to keep down to a bare minimum—I feel her looking at me with these little peering eyes. We might be eating and talking and laughing and having a good time, then I'll look up at her mother across the table and she'll be staring at me. I can just imagine what she says to Paula when they're alone. We got into a fight last week. Paula was going to visit her mother and I wanted to go along with her, just feeling that if I wasn't there her mother would say things to her about me."

He laughed shortly. "Her boss is another one. He's a bachelor and good-looking to boot. I caught him flirting with Paula at a party and I'm sure he wants to have an affair with her. He tried to promote her so they could work more closely together but I put a stop to that. I've been working on getting her away from him."

"Is there anyone else you're concerned about?"

"I was about Judith. She's my ex-wife. She was telling Paula all these things about me. These lies to break us up. But I took care of her." He faltered a moment, then added quickly, "I got restraining orders against her. If she ever comes near Paula again I can have her arrested. Paula won't listen to her anymore."

"How would you feel if Paula left you, Hugh?"

Hugh looked up sharply. "It would be disastrous, Doctor. Because if Paula leaves me she'll die."

"Why will she die?"

"Because . . ." Hugh lowered his eyes and worked his hands nervously. "Whenever people leave me, they die. My father . . . the children. I don't know what it is, but when people leave me they die."

Grolier looked at him, surprised.

"Paula doesn't like it when I watch over her, but I have reason. I'm afraid of what might happen to her if she left me." He looked imploringly at the psychologist. "Maybe we can work on this, Doctor. Because I can't stop feeling this way. Paula doesn't like my being possessive of her, but I just have to be."

"Yes," Dr. Grolier said. "We're going to work on it."

Hugh couldn't wait to tell Paula about his visit to Dr. Grolier. "Believe me," he said excitedly, "when I finish with this guy, I'm never going to be possessive of you again."

"Maybe just a little bit?" Paula asked.

They made love that night, snuggled next to each other, and made light talk about their day, neither wanting to give way to sleep. Then Paula yawned and stretched. She kissed Hugh good night and they exchanged vows of love, then she rolled onto her side. Her hair was splayed out across the pillow and Hugh watched her intently as a faint band of moonlight softly caressed her face. She was so beautiful. So loving. All his.

And he was afraid.

Which was why he couldn't sleep.

He had stated it all today. Clearly. Succinctly. All of his feelings. His fears.

People were trying to get her to leave him. Her mother. Her friends. Her boss.

All threats.

Because if Paula ever left him, she would die. It was a—power he had. That was the word for it. He had always intuitively known it was something like that, just had never articulated it before. But that's exactly what it was. A power. A terrible power.

A curse.

Hugh told Dr. Grolier about his mother abandoning him and his father when he was only a child, remembering the day vividly. He and his father had been out at a local high school basketball game. They had cheered the players, eaten popcorn, and drunk soda. When they got back to the house his mother wasn't home. They saw the piece of paper taped to the refrigerator—where his parents often passed notes to each other.

"My father's face went totally blank as he read the note. Even though I couldn't read yet, I knew then that something bad had happened. My father sat me down and explained that my mother had had to go away for a little time. It wasn't until months later, when I was five, that I fully understood she had left for good.

"My aunt came to live with us and take care of me. But no one could watch over me during the day when I was at school and on my own.

"I don't know how it happened, but I somehow angered a group of neighborhood toughs. Either I inadvertently insulted someone's mother, broke into their stickball game, or they just didn't like my face. But after that the trouble began.

"I was beaten up and became afraid to go to school for fear that the gang members were waiting for me. And if not beaten up, jostled, my homework taken or dirtied.

"My father reported it to the principal, who warned them to leave me alone, which of course made them want to attack me more. So my father picked me up after school for several days. One afternoon I spotted one of the guys who picked on me. I'll never forget that moment." Hugh smiled. "It was terrific. My father charged after the kid, grabbed him by the collar, and lifted him off the ground. Now you have to try to visualize my father. He was a pretty stocky guy and had lips which could really curl up into a mean face if he wanted them to, and a deep, booming voice. Well, he screamed directly into this kid's face" —Hugh rounded his own face and deepened his voice to mimic his father—"that if he and his punk friends didn't leave me the hell alone he was going to come after each and every one of them and stomp them into the ground." Hugh laughed. "It sounds funny now—'stomp them into the ground.' But back then it wasn't funny. The kid was scared shitless. Then my father gave him one of those Marine things—repeating 'Do you understand?' over and over, louder and louder, forcing the kid to yell back, really terrifying him. I guess I did the same thing when some bigger kids picked on my stepson, Jeremy."

"So what happened?"

"Things went okay after that. They gave me looks but they left me alone. I guess my father successfully put the fear of God, and him, in them.

"And I walked a little more easily knowing I wasn't going to get creamed. But then one day my father announced that he had to take a business trip for his company and would be away for a month."

Hugh exhaled and tightened his lips thoughtfully. "I don't know . . . I guess his needing to go away hit me pretty badly. A month seemed like forever and I kept thinking to myself— my mother went away and never came back. What would happen to me if my father went away and never came back. And, what was going to happen when the gang found out my father was gone. There went my protection. So, needless to say, I was pretty frightened by the thought of my father's leaving. I put up a really big fuss, but he told me he had to make the trip and I had to be a man. He let me and my aunt take him to the airport." Hugh paused and looked down at his hands. "Of course he never made it to the airport because we got into the accident."

"Can you tell me about that?"

Hugh shook his head. "Not entirely. I don't remember everything about it. Certain things yes, others no. This is also something that has been troubling me. It was a warm day. We were riding in the convertible with the top down. I was in the back seat and was thrown free. Although I don't really remember what happened in the car."

He leaned in toward Dr. Grolier. "When we were in Vermont two weeks ago, I was looking at the fire, sleeping, drifting off, thinking about the accident, and I just said something like 'I didn't mean to do it, Daddy.' But like I told Paula, I don't know what I didn't mean to do."

"Do you feel what you can't remember is significant?"

Hugh shrugged. "I don't know. I know I've been struggling to recall the accident. Again, some things I can see and hear so clearly—being on the ground and watching them try to help my father and aunt, the slam of the ambulance doors. The sights and sounds are so vivid even now. Other things, nothing at all."

Dr. Grolier changed gears. "Tell me about the night that Judith left you."

"Judith wasn't happy in our marriage. She wasn't fulfilled," he said dryly with a turn of his lips. "I was a best-selling author, doing the talk shows, making loads of money, and she was a housewife and mother—not that there was anything wrong with that. I was happy and proud of her. But she wanted more and went through this thing about finding herself. One day I came home—just like my father did, you know?—and found a note in our bedroom that she had taken the children to Cape Cod. She needed several days away from me just to think."

"What did you do?"

"I called her and told her to come back home, but she refused and hung up on me."

"And then?"

"Then?" he shrugged. "I can't remember. I was in a bit of a fog—my wife had just left me. I might have tried to work, I might have paced the house, watched TV, I really don't remember what I did that night. Until the phone call."

Grolier's look told Hugh to continue.

"It was four, five in the morning. I was asleep. It was the police, telling me there had been an explosion and fire at our Cape Cod house, and"—he looked away sadly—"the children were dead."

"I see. And Judith?"

"She was burned somewhat, mostly on her hands, but not hurt badly."

"How did you feel?"

"Numbed. I still loved Judith, I couldn't hate her. Although I had to struggle to forgive her. The deaths were—what's a good word?—unnecessary. She had to pick *that* night to *find* herself," he said sarcastically. "I could have blamed her for the accident, but what was the point? I tried to continue the marriage, but it was over. The shock had been too much for Judith and her mind snapped. She accused *me* of being there and setting the fire, she stopped going for therapy, and we divorced."

"Do you ever see her now?"

Grolier watched Hugh shift uncomfortably for a second and wondered why.

"No. Just in court for the restraining orders."

"Well, Hugh," Dr. Grolier said, closing his notebook, "there seem to be a lot of things that you can't remember that I'm going to help you try to. Next time you come here I'd like to put you under hypnosis. Even though your conscious mind can't recall certain times in your life, your unconscious has everything logged into it. Practically frame by frame, like a motion picture camera. By putting you into a deep hypnotic trance, I'll be able to speak directly to and probe your unconscious. That will tell us what you can't remember and maybe we can find out if it's significant or not."

Chapter 19

PAULA AND NATHAN BLUME SET UP EASELS AND storyboards in Dwight Hempster's conference room. They had spent weeks finalizing the campaign for Hempster's products aimed at women, and had put together advertisements for print media, radio, and television. The conference room had an oval table with leather-covered chairs. There was a raised tier and more chairs for subordinates who might have to attend a meeting. Behind a curtain was a movie screen, and a projection room was hidden behind a windowed wall.

Nathan was pacing nervously.

"Relax," Paula said. "Why can't you be as calm as I am? After six Valiums you can be," she joked. "Besides, Nathan, you came in late on this thing; I've done most of the work on the campaign. If he hates it, it's my doing." But the work was good and she really didn't expect him to hate it.

Hempster strode into the room. "Let's get on with it," he said with no further greeting and took a thronelike chair at the head of the conference table. He was followed by a half dozen others, all similarly dressed in gray suits, while the boss wore open-collared plaid. They were all Hempster's yes-men who silently sat in prescribed seats around the room. Although Paula didn't suspect they would offer anything, except to echo the boss. This was Hempster's room, Hempster's show, and he would singly approve the campaign. What was it that Darryl Zanuck was known for saying? "Don't say yes until I've finished speaking." Another case in point, she smiled to herself.

Nathan reviewed the concept of the campaign. Hempster puffed on a cigar, drummed his fingers impatiently on the table, and kept glancing at his watch. Finally he huffed, "I know the concept. It's *my* concept. Get on with the specifics."

Paula took over and led them through the storyboards of the television commercial first, explaining each picture, the visuals as well as the voice-over narration and dialogue, trying to bring the flat pictures to three-dimensional life through her verbal presentation. They had come up with a catchphrase that would be used in all of the advertising—"The Handy Hempster Woman." She would be a *Vogue* model, Paula explained, but with her hair slightly out of place—she had been working in the house.

When she was finished she looked toward Hempster, who angrily threw his cigar across the table, scattering ashes all over the wood and into the laps of two yes-men within range.

"It stinks, Paula!" he flared. "It's lousy, no good, and so boring I wouldn't shoplift the products let alone buy them. Do you hear me?" He glowered for emphasis. "Your work is worthless!" He picked up the conference table phone and dialed Arthur Witt's private line. "I don't know if it's burnout or what with Paula," he yelled into the phone, "but I don't know how she could even present this shit to me. I don't care if you have to pull her and Blume off it and rehire Glenn, but I want the campaign completely redone. At your cost!" And with that he slammed down the phone and left the room. Followed by his six silent yes-men, who barely gave Paula a glance.

Paula stared stiffly after them. At first she was frozen, too numbed by Hempster's outburst to react in any way. Then the tears started to form—of hurt, humiliation. Her breath came in spurts, her stomach started to heave. She felt like two cents. Less. She knocked into an easel and sent it sprawling to the floor with a loud clatter. The oak-tag storyboards fell in a heap. "Goddammit!" she exploded. "That stuff is good. He doesn't have the right. He doesn't—" She broke off, as the tears came. She knew advertising was a tough game; she thought she was stronger, but suddenly saw she wasn't.

Nathan was at her side, his arm around her. "It's a good

campaign, Paula. I wouldn't have done anything differently. In fact, I didn't. I liked it as much as you did. His criticism is as much mine as yours."

"It isn't, Nathan. I told you what I suspected he would go for. It's all my doing."

"Well, just forget it. He's an ogre and not worth getting upset over. Which you already know. And I repeat, Paula. The campaign is good. It couldn't have been any better"—he tried a joke —"if you had done it all in iambic pentameter."

"No, it isn't a good campaign," she yelled back tearfully. "Unless the client likes it, it's nothing, it's garbage."

Hugh was reading in the den when she came home. She had kept back the tears all afternoon, but once in his arms they came cleanly.

"He's so impossible," she cried. "I've never been so humiliated. The way he spoke to me in front of all those people. In front of my boss!"

"That's terrible, Paula. Somebody should cut that Hempster down to size," Hugh growled.

"Yes. Somebody should. But he's so goddamn independent. He does whatever he wants. Nobody ever stands up to him. Oh, Hugh, let's forget it." She shivered. "I hope I never have a day like this one again. God, that man is so infuriating."

Hugh held her in his arms and stroked her head. "He had no right to say those things to you. What did Arthur say when you got back to the office? He didn't fire you, did he?"

"Oh, no, of course not. He knows Hempster's an ogre as much as anybody else. In fact, he felt very sorry for me and couldn't have been nicer."

"Like what did he do?" Hugh asked, a slight breaking in his voice.

"He took me out to lunch and told me how much he liked my work, and that he was not going to take me off the account."

"Well, that was good," Hugh said.

"Then I think he tried to get me drunk so I would forget the morning." Paula smiled.

A nerve jumped in Hugh's cheek, a tic at the corner of his lips—

"While all I really wanted to do was come home."

—and he relaxed.

"And now you're here," Hugh said soothingly. "Everything is all right, Paula. You still have me. No matter what happens with that job, you'll always have me."

"I know, Hugh." She touched his cheek and smiled. "And believe me, I'm grateful." She exhaled to cleanse herself of the day. "All right, enough of the Ogre. How was your day? Is the new idea working?" He had come upon an idea that was barely crystallized. She prayed it had finally jelled because Hugh was happiest when he was writing, miserable when he was in between books. Like now.

"It fell apart," he said. "It wasn't working so I had to junk it. I guess we both had lousy days. At least it shows we're on the same wavelength."

"Oh, that's too bad about the idea," she said disappointedly.

"Not too bad. It gave me some time to go out shopping today. I got you a present."

"You didn't." She smiled. "Why? What's the occasion?"

"No occasion. Just because I love you. And love getting you things."

He gave her the jewelry box to open. It was an eighteen-karat Baume & Mercier watch, with an oval face and delicate ribbing along the band and face.

"Oh, Hugh," Paula sighed. "It's absolutely exquisite."

He beamed. "So you like it."

"I love it. But it's so expensive."

"Paula . . ." he admonished jokingly. "We have the money. And believe me when I say I want to spend it only on you."

She wrapped it around her wrist. "The band is too long. I'll have to take it in to the jeweler's tomorrow to have it cut."

"Can I come with you?" Hugh asked.

"Of course you can."

"I was hoping it would fit because I wanted you to wear it tonight. I had planned on our going out to celebrate my new idea and your successful campaign, but since we don't have either thing to celebrate, let's just go out and celebrate each other."

"Oh, Hugh, I'd like to, but I'm meeting the girls for dinner tonight."

"That's right," he said broadly, and dropped his arms to his sides. "I had forgotten." Then his cheek twitched uncomfortably and he turned away so she wouldn't see, and fought the urge to say anything else to her. He had hoped the watch would have gotten her to stay with him. But he couldn't press. He must not smother her, he knew.

And when he went upstairs and watched her as she changed into her casual clothes, he couldn't help but begin to feel a little out of control. Even with the new watch, she was still going out with her friends tonight.

The women met for dinner at a Japanese restaurant along the Boston waterfront. The restaurant was once part of a deserted warehouse on the wharf that had been converted into a shopping arcade and condominium apartments. Paula, Joan, Maggie, and three others had a large round table near the front window of the restaurant, visible to the street and to the person watching from across the cobbled mall.

Hugh knew what was happening inside. Paula's friends were all talking about him, trying to convince Paula to leave him. While he couldn't hear the actual words, he felt certain about what they were saying. And stacked against five of her friends, and her boss, even the expensive watch he had gotten her paled in comparison. He would not be able to compete with all the women, not be able to keep Paula from leaving him. He paced up and down the street, oblivious to the shoppers and strollers out enjoying the springlike weather of the late March evening. He brushed against a man who looked at him strangely but continued on; he had the face of someone not to tangle with. His arm jumped spasmodically, almost uncontrollably; he couldn't calm himself, free his mind. His stomach was in knots, his palms clammy. He hadn't even been able to eat the dinner she had left him. He was too concerned about the future. Frightened. Things were getting away from him. What would happen to Paula. To him. If . . .

He felt he might jump out of his skin. He had to do something.

He thought briefly about rushing into the restaurant, grabbing her by the wrist and taking her home, but he knew he couldn't do that. It would be humiliating, she would say, and she would accuse him of trying to own her; she might leave him even more quickly. No—it was a bad idea. He had learned his lesson. He couldn't rush into the restaurant, nor could he let her see him outside. That would be just as bad.

Like the other time he couldn't let her see him.

The night in the parking garage.

Hugh clearly remembered that night. Paula had called him to say she was working late and wouldn't be home before eleven. He remembered how he had felt—much the same as now, rejected, nervous that perhaps Paula wasn't going to come home to him at all, that working late was just an excuse, she was leaving him. While one part of him suspected that that couldn't be so, another part of him *had to know*. He had paced the house, looking at the clock every few seconds. *Where was she? What was she doing? Was she going to come home to him? When?* Pinpricks jabbed at his brain, white noise rushed through his ears. The pressure built. He couldn't relax. He could almost feel himself ready to explode. He had to be close to Paula. If only he could be near her, he could reassure himself that everything was all right. *If only he could see her,* his mind had tortured him. Even that would be enough.

He knew where she parked. So he had gone to the garage to wait for her, climbing up the drafty ramp to her car, taking refuge behind a delivery van. Then he had gotten the idea—although it was a terrible idea, he should never have done it. But he didn't know that then. He had disconnected the ignition wire, thinking her car wouldn't start and he would come out of the shadows to rescue her. He was there with his car, they could go home together.

So he had disconnected the coil and waited for her. And then he saw her, scrunched into herself against the rain and cold. His heart had leapt with joy—she *was* coming home, she wasn't leaving him. She had tried to start the car, but of course wasn't able to. He watched from the shadows as she struggled and struck the steering wheel, felt her anger, her fear. Then she was out of the car and had started down the ramp and he was just about to surprise her and make his presence known when he stopped and pulled back. He saw how frightened she was alone in the dark garage, and knew he had made a mistake. He couldn't just appear to her and tell her what he had done; she would be so angry that she indeed might leave him.

Everything might backfire; he had panicked. He had to get out of the garage and home before she did. He knew he was frightening her even more by running down the ramp after her, but he couldn't take the chance of her getting home first because then she would know he had been there.

There had been only one close moment, when he had run out of the garage and she had still been in sight. But she had been too far away to see him. He had made it home ahead of her and had been properly loving and concerned when she finally did arrive.

He had even turned that night into his advantage, he remembered. She had been so frightened that he could easily tell her he didn't want her to go anyplace by herself.

But he didn't yet know what to do about tonight.

If any good could come of it at all.

He watched Paula and her friends through the window. Paula was laughing, no longer upset by what had happened with the ogre. Her friends made her laugh. She needed *them* tonight, he thought bitterly; that's why she hadn't gone out with him.

It was only a matter of time until she listened to them.

Like she had been drawn to Judith, and had been ready to listen to her.

He had to do something. He couldn't lose Paula. He couldn't be left alone.

He had to think of a way to keep Paula away from the others. *And he would.*

And just thinking that made him feel infinitely better and in control again.

Chapter 20

THE CURTAINS WERE CLOSED AND THE LIGHT THAT TRICK-led into the psychologist's office was muted, a sunless daylight gray. Hugh was sitting on Dr. Grolier's couch. The psychologist was perched in front of him on the cable-wheel coffee table with a small penlight, which he shone into Hugh's eyes. Although the flashlight was only a prop, like a pendulum or a watch. First-time patients expected a sideshow like that. After they'd gone through several sessions Grolier would be able to hypnotize Hugh by voice alone, and then by mere suggestion.

He passed the light slowly before Hugh's eyes and bade him focus on it.

At close range the ball of light flared with a rainbowed aura. Hugh defocused his eyes and lost himself to the fluorescent glow and the psychologist's voice, relaxing, soothing, as he coaxed each part of Hugh's body to become heavier and more tired. His eyes rolled upward in their sockets, his lids fluttered and dropped.

He was a good subject. He had attained the trance state quickly, was cooperative and eager. A patient could block hypnosis if he wanted to, through will or subconscious fear that something painful or traumatic might be recalled—what had been repressed for just those reasons. But Hugh had chosen to put himself in his therapist's care.

"We're going to go back a little in time, Hugh," Grolier said. "You are now a man of thirty-eight, but I want you to see yourself at your college graduation. Can you?"

A pause, then the answer. "Yes."

"Tell me what you see."

"A field of caps and gowns . . ." Hugh's words came slowly, disjointedly, typical of the hypnotic state. "Hubert Humphrey is the guest speaker. . . . He is campaigning, speaking about the war in Vietnam, his plans for peace . . ."

"Can you see yourself on your sixteenth birthday, Hugh?"

". . . yes . . ."

"On your tenth birthday?"

A longer pause as Hugh's forehead tightened and he seemingly searched his memory. "Yes."

"Who is there?"

"Friends," the labored voice said. "My aunt—"

"Is your mother there? Do you see your mother?"

The hint of struggle on his face. A slight twitching of his nose, squinting of his eyes.

"No . . . she isn't there. She left when I was only a child. . . . Never saw her again."

"Your father? Is he there?"

Hugh shook his head. "My father is dead."

"Tell me, Hugh," Dr. Grolier edged in carefully. "Do you remember how your father died?"

He was in a deep hynotic trance, his body relaxed, his breathing heavy and even, a wind tunnel echoing as he inhaled and exhaled. The screech of brakes and the blast of a car horn were heard outside but Hugh didn't react at all to the sound, lost to his memories and to the therapist's voice.

"How did he die?"

". . . accident . . ."

"That's right. Now what we want to do is go back to that day and try to remember everything about it. From getting up in the morning to leaving for the airport, everything up until the accident. We're going to calmly go through the morning without getting excited or experiencing any pain. Do you think you can do that?"

The swallow was noticeable, the slight tic at the corner of his mouth, the paling of his skin. His subconscious mind was prepared to battle the doctor, be protective of what it had repressed. Although his answer came as before. "Yes."

"Now just remember, Hugh, if things become too stressful for you, I will ask you to leave the memory and we can go somewhere else. Do you understand?"

The color returned to Hugh's face. "Yes."

"Let's go back then to that day, Hugh. Can you remember that morning and tell me what you see?"

He swallowed again, knowing he was starting down a road of memory and pain. There was a brief involuntary flex of his arm and a momentary flashing fear. "I see my father in his bedroom. His suitcase is laid out on the bed. He's packing. I'm watching him pack."

"How do you feel as you watch him pack?"

"I'm frightened."

"Tell me why." Dr. Grolier's tone was gentle, nonthreatening. "Just relax and tell me." Constant reassurance was essential.

"Because he's leaving me," Hugh gasped. "And I'm afraid he'll never come back." His voice was becoming more animated and starting to strain. Tension lines crossed his face as he struggled against the recall.

"Did he ever give you any reason to think he wouldn't—?" Grolier started, then abruptly broke off as tears formed in Hugh's eyes and his expression changed, his face taking on the look of a terrified eight-year-old. "Don't go, Daddy," he cried suddenly in a high-pitched whine. "Don't leave me. I'm afraid —" His body came alive. His fists clenched and unclenched as he worked his arms hysterically, as he had in his father's bedroom thirty years before, a child whose world was about to crumble. He was no longer just an observer to his past, reporting. He had thrown himself back into that morning, spontaneously regressing himself to his time of trauma.

Dr. Grolier touched his leg. "It's all right, Hugh. This memory can't hurt you."

". . . afraid . . ." His head wobbled fragilely; he rocked back and forth.

"Now tell me what is happening."

Hugh sniffed back his tears but his voice remained stressful, troubled, the words coming from high in his throat. "My father is still packing. He's telling me I have to be a big boy. He has to go on the trip. Now he's asking if I want to drive with him to the airport. I do. I need to hold on to every moment we could be together."

"Do you remember the trip to the airport, Hugh? Being in the car?"

The swallow again. The pause. He had entered a long, dark tunnel. Fear of discovery held him back; a need to understand propelled him forward. "My aunt was sitting in the front seat next to my father and I was in the back. I loved riding in the convertible with my father with the top down and the wind on my face and hair but that day I couldn't sit still. I was afraid. I stood up behind my father. He kept telling me to sit down, that I was blocking the rearview mirror and he couldn't see. But I was too keyed up to sit down. I kept thinking he wasn't coming back. He was abandoning me. Like my mother did. I would never see him again. I would get beaten up . . . be all alone . . ."

Perspiration had broken out on his forehead and under his arms, staining his shirt. His breath quickened as the memories came. More than just the memories, his actual feelings and emotions of the moment. There was tension on his face. His nervous tic was more pronounced. His eyes were squeezed tightly shut as if he was trying to blot out the vision—a child's game, if he closed his eyes and didn't see, all the bad would disappear.

"I saw the sign for the airport. We were getting closer and I felt panicked. . . . Once we got to the airport my father would be gone. I had to stop him. I couldn't let him get to the airport. I—had—to—stop—him!" he seethed. "Do—something—to—stop—him!"

Dr. Grolier studied Hugh's internal struggle and chose to let him continue. He knew they were getting to what Hugh had repressed, although he remained ready to pull him free if the abreaction became too intense.

"To stop him!" Hugh repeated, and his hands started to move spastically, uncontrollably, almost as if he were playacting a scene in front of his word processor. But he wasn't playacting, Dr. Grolier knew. He was back in the car, reliving that terrible morning.

Suddenly Hugh thrashed stiff-bodied on the couch, trying to escape the memory. "Can't . . . don't want to . . ."

"What, Hugh! Tell me!"

"I'm standing up in the backseat." Hugh's chin was high, jutted forward, his neck muscles thick and corded. His words came furiously. The recall was flooding his mind and he was talking quickly, spitting it all back as it opened to him mercilessly, his breath short and gasping. "Have to stop my father. Stop the car. Turn it around. I'm standing behind him . . . my arms are on his . . . trying to—must force him to turn the steering wheel, to go home. . . . He's yelling at me to stop, to leave him alone . . . he's trying to push me away from him . . . my aunt is trying to break my hold on his arms. . . . But I'm fighting them . . . have to turn the car around . . . have to . . ." he cried, his voice plaintive, frantic. Hugh's arms stretched out in front of him again as he struggled for control of the steering wheel.

There was a change. Hugh's eyes widened in terror. It was as if he were looking at something horrible in the room with them, rather than staring deep inside himself.

"The car is swerving!" he screamed. "My father doesn't have control of the car! We're going off the road. No . . . !" He threw his hands up instinctively to protect himself. "We're hitting a rock! It's jarring the underside of the car. We're tilting, off balance! I'm being thrown out of the car." With a sudden screech he wrested himself off the psychiatrist's couch to the floor and rolled to the center of the room. His breath came in short, shallow spurts, his nostrils flared. "I'm all right. I've landed on a soft grassy spot. I'm not really hurt, although my arm hurts where I landed on it. But I can see my father's car is upside down, the windshield is shattered, broken glass is all over the place . . . *'Daddy?'* Louder. *'Daddy.'* Then a desperate shriek. *'He isn't getting out!'* "

His cry was like the wail of the damned, delivered in a sudden onrush of escaping emotion at the realization. "I caused the accident. I fought with my father, made him lose control of the car! *I didn't mean to do it, Daddy, I didn't . . .*"

Hugh scrambled forward on his hands and knees, trying to go to his father.

"Daddy?" he cried again. He started to kick his legs and move his arms again, fighting off unseen figures. *"Leave me alone. Leave me—"* He flailed and stamped. People were trying

to help him, Dr. Grolier surmised. *"Daddy!"* the child cried. *"Save him. Save my father!"*

He ceased his struggling. His arms were stiff and bent at odd angles. The angle they would be if someone were holding on to him, restraining him. He was crying.

"What do you see now, Hugh?" Dr. Grolier asked very softly. "What is happening?"

"There are sirens," Hugh sobbed. "I hear sirens. The police are coming. *'Save him!'* " he yelled. " *'Get him out of the car. I'm sorry, Daddy. I didn't mean—'* "

"What now, Hugh?" Grolier pressed.

"They're pulling my aunt out of the car. There's so much blood. Her face. Her arms. Covered with blood. Now my father —Daddy!" He grew more excited and hope entered his voice. *"He's going to be all right."* Then quickly left it. *"He isn't moving!"* More desperate, croaking. *"They're checking for breath. Feeling his wrist for pulse—"* Even more. *"They're shaking their heads, looking at me. No—"* the child moaned. *"Save him. Save him."* Hope again. *"An ambulance is coming. They're putting him onto the stretcher. . . ."*

Suddenly Hugh sat bolt upright on the floor, his eyes bulging in understanding and final realization. *"Daddeeee!"* A black voice stripped by terror rose from deep within him. It was a scream, loud and fierce, fraught with loss and utter hopelessness. *"They're covering his head with a sheet! He's dead!"* A forced choking sound emerged from somewhere in his throat, as if his voice box had been removed. *"AND I KILLED HIM! I—KILLED—MY—FATHER!"*

It was enough. Time to pull him away from the memory. "Hugh!" Dr. Grolier ordered sharply. This was what had been repressed, triggered anew by the recent car accident. The knowledge that the child had killed his father had been too traumatic and he had protectively wiped it from his memory. All he had consciously remembered was that there was a car accident, nothing of his participation. "You will leave this memory, now, Hugh. You will leave it and go to a happy time in your life, the time when you met Paula." The psychologist was perspiring. The session was exhausting.

"Dead!" Hugh continued to sob.

"When I count to three you will leave this memory," Dr. Grolier repeated.

"I didn't mean to do it." Hugh had rolled himself into a ball on the floor. Tears of anguish, of despair rolled down his cheeks. It was a situation from which there was no escape.

Grolier slapped his hands together and Hugh was quieted, his body uncoiling, relaxing again. And after the power of the recall, the silence in the room was sudden, like a plug had been pulled.

"Come back on the couch." Grolier reached for Hugh's arm and lifted him up. There was no fight left in him; he did not resist Grolier's touch as he had the hands of those who had come to his assistance during the accident.

"I'm going to deepen your trance now, Hugh, and we're going to talk to each other. You have just learned something about yourself, something painful. . . ."

Hugh's body seemed to sway, overwhelmed by memory and remorse, guilt.

"But something we will get through together," Grolier reassured calmly, preparing to instill in Hugh a sense of well-being and support to lessen the impact of his new reality when he awoke. There was no excitement to his voice; it was cool and professional. "I know this is difficult for you, Hugh, but I'm going to make it easier. It's important that it all has come out. This way it can't torture you anymore because you will be in control. You were only a child when all of this happened. Desperate and frightened. You were struggling to hold on to your father. You had lost your mother and were terrified of losing your father as well. You are not a bad person, Hugh, you were just frightened, and your actions were prompted by that fear. It's now thirty years after the accident, a lot of time to suffer and punish yourself and fear for those you love, and time enough to be over it and free of the past. And while your deed cannot be undone, it can be justified, and together we will use that knowledge to help you understand your possessiveness of Paula and your fear of her leaving you and something happening to her. Then we will work together to remove that fear."

His hands struck together sharply, Hugh blinked twice and looked up. Then he covered his eyes and wept, an overflow of emotion and guilt, although tempered by the psychologist's hypnotic suggestions.

* * *

It was an hour later when Hugh left the office. Dr. Grolier had reiterated over and over that he had been a frightened child, caught up in circumstances, that he had reacted defensively, not at all maliciously. "You didn't mean to hurt anybody and can't blame yourself for your father's death. It was only a terrible, terrible accident."

Hugh leaned on the psychologist's words and left for home feeling better. He knew he could almost accept what he had done if using that information would keep Paula from leaving him.

But he still felt troubled. The visit to the psychologist *proved he really did have a power.*

They'd have to talk about that next time.

He wondered why he hadn't mentioned his power to Dr. Grolier before.

Chapter 21

THE DAY WAS GLORIOUSLY SPRINGLIKE, THE SUN HIGH IN A cloudless sky, and it seemed that everyone had been outside at lunchtime taking advantage of the weather. Paula went window-shopping along Washington and Summer streets, browsing through the first floors of Filene's and the Jordan Marsh Company, where she bought their famous blueberry cupcakes for lunch. She returned to work at a quarter to three. "Arthur wants to see you," Amanda said.

Paula checked in with Arthur Witt's secretary and was surprised by the look that Helen gave her—a hurried glance, then she turned away.

"Come in, Paula," Arthur beckoned, and motioned her to a chair opposite his desk.

"What's up?" she asked.

"I don't exactly know how to say this," Arthur started. "But I got a call from Dwight Hempster before lunch—"

"We're reworking the presentation. He can't expect—"

Witt held up a hand to stop her. "It wasn't that. He knows we're on it."

"So, what?"

"So"—he paused—"Hugh called him."

Paula leaned forward in the chair. "Hugh?"

"Apparently Hugh screamed at him for having screamed at

you at the presentational meeting, said he had no right to treat you like he did—which I agree—called him all sorts of names, questioned his lineage, I understand, and threatened him with I-don't-even-know-what. Hempster was almost apoplectic when he called me. I don't think I've heard him this angry before. I can just imagine the color of his face and how high into the triple digits his blood pressure went."

"I can't believe Hugh did that," Paula said, shocked. "I don't know what to say to you, Arthur. I'm so embarrassed. I'm sorry."

"From what I understand"—Arthur managed a smile—"he really laid into him—and for that he has my admiration. He did something we've all been wanting to do for years, but because of little things like economic security never got around to it. That, and doing our share for the tranquilizer business," he joked and paused.

"There's more, isn't there," Paula said more than asked.

Arthur nodded. "Yes. There's more." He jumped off the desk and walked to the window. Traffic moved haltingly below on Beacon Street and he followed a stretch limousine as it rounded the corner and disappeared from sight. "He demanded I fire you. Or else he would be out of here immediately."

"Oh, no . . ." Paula sighed.

"Paula, you are a damn good advertising woman. You can conceive a whole campaign. You can do everything. I think you know I think that of you. You are invaluable to this company and you've got my total support. Besides, no client is ever going to tell me who to fire in my company. Jeff feels the same way. I've talked to him and we're united on this. So I'm going to take a stand, apologize for Hugh's call, which was completely unauthorized and unsolicited—an irate husband whose wife was slighted—but tell Hempster that my best employee stays."

"And he'll be out the door in a minute." Paula held up her hand. "No, Arthur, I won't let you do that. I appreciate this, but I'm not going to let you jeopardize the account. Hempster's a stubborn mule. He'll walk and you know it. We have too much into that account and too much riding on its success to lose it now. Besides, you'll have to let people go and I don't want to be responsible for that. *I'll* walk, Arthur. Hugh did this, and I'm the one who's going to leave."

"Paula—" Arthur started.

"No. Don't say anything. Just get on the phone and tell Hempster you fired me, that the situation is under control. Then call some of your friends and tell them your best damn employee ever just quit and needs another job. It's all right to tell them the circumstances. So they'll be getting a copywriter with a passionate, protective husband." She smiled, although her eyes were clouded with tears. "Do you want my desk cleaned out this afternoon or will I have time to Xerox my successes and copy the Rolodex?"

"Oh, Paula," Arthur sighed.

"I'm going to miss you too," she said, cutting him off.

"This will blow over," he promised.

"No, it won't for some time," Paula said, but she wasn't thinking about her conversation with Arthur Witt, rather, her confrontation coming up with Hugh at home. Now he had overstepped.

"You'll have no trouble finding another job," Arthur assured her.

"No, I don't think I will. And I'm going to make certain I find one immediately," she added pointedly.

"What are you doing home from work so early, Mom?" Jeremy asked as she came through the door.

Hugh was sitting with the children in the living room. She glanced at him quickly, then turned her gaze to Jeremy and Michelle and summoned a smile. "Oh, I decided to take the afternoon off. A touch of spring fever." She hung up her raincoat in the closet.

"Now you're getting with it, Mom. We were just going to go out and toss a softball. Want to play too?"

"No, I don't think so." She met Hugh's eyes neutrally. "You three go out, I've got to make some phone calls."

"It's good to have you home early, Paula," Hugh said.

"Yes," she said coolly. "I'm sure it is."

Then without saying anything more to him, she swept past him and toward the kitchen.

He came back into the house ten minutes later.

"I left the children playing outside. I wanted to be here with you."

She stiffened when she heard him come in. She was standing

at the sink cutting up potatoes for dinner, expending nervous energy. Her back was to the door. On the way home she had gone over in her head a dozen different ways to tell him how she felt, turning her thoughts over and over to the point of distraction where she had almost caused an accident on the turnpike. Now all the rehearsed words flew out of her head. She just turned and faced him.

"How could you do that to me, Hugh? How could you have made that call to Hempster?"

A nerve jumped in his cheek. His arm twitched. "He—he had upset you," he said. "You were so angry when you came home because he had humiliated you. I wasn't going to let anyone speak to you like that and get away with it. You're my wife and I love you and I have to stand up for you." He was poised at the edge of the kitchen table. He wanted to move closer to her, but her posture made him afraid.

"You just didn't have the right," she said angrily. "That is my career, my life—"

"But you even said that someone should talk back to him."

"I didn't mean for *you* to do it, Hugh. And you had no business tampering with my job without first checking with me."

"I—I didn't think to talk to you first. I guess I should have. I thought I was doing the right thing . . ." His hands turned nervously against each other. He hadn't considered she would be angry with him. He hadn't thought everything out.

"Well, it couldn't have been more wrong. Because I got fired."

"Paula, no!" he said, shocked. He had to sound surprised, outraged. She should never suspect his plan. "Arthur had no business—"

"Oh, Hugh, stop it. What did you think was going to happen? Hempster was going to thank you for pointing out to him he was a bastard and then Arthur was going to give me a raise? How would you feel if I phoned Jason and called him whatever it was you called Hempster? What do you think would happen there? How long do you think you would be with that publishing company? And Arthur said you even threatened Hempster? How? Bodily? You're probably lucky he didn't file charges against you."

"I—I didn't mean—" he stammered. He couldn't get the

words out. His entire body was shivering in the face of her fury. He had never considered it would be like this.

"I was with those people for years. I loved them like family. Joan came into my office after I left Arthur, took one look at me, and burst into tears. I couldn't even talk to her. Even Nathan, who I just met—" She brushed off the thought with a wave of her hand. "And besides my getting fired, couldn't you realize how humiliating it was going to be for me. Calling our biggest client? In my *defense?*" She curled her lips at the word. "Even it that were so, I'm not a child, and won't be treated like one."

"Never," he promised. "I just thought that maybe I could set him straight . . . so he'll never do that to you again. . . . It hurt me to see you hurt like that. . . ." He was fumbling with his words, grasping.

"Look, Hugh," she said. "I'm pretty angry with you now and I'm going to say this. I don't believe you called Hempster for my feelings or honor, okay? I just don't believe it. We had this discussion when I went to my mother's house and you wanted to come along. I think you did what you did today to be controlling, manipulative. But I said I wasn't going to be smothered, Hugh, and I meant it. That's what made you start going to see the psychologist."

"And he's helping me. I know he is. It was a rough day today, but—"

"All right. Good. I'm glad. But you tell him what you did and see what he says. I've overlooked a lot, I've given you the benefit of the doubt on some things, I've convinced myself I misread other things, but I just think that this was an attempt of yours to get me out of the work force and home. I know you want me here. You've made that clear enough to me, but I told you that I wanted to work now and I meant it. I gave up a lot for you, Hugh. I could have been creative director of the company, but I gave up that job because you wanted me to—"

"Only because I was afraid it would take too much time away from us . . ." he stammered.

"That was a compromise I made for you. And I gave up that trip to Atlanta, and another trip I didn't even tell you about. I just told Arthur no, I wasn't going to go. I don't even think he'd ask me to go anywhere for the company again." She laughed shortly. "Not that there is even a company for me now.

But that was another compromise for you. And all I wanted in return was your respect for my working."

"I do respect your working, Paula."

"Look, I know that you have lost a lot of people in your life, Hugh, and for that you have my sincerest sympathies. I can understand why you want to be close to me and have me close to you, but it's just too much. I won't live this way."

His eyes flickered nervously.

"Your possessive nature drove Judith away from you, and I'm just warning you if you don't stop it now, as much as I hate to say it, it might make me do the same."

"Paula, no!" he said frightfully. "You can't leave me too. I have this pow—" He broke off and started another way, speaking quickly, needing to hold on to the conversation, *her*. "I love you too much. I'm sorry for what I did today. Yes, I hated the way Hempster embarrassed you—I guess I'm so independent in my work that I can't conceive of anyone speaking that way to me. But believe me, I didn't want it to turn out like this—your getting fired, hating me . . ."

Hugh was struggling with his words, trying to make her believe them. But there were so many distractions. The session in Dr. Grolier's office was still fresh in his mind, the knowledge of what he had done when he was a child . . . the power he had. . . . He had to be careful of Paula, not to possess her, not to drive her away from him. At the same time he had to be careful that she wouldn't leave him. There was so much to look out for. His head was starting to pain him, he didn't know what more to say.

"Hugh, the compromising is over. I've asked Arthur to make some calls for me to other agencies. And I'm going to do the same. I have an appointment set up tomorrow morning with a headhunter. I'm going to find another job. And one with more responsibility if I can. If anybody will have me as creative director or account exec, that's a job I want now. And if our time together has to suffer, then I'm sorry, it will have to suffer and we'll have to live with it."

"You know I love you, Paula," he repeated, a mounting desperation in his voice. There was a buzzing noise in his head. His hands were sweating and he felt afraid. He just didn't know what was going to happen. He wanted to reach out for her, sweep her up in his arms, hold her, protect her, never let her go from him, but he knew he couldn't do that now. He had made a mistake, a terrible mistake. He swallowed tightly. "Do you still love me?" he asked, his tone strained and frightened.

The phone rang. Paula reached for it. "Joan!" she said, an upward lilt to her voice. "Okay . . . I'm doing all right . . ."

Then she turned away from Hugh and cradled the phone.

He was almost afraid to leave her alone in the room. He stood immobile, watching her, lost to his private thoughts, not even hearing her conversation, only jarred back when she glanced over her shoulder at him. He looked at her hungrily, wide-eyed, but she turned away from him again.

Hugh spent the evening with the children, helping Michelle with her homework, playing Asteroids with Jeremy, letting him win. Paula was up in their bedroom going through an advertising contact book. She came out only to put the children to sleep, then went back in again.

Hugh didn't know what to do. He wanted to get into bed with her, even if only to read. But he was afraid of her reaction —would she think he was being too possessive of her just because he wanted to spend the evening together? He ended up pacing the first floor of the house. The television was on. He pretended he was watching for Paula's benefit—to show he didn't have to be with her, wasn't being possessive of her—but he didn't even know which channel he was tuned to. Nor did Paula come downstairs.

When he went upstairs after the eleven o'clock news, she was already asleep. The hall light rushed in, beating a triangular path to the bed. She was wearing a nightgown and lay half under the covers, half exposed, her arms folded over her chest defensively; *keep away* was the message. He quickly closed the door so the light wouldn't disturb her and tucked the blankets carefully under her chin. *She shouldn't object to that,* he thought. She stirred but did not awaken.

Hugh got under the covers but couldn't unwind and fall asleep. His mind was clouded, his thoughts folding, shifting. He twisted and turned, searching for a comfortable position, then afraid he would wake Paula, he threw the blanket aside and sat on the edge of the bed, his head in his open hands, his fingers playing over his eyes, trying to stop his thoughts, clear his head. There was so much confusion, so much pressure building inside of him, a rush in his ears as if they were clogged, a murky blur. It had been one of the worst days of his life. He had learned something terrible about himself at Dr. Grolier's office, and had just had a major fight with Paula in which she even threatened to leave him.

He had never felt this confused before. This frightened. His hands were shaking, his palms damp and cold, and he rubbed them against each other trying to warm them.

He wished he could just fall asleep and forget everything, but there was too much turmoil raging inside of him. The buzzing through his head had picked up, a roaring sound, pounding surf.

He needed to have Paula totally to himself, but now things couldn't be worse *because she threatened to leave him.*

His forearms jerked involuntarily just below the front of the elbow, as if he had been electrically shocked.

Everything had gone tragically wrong. He had made a terrible mistake doing what he had with her client. He saw that now, but now it was too late. He had never considered she would be so angry with him. And now he was going to lose her.

The reflected light on his dresser caught his eye, a golden sheen melting into shadow.

The night sky was cloudless, the moon full. The window shade was only three quarters drawn, and pale orange light passed into the bedroom and fell across the polished surface of the dresser . . .

. . . and over the small pocket knife lying next to his and Paula's wedding picture in a standing frame.

The feelings he had now were familiar, he thought. He had felt this way once before, he recalled vaguely, but couldn't quite remember when.

The penknife beckoned him. He blinked twice and cocked his head, oddly drawn to the slit of flared light. He had kept that knife in his dresser for years and had used a knife blade the previous evening to tighten something for Jeremy, not wanting to go downstairs for a screwdriver. He hadn't put the knife away afterward. It was beautiful the way the bronze handle captured the moonglow. Almost hypnotic.

Then he identified his feelings as the same as the night that Judith had left him. He had sat right here on the bed after he had talked to her on Cape Cod and she had refused to come home, filled with the anguish he was experiencing now.

Judith had put him through such terrible pain that night.

And now the pain was even worse than it had been with Judith.

He didn't want to go through the hurt and rejection again, the fear of being left alone.

He couldn't go through it again. He began to panic. His fists clenched, his forehead tightened, pain sliced behind his eyes, and he almost lost his balance and toppled from the bed.

His mind churned, images sifted. He loved Paula so much, but she was just going to turn around and hurt him. Like she had tonight. Threatening to leave him, not telling him she loved him. *Because she didn't! She was getting ready to leave him just as Judith had!* his mind pulsed and warned. That's why the similarity of feeling. Her friends had gotten to her, her mother.

Hurt or be hurt—the fleeting thought teased suddenly with solution.

He couldn't let Paula leave him. It couldn't happen to him again. His body was trembling. He was cold, so cold, so afraid.

But there was a way out of his pain. If Paula was dead, then she couldn't leave him.

He moved his hands in front of his face to banish the thought. He couldn't even dare to think such a terrible thing. Paula dead? He twisted around on the bed to look at her. She was curled up on her side in the fetal position. He thought about how he loved to lie in bed propped up on his elbows watching her sleep. She never knew about that because he had never wanted to spoil his pleasure by having her suspect he was watching her. So many nights he had just lain in bed watching her, listening to the faint wisps of her soft breath. She was such a beauty in sleep and he loved her so much—

It wasn't accidental the pocket knife was there. It was there for a reason.

There was something haunting about the way the moonlight glinted off the metal of the knife; the reflective glow was almost surreal.

He was meant to use it, a voice inside of him cried.

To kill Paula.

That's what he had to do.

The pressures inside of him mounted. There was no escape

from his feelings. From the pounding. The knotting. From his terrible fear of being abandoned again.

He remembered he had felt this way, too, when his father was leaving him.

And he had killed his father.

But then it had happened again with Judith. She had left him. And now with Paula. She was going to leave him too.

The realization came explosively: *He could kill Paula, then kill himself. That was the way out. That way he wouldn't have to experience these torturing feelings again and again.*

That was the solution.

The was *the power,* he thought triumphantly.

He understood it now and didn't need the psychologist anymore.

Dizzily, he got up from the bed. The slight movement made Paula stir. He froze. She shouldn't see what he was doing.

From a different angle, standing over the penknife, he could see it was completely illuminated in the moonlight. It even seemed to be twitching with life, beckoning him.

He lifted the knife from the dresser, weighed it in his palm. It was talking to him, telling him to open it up, that this was the way out. If he wanted to free himself of all pain, this was the way out. *The only way out.*

He flipped open the knife and ran his finger along the flat of one of the blades. There were tiny indentations where it had been scraped and gouged. It wasn't a sharp knife, he had never kept it up. But one thrust was all he would need.

He held the knife in his right hand and ran his left up and down his bare chest, sticky with perspiration. His skin was alive and crawling, rough, goose-bumpy. He felt a weakness in his stomach, a nervous fluttering. A new feeling veiled him—a new memory was trying to come through, he thought distantly. It was just on the edge of touch and discovery, calling to him. There was something else he had to remember, like what had happened with his father. Another time when he had felt just like he did now. But he didn't want to try to remember it now. Now he had to kill Paula because she was going to leave him.

He walked closer to the bed. The knife felt comfortable in his hand. His knees pressed flush against the mattress, his arms at his side. All he had to do was reach out toward her—

It would be easy. And the end result so blessed. He would never have to go through this terrible pain again.

One quick thrust.

Then another.

First Paula, then himself.

She breathed easily right below him. She looked so beautiful lying there he just wanted to cradle her in his arms and forget everything else except her. His fingers weakened, the knife was loose in his grasp, balanced gingerly in his palm.

You have to do it. The voice was sharp, controlling.

No— He struggled, he couldn't. His head lolled loosely on his neck and he strained to open his hand and drop the knife. Something felt wrong. A piece was missing. He didn't know what. But he couldn't think clearly or fight the pressure anymore. There was no way to ensure her staying with him; he couldn't protect himself.

Do it!

His hands were shaking but he tightened his fingers around the handle and raised his arm to its full extension. He squinted fearfully, hesitated.

Do it! the knife and his mind screamed simultaneously, a clear, commanding voice through a rush of sound and confusion.

Do it, do it, do it. The chant inside of him accompanied the movement of his arm, a smooth, unbroken downward arc, a quarter circle. *Think of the relief. You can never be hurt again. First Paula. Then yourself. It's easy. Easy. Easy. EASY!* The voice grew to deafening intensity.

Yes!!! he shrieked almost madly.

He brought his arm down stiffly, touched the blade to the covers ready to plunge through when the new thought wrenched through him and he stopped, his arm frozen right-angled in front of him.

It was the missing piece.

He frowned.

If he killed both Paula and himself, what would happen to the children?

Jeremy and Michelle would be abandoned by both their parents, doomed to what had happened to him as a child. Everything would repeat itself. He couldn't do that. He couldn't cause the children to suffer all that he had. They would grow up to be like him.

His arm dropped limply to his side. He inhaled slowly, deeply, let his body shake, then relax. *What he had almost done!* Then he closed the blade in the handle, watched it nestle smoothly, soundlessly among the other blades, and put the pocket knife back into the top drawer, out of the moonlight. He covered it over with T-shirts. He wouldn't be able to see it, or hear it.

He closed the drawer lightly so it wouldn't make a sound and disturb Paula. Then he got back into bed and snuggled in next to her, rubbed his chin against her soft flesh, breathed in her sweet chypre scent. Just holding her filled him with a heady sense of relief. He was feeling better already, more sure of himself.

But he didn't know how long he could hold out. How much of this pain he could endure before he—

She was the key. If he could only keep her with him. . . .

"I love you so much," he whispered tenderly, his voice barely audible, his words little more than thoughts. Tears brimmed in his eyes. Of love. And fear. For both of them.

Then he begged her. "Please don't leave me, Paula. Because I don't want to have to hurt you."

Chapter 22

HUGH WOKE UP AND REACHED OUT BESIDE HIM FOR PAULA.
She wasn't there!

His eyes shocked wide and he twisted himself on the bed, his mind alert and spinning. The worst had happened. She had left him!

Then he heard the sound of running water and lay back and calmed himself. It was all right. She was in the bathroom washing up, getting ready for the day. But what was her plan? he wondered fearfully.

The bathroom door opened and she came out. Through eye slits he watched her, pretending still to be asleep. Then to be just awakening. He rustled the covers, yawned, and stretched. *He must be careful not to be too possessive of her. That was the most important.*

"Good morning." He strove for evenness of voice.

"Good morning, Hugh." She was putting on her slip, reaching into the closet for a dress.

"Where are you going?" He swallowed and tried not to let his nervousness show.

"I would be going to work. But instead I'm going to look for work. I have an interview this morning. Is that all right with you?"

She was being cool with him he knew, but it was all right because she was still there.

"Yes, of course. I won't repeat what I did yesterday," he promised.

"Hugh, I really hope not," she answered.

The children left for school and Paula for her appointment. Hugh went up to his office and started to work on his new idea, convinced that everything was under control, last night an aberration. Paula had no plans to leave him.

He looked at the clock.

It was ten-fifteen. She had been gone for more than an hour. Surely that was enough time to have a meeting, then come home, wasn't it? Had anything happened? Could she be hurt?

He shook off the worry, but then a voice deep inside of him questioned, *What if she wasn't coming home? What if she had left for good?*

He rolled his shoulders as if warding off something irritating his neck, then tried to focus in on his new idea, but overwhelmed by distraction he couldn't work. He turned off his computer and stared out the window. He was able to see the main road at the end of the cul-de-sac. Cars roared by. He was hoping to catch Paula's car turning into their street.

He was starting to feel unsettled again. Itchy. He rubbed his arms nervously; his flesh was raised and cool. He tried to buffer himself against unwanted, surfacing fears. He couldn't. Then his thoughts exploded with certainty: *She took the children and left him. He would find a note saying she wasn't coming home. It would be just like his father and Judith all over again.*

He had to find the note. He had to know. The uncertainty was torturous. He went downstairs to their bedroom and hastily scanned the room. There was nothing left for him on the dresser or pillow. To the kitchen next. Nothing on the refrigerator door, no note on the table. *No note,* he breathed, tensed as he sniffed the air, an alert and prowling animal. But that didn't make him feel any better because she still might call him. His breath was coming faster and he felt his heart racing. He was all alone and frightened. A white rush filmed his eyes.

He should have killed them both last night.

He began to pace the house anxiously. Living room, kitchen, dining room, den, panther steps, short, quick. If only he knew where she might have gone, he could go after her, find her, bring her home—

The phone rang. He pounced on it.

"Paula . . ." he gasped. "Where are . . . ?"

"Is this Mr. Hugh Tolson?"

Confusion. It wasn't Paula. It was a man's voice. "Yes. Who is this?"

"This is Detective Nicholson with the Cambridge Police Department. I'm sorry, but we've just discovered the body of your ex-wife. An apparent suicide. She's been dead close to a week. Would you mind coming down to the morgue to identify her for us?"

"What?" he asked blankly, then added hurriedly, "I'm sorry, I have to keep this line free now . . . I'm expecting a call."

"We'll just need you for a few minutes."

"Yes. All right. Later today."

"About three?"

"Yes. About three."

"Is there any other family—?"

"I can't stay on the phone now. I'll see you at three." And he hung up.

He heard the sound of a car and flew to the window. But when he peered out he saw it was only the woman who lived across the street, now driving into her garage, closing the door automatically behind her. The street was quiet again. He flung open the front door and stood outside in the entranceway, as if his being out there would make Paula come home faster. Then, afraid he might miss her phone call, he went back into the house. He didn't know what to do with himself. He stared at the phone, willing it to ring. Then he searched the house another time looking for a note. He felt like he wanted to crawl out of his body, escape the mounting tension he was feeling again. She wasn't coming home. He was being abandoned.

He had lost all track of time when he heard her car pull into the driveway. Relief flooded through him; weight lifted from his shoulders. He struggled for composure. *She couldn't catch him worrying about her.* That would certainly drive her away.

He raced upstairs to his office, hurriedly turned on his computer, and with trembling fingers inserted his system diskette into the disc drive, typed some words on the screen, pretended to be working. All for her benefit if she came upstairs. She shouldn't know he had done anything else that day. She came into the house. He heard the rustling of packages in the kitchen, the slam of the cupboard door; she must have gone shopping. Then she was on the stairs.

"Is that you, Paula?" He tried sounding casual. As far as she would know it had just been a day of work for him, without worry or care.

"Yes. I'm in the bedroom."

"I'll be right down. I just want to finish a paragraph."

"All right."

He desperately wanted to be with her and it was agonizing to wait two full minutes, but he carefully counted out the time. He smoothed his clothes, his hair. Then, relaxing his body, he walked down the steps. She was hanging up her work dress, changing into a jogging suit.

"How was your day?" he asked. He set his muscles in an easy smile.

"I have two interviews set for tomorrow. I think I'll get an offer. At a lot more money than Arthur was paying me," she added with a surfacing smile.

"I didn't think you'd have any trouble. You're so talented. And you'll have no ogre to deal with . . . although I know that isn't the point." A pause between them, then he stammered, "I'm sorry again for what I did. . . ."

She looked at him evenly, tensed her lips, and shook her head. "I know you are and I don't want to stay angry with you, Hugh. . . ."

His heart leapt excitedly with promise. "And I don't want you to be angry with me either." Just a few words from her and things were looking better, his fear subsiding.

"Okay. I think we understand each other now. I think you know what I want and need from you."

"Yes."

"We'll forget yesterday. Like it didn't happen. Okay?"

He wanted to grab her and hold her, but he played it cautiously. "Like it never happened."

"When's your next appointment with the psychologist?"

"Tomorrow."

"All right. Tell him I'm with you all the way. I want to be friends again."

She let him take her in his arms. He enveloped her and closed his eyes, shivering with the purest of joy. She wasn't leaving him.

But his feeling of ease was short-lived, elusive, and he grew frightened again. As relieved as he felt now, he didn't know how long she would stay. Because he knew from last night he couldn't be positively certain of her and didn't know how to ensure himself she would always be there. How could he spend day after day after day staring at the clock, trembling with growing fear, waiting for the moment she would come home, agonizing that she would not?

He couldn't.

He went to the morgue to identify Judith's body. It had been the decaying odor of the body that had prompted her neighbors to call the police. Detective Nicholson told him that the physical evidence in the apartment indicated she had ingested a combination of pills and liquor in a fatal combination. Given her unhappiness and mental illness, Hugh nodded solemnly, he could understand. If only he had seen it coming. . . . Procedure required an autopsy be performed, but no one was expecting to discover any foul play. It was suicide, pure and simple.

Which was how he had planned it, Hugh knew, remembering how he had poured the liquor and pills into her mouth, and scattered the empty bottles and vials as she might have. The ether he had used had long since disappeared from her system and would not be in evidence. Nor had there been any bruises from her fall down the stairs; he had inspected and found nothing. He had also carefully vacuumed all flakes of plaster and shards of glass, and hung a picture over the wall to cover a newly plastered crack. There was no evidence of any struggle in the apartment; he had covered his tracks.

After he left the morgue he smiled. This would not be a worry and Judith would never interfere with their lives again.

That night Hugh took Paula and the children out to a French restaurant on Arlington Street, overlooking the Boston public garden. They came home, put Jeremy and Michelle to bed, and made love. Afterward, Paula drifted off to sleep in his arms and under his protective gaze, and Hugh couldn't have been happier.

But then, as always happens when one is content and ready

for rest, in the twilight zone at the edge of wakefulness, Hugh's mind clouded and grew active and punishing, and night worries began to prey on him mercilessly, refusing to release him to sleep. He lay awake in bed, his eyes sprung open and staring blankly, unblinking at the shadowed ceiling, his body taut and filmed with the clammy kind of perspiration that comes only from terror. And as the clock swept forward from late night toward early morning there was no escape from what coursed relentlessly through him—all of his terrible fears of abandonment and loneliness—from which there appeared to be no resolution.

Except one, he knew, as he finally found his peace through exhaustion.

There was only one resolution to Kate Forest's problem too. She had to just boldly pick up the phone, call Hugh, and tell him how she felt. The time for subtlety was long gone; she could no longer wait out Hugh's pace. If she wanted him she would have to act. What she should have done long ago, she knew now.

All of the nights she had cried herself to sleep thinking of Hugh, all the evenings she had driven to his house, parked her car at the end of the cul-de-sac, and approached on foot so the motor sounds wouldn't call attention to her presence. Then hid in a clump of tall trees watching the bedroom and the two figures silhouetted behind the shades, envisioning them holding each other, loving each other, when it should have been she who was upstairs in Hugh's arms. Instead of becoming cold and having to return home to her lonely apartment and her empty bed.

Her body ached to be touched by Hugh, possessed by him. There was a stinging longing inside of her that had gone on for too long. A dull pain without end. She no longer enjoyed eating, nor even her work.

. . . *if only I wasn't married* . . .

No! She had lived too long with those words. It was time to declare her love for him, convince him to leave Paula and marry her. Which he would do, she was certain. She had seen it in his eyes when he had come to the office, heard it in his voice, read it in his words to her, in his body when they had danced. She had feared his rejection and that had kept her silent. But now she resolved to risk it, because there was no risk.

He was waiting for her to come to him.

Chapter 23

PAULA WENT ON A CALL-BACK INTERVIEW ON WEDNESDAY. Hugh desperately wanted to go downtown with her, but fought the urge and instead stayed home and tried to conquer his new idea, create a sense of normalcy and ease. But he remained too distracted and tired to work effectively. He was sleeping only fitfully, plagued by his guilt of the past and fears of the future, afraid that if he dared to close his eyes, he might wake up to find Paula gone. He passed the night thrashing and twisting on the bed, unable to find a comfortable position or escape his torturing thoughts. He skipped his appointment with Dr. Grolier, begging off because of the flu. He couldn't bring himself to be hypnotized again; he distrusted himself. What he learned from his last session with the psychologist was very disturbing and frightening. Even though what he did to his father was accidental, defensive, he couldn't stop puzzling: If he did that he didn't know what else he had done. He knew that he had killed his father, he was divorced and his two children were dead. He began to wonder whether the incident with his father had anything to do with what happened to make him lose his wife and children. If he had done anything else. It was all very complicated, and what was complicated was threatening, overwhelming, and he was afraid to find out anything more. He needed order about him, to eliminate the tensions he was feeling, to make certain that Paula wasn't going to leave him. That's why he did what he did that Wednesday afternoon when Paula had a late appointment in downtown Boston.

Paula had a final meeting with an agency on Thursday morning, the last step in the hiring process. Hugh didn't even try to work. For a third night he hadn't slept and his mind was dulled, distracted, almost as if he had been drugged. He couldn't concentrate on anything. From the moment Paula and the children left he paced the house, not knowing when she would be coming home. And when she finally did there was the pressure of trying to keep his distance from her so she wouldn't think he was being too possessive. He didn't know how long he could keep living this way until something gave.

The phone rang. "Mr. Tolson?"

"Yes. Who is this?" It wasn't Paula.

"Mr. Tolson, this is Kate. Kate Forest."

What did she want? He had to keep the line open in case Paula was trying to reach him.

"What is it, Kate?" he asked impatiently.

"Mr. Tolson, I . . ." She hesitated. The moments Hugh waited for her to continue stretched out. "I wanted to tell you that I . . . I . . ." There was struggle in her voice, Hugh heard. He ran his hand through his hair anxiously: What did she want to say to him?

A car pulled up outside. Through the parted curtain he saw that it was Paula. He frowned uncomfortably. She had stopped in front of the house, not driving into the garage like she usually did. Something was wrong.

"Kate, I have to go—" Now Paula was almost running up the front walk. There was anger in her steps. He started to put down the phone.

"I think I have a new idea for you, Mr. Tolson," Kate blurted out. "Can I come over and tell you about it?"

Paula was inserting the key in the lock, opening the door. Hugh's forehead started to bead perspiration and he wiped it away with his sleeve. He smiled at Paula as she came in but she slammed the door shut behind her, whipping a breeze through the room. He had to end this conversation with Kate. Something was very wrong.

"No. I'm busy now. I can't."

"When, Mr. Tolson?" Kate pressed. "I need to see—to tell—I love—" Paula's hands were on her hips, waiting for him to finish the call. There was fire in her eyes.

"Next week."

"Tomorrow."

"Sure," he said hurriedly. "It doesn't matter." Then he put down the phone. "That was Kate. She has a new idea for me."

Paula was on top of him challengingly. "I don't believe you could do such a thing to me, Hugh. I just don't know what to think anymore—"

"Why? What's the matter?" he asked as fear suddenly twisted his stomach. His arm twitched and he grabbed it and tried to control it.

"After everything we had talked about. Everything you had done, which I told you I was willing to forget about. To—"

"What is it, Paula? What's the matter? What did I do?"

"You don't know, Hugh?" she asked, amazed. "You close off our bank accounts so I can't take any money out and you ask me 'What's the matter?' "

That.

"Do you have any idea how embarrassing it just was for me at the bank? But forget that—how could you do it?"

His face flushed a deep red. "I—I had thought it might make you a little angry," he stuttered, "but I also thought that after you thought about it, you might like it better this way."

"How, Hugh? How would I like it better? Tell me."

"I—I would be like Daddy, taking care of you. Believe me, Paula, there was never any problem with my giving you money. I like to give you money. As much as you want. Come. We'll go down to the bank together now. Whatever I have is yours. I love to buy you things. That watch—you love it so much—" He reached out toward her but she pulled back disgustedly.

"Oh, Hugh, that isn't it at all. You just don't understand me and I guess I can't understand you and this insane, pointless possessiveness you have. I know all about your past and losing the people you love and I've really tried to accommodate myself. I've altered my life to respect your loss and cater to your fears and I honestly don't know what more I could do. Look—" She stepped back from him and held up her hand, having made up her mind. "All that notwithstanding, I think I need a little time away, okay. Maybe we could both use a little separation period so we can think of the needs of the other."

"Paula, no—" he said horrified. "You can't leave—"

"I'm not leaving you, Hugh. I'm just going to give us both some time—"

"You can't!" he cried. "I don't want to be possessive of you. I just can't help it. I'm seeing a psychiatrist—"

"And you'll continue to see him, but in the meantime—"

"He's helping me learn about myself," he rushed. "He made me remember how my father died. I caused the accident, Paula. I was afraid and grabbed the wheel. But I didn't mean to kill my father. I was only a frightened child, acting defensively. That's what Dr. Grolier brought out during the hypnosis." He hurried to the phone. "I'll call him right now. You can talk to him if you want. And I'll make another appointment." The pain was starting in his head, just above his eyes, a boring pang that went deep. He didn't know if he would be able to control himself or what might happen because *the absolute worst was happening.* It was worse even than last night. He was feeling brittle, on the edge.

"I—I didn't go to Dr. Grolier yesterday. I wasn't feeling well. I know I told you I did go but I just didn't feel like it—I don't know, I guess what I had learned about myself was pretty terrible and I needed some time off. But see, I'm making another appointment right now. Dr. Grolier's helping me, I know he is. . . ."

Quickly Hugh punched the numbers. He tried not to take his eyes off Paula and fumbled the last digit and had to dial again. Paula was mesmerized by him, watching his fingers frantically working the phone. He was a stranger to her; she didn't understand what she was seeing in her husband. Yet she really did, and it spurred her in her decision.

Dr. Grolier's answering machine clicked on. The psychologist was in session with a patient.

"Damn!" Hugh clenched his fist and tightly left a message to please call him back about scheduling another appointment. But when he turned around Paula was past him and partway up the steps.

"Paula, no!" he screamed, a rasping sound that frightened her and made her stop. He was standing at the bottom of the steps looking up at her pleadingly. They were two statues, frozen in time. "Wait till Dr. Grolier calls back. He's only with a patient now. He'll call right back and then you'll talk to him."

Paula watched Hugh work his hands against each other, one hand rubbing his fingers, his palm, his wrist.

"I don't understand it all yet," he said. "But I have this—this power. I didn't even want to tell you about it. We're working on it together, Dr. Grolier and I, and we're going to lick it. A power that whenever people leave me they—they—die." His laugh was nervous, high-pitched, a whimpering giggle. "I can't explain it"—his head was cocked, his palms open, his shoulders shrugged almost humbly; this was something out of his control —"it just seems to happen. It's something I was cursed with. And I'm really afraid, Paula, that if you leave me all alone something will happen to you too. Because of the power you'll die too." His face saddened imploringly. "You have to stay here. At least until Dr. Grolier and I understand what's going on."

Hugh continued talking, his words blurring, becoming indistinct. He was repeating what he had said about his power, about having caused the accident that killed his father, the trauma, the repression, everything that the psychologist had said to him.

Fear touched Paula. Cold. Gripping. A chill starting at the base of her neck and fanning throughout her body. It was not only what Hugh was saying but how he was saying it. *If you leave me, you'll die. Just like the others.*

Judith's warning came back to her as well:

You'll want to leave him, but then it will be too late. He'll kill you first.

And Paula understood why he knew that if she left him she was going to die. *Because he was going to kill her.*

That was his power.

And she knew without a doubt that her husband was dangerously insane.

She stifled an intake of breath. She was paralyzed for only a second and then the idea came. She knew what she had to do. She had to deflect him, play this out cautiously.

She ran down the stairs to Hugh and threw her arms around him, her fingers caressing his back.

"Oh, Hugh, I'll never leave you," she sighed. "I love you so much. I'm sorry I yelled at you before, I didn't mean it. . . ." She hoped her voice sounded genuine. To her ears she rang false, unconvincing, and prayed Hugh would not pick up the deception. "I love when you buy me gifts. See—" She flashed her wrist where the gold watch glistened in the afternoon sunlight. "I show this to everyone and tell them it was my wonderful husband who bought it for me." She watched his eyes start to brighten, an incredible instantaneous transformation, confirmation of his madness.

"And you know what?" she continued openly. "I was thinking about not going back to work. I thought maybe I would stay home with you and work on my book. It is good, isn't it?" she asked, ringing a childish eagerness and naïveté into her voice. He was Daddy, taking care of her. "You weren't just saying those things to me because you wanted to boost my ego?"

"Oh, no, Paula! It's terrific! You have such natural talent for writing. Especially your dialogue."

She stifled a hysterical laugh. Her dialogue with him was absolutely inane. There was no sense of reality to it, but it was just what he wanted to hear. So she fed him more.

"Maybe I can get a word processor for myself, too, and work up in your office with you. Put another desk in there. That would be all right for you, wouldn't it? It wouldn't be too crowded in there?"

"Too crowded?" he scoffed. "Paula, it would be wonderful being able to work so close to you. We can share ideas, I can help you with your writing. Oh, just the thought of having you up there with me all day . . . I'll admit I haven't been working very well the last several weeks . . . I've been so worried about things, but now I'm sure I'll be able to come up with a new idea in a flash. Oh, you don't know how happy this makes me feel. Now we don't have to worry about the power at all. Although I'll still go to see Dr. Grolier, I promised you that."

"That's good, Hugh." She smiled, then glanced quickly behind him at the clock on the fireplace mantel. It was nearing three. The children would be home from school soon, subject to danger as well. Who knew the limits of Hugh's stability? She had to get her children far away from him. *Just like Judith had warned her before they married.*

"I have an idea, Hugh," she said. "Why don't you go up to your office—or should I say 'our office'—and see where we can put another desk? I left something in the car. Let me get it and join you in a minute."

His face absolutely beamed, a child on Christmas morning. "Paula, this is going to be so wonderful. I knew it was only a matter of time until you saw it could be better this way. . . ."

She watched him go up the stairs. Then she moved to the phone, quickly flipped open her address book to the intermediate school, and dialed the office. She spoke in hushed precise tones to the secretary. "This is Paula Weller. My son, Jeremy, is in sixth grade. There has been an emergency at home and I have to come and get him. Would you please make certain he waits in the office and leaves only with me? I'll be there in a few minutes."

"Yes, Mrs. Tolson," the secretary said.

She depressed the receiver button and flipped her address book to the elementary school. She listened, but there was no dial tone. She flicked the hook down twice, tried to get a tone, but all she had was air. She tried once again, and then with a lurch of panic she understood what was wrong—the upstairs receiver was off the hook. She gasped. Hugh had heard her conversation. He knew what she was going to do. Now she had to do it fast. Dropping the phone, she started to run for the door. She heard him behind her on the stairs. An involuntary noise escaped from her throat, a keening sound. She didn't know what he was capable of. She closed her fingers around the doorknob and pulled. But he was on top of her, and in one motion his arms were around her—"You can't leave me!"—and with a grunt he spun her away from the door, pinning her arms behind her back—"I have this power!"—and slamming the door shut with the flat of his palm and a resounding crash that shuddered the room.

Paula gasped. Hugh's eyes were glazed, disoriented. Did he know what he was doing? she wondered frantically.

"Let me go, Hugh." She struggled and fought against him, trying to break his hold on her.

"I can't," he cried—real tears, his confused look solidifying into cornered fear, a flaring of his nostrils, a widening of his mouth. She felt his arms around her, shaking as if he was cold. But he wasn't cold, he seemed deathly afraid, his skin pale and wan. Now he was twisting her arm behind her back, causing her pain.

"What are you doing, Hugh?" she cried out. "You're hurting me."

"You can't leave me. You can't!" He was starting to drag her across the room. "You have to stay here with me so we'll be all right."

"Where are you taking me!" She tried to wriggle out of his grasp but he tightened his hold on her, clamping her wrists together with one hand and using his other to twist open the basement door. Now stumbling down the stairs, pushing her ahead of him. She resisted, tried to break free, but, stronger, he steered her across the floor.

There was a large storage room in the corner of the basement. When she had first moved in Hugh had shown it to her. There were no windows in the room, no lights. The room was filled with junk—old outdoor furniture, slatted, splintered wooden chairs with tombstone backs, metal flowerpots, rusted, broken gardening tools. Now surprisingly, as he opened the storage door, she saw the room was mostly empty. Only some scattered debris. It had been virtually cleaned out. *When had it been done? Was all of this planned?*

Then he spun her away from him. She half stumbled across the room, righted herself. She stood facing him, gasping for breath, her chest heaving. He was at the doorway.

"What's the matter with you, Hugh? What are you doing to me?"

"Paula, you have to understand—"

"No, Hugh. I don't understand. I don't understand at all."

"It's the power, Paula. I have to protect you—"

"Let's go upstairs and call Dr. Grolier. Maybe we can go and see him together now."

"You'll leave me," Hugh sobbed. "And something will happen."

"No, I won't, Hugh, I swear it. We'll go together right now. You can drive if you want or we can call a cab. But we'll always be together in each other's sight."

He was shaking his head fragilely. "Can't trust you . . . can't trust—" He frowned, then more mouthed the word than said it, his tone confused, uncertain: "Myself."

Paula smiled her warmest smile and held out her hands to him. "Come here, Hugh. I want to feel your arms around me. I want to make love to you. I just love it when you touch me, hold me—"

"And I love it, too, Paula!" he cried. "But not now. We can't do it now. I have so much to work out first." He held his fists to his head. The pain had returned.

"Are you going to leave me down here, Hugh?" she asked in a small, girlish voice. *This isn't happening. Dear God, it isn't!*

"Just for a little while. Just until I have time to think."

"Okay." She shifted gears suddenly and readily agreed. "I'll stay down here. But you send the children to my mother. Let her watch them, okay?"

He shook his head. "We all have to be here together. We're a family and we have to stay together. No one can leave that way. You'll all be safe."

"Please, Hugh," she begged. "They're not going to go anywhere."

"I can't risk it. I don't know the extent of the power. I don't know if they're in danger too."

He set the fire. He killed the children. He's going to kill you all too. The memory of Judith's words chilled Paula.

"No, Hugh, I'm sure they're not. And it will be so much easier if I'm here all alone, wouldn't it?" Her voice was naked, stripped by fear. "You can always ask Dr. Grolier what he thinks and go get them if you need them."

He shook his head and swooned. There was too much to think about, too much was happening. The simplest solution was the best.

"No, they have to be here too!" he roared. "I don't want anything to happen to them!"

"Why don't you come in here and let's sit together, Hugh. Then we can talk about how much we love and need each other, how much we mean to each other, and how neither of us will ever leave the other."

She saw the flickering in his eyes. He was tempted. If she could coax him to this side of the room, perhaps she could outwit him, somehow push out past him.

He took a step closer to her, then his face darkened again. "Jeremy's still at school. I have to get him. And I'll pick up Michelle too—"

"Hugh, wait," she cried, but he had already left the room, slamming the door shut behind him, plunging the storage room into darkness. "Hugh! Hugh!"

"I'll be back in a few minutes," he called through the closed door.

She heard the play of metal outside the door. He was wrapping a chain around the door, locking it.

"Hugh, wait! Let's go together. That's the only way I can be safe from the power, if we're together. If you leave me here alone, the power could . . ."

But he was gone.

She pounded on the door with her fist. More in frustration than from any hope of anyone hearing her. That was why she didn't even try to scream. The storage room was in the rear of the house, windowless. The nearest house on that side was separated by a thick line of trees now greening, and there was no neighbor for an acre behind them. No one would hear her cries. No one. She was trapped.

"Judith . . ." she moaned, and slumped to the floor. If only she had listened . . . if only . . . if only . . .

Upstairs the phone rang. It must have been Dr. Grolier calling back, Paula thought hysterically. It sounded seven times, then was silent.

She heard him return a half hour later. She was slumped against a wall and sprang to her feet. The children were with him. They were crossing the basement, coming closer to the storage room. She wanted to scream out to them, "Jeremy. Michelle. Run." But they wouldn't understand what was happening. They would become afraid. Frozen. And she didn't know what Hugh would do to them. Patience, she decided. That was the watchword. She heard him fumbling with the metal chain, heard Jeremy question what he was doing. Patience. Something would happen. She would catch him at a vulnerable moment. He might tell Dr. Grolier what he had done. Someone would come looking for her—her mother would demand to know where she was. For the time being she would just play along.

"What are we doing down here?" Michelle asked, and Paula could almost envision her little girl's head cocked to the side, her hands on her hips demandingly.

Then the door was opening, light was streaming in. She blinked at the sudden onslaught of light and then mother and children were staring at each other, the children's faces uncomprehending masks.

They were still uncomprehending as Hugh pushed them all into the room and slammed the door shut behind them.

"Now you'll never leave me, Paula," he said.

Chapter 24

"I'M COLD, MOMMY," MICHELLE WHIMPERED.

Paula and the children were huddled against each other on the damp tile floor of the basement. Water from a recent rainstorm had seeped in through the concrete and a slight musty smell filled the room. Paula's arms were draped around their shoulders, hugging them tightly to her, telling them to be brave, but Michelle tried to burrow in even closer to her mother. Paula felt the little girl shudder and rubbed her arm. In her short-sleeve spring dress her skin was raised and prickly. "I'm cold," she repeated. But what the child was really saying was that she was afraid.

Paula was afraid too. She didn't know exactly how long they had been down there but estimated it had to be at least four hours. Nor did she know how much longer Hugh planned on keeping them locked up, or even what his plan was. Besides being cold, the children were hungry and had to go to the bathroom. Paula had tried to remain strong for them. They played word games and sang round-robin camp songs until becoming tired. Michelle had fallen asleep for a while then awoke with a jerk, crying out and clawing at the blackness that surrounded them. Paula had rubbed her forehead to soothe her and wipe away the perspiration. The bottom of the door was an inch from the floor. The space let in a band of the afternoon sunlight, giving them some grasping comfort, but then the sun had set, plunging the room into total darkness, causing disorientation, a dizzying white-out effect.

The phone rang several times, seven, eight rings; the minutes that the average person lets a phone ring before hanging up. But Hugh didn't pick up. Nor did she hear his footsteps on the kitchen floor above them; he probably wasn't home. The sound of the phone was urgent, alarming, as tension seemingly mounted with each ring. It was hard to listen to a ringing phone without answering it.

When Hugh had closed the storeroom door on them, Paula had banged on it, demanding that they be let out—angrily, not hysterically—hoping that the fury of her voice would shock him into action. When it was clear that he would not respond she turned to Jeremy and Michelle and tried to explain to them what was happening. In the dimness of the room and their uncertain fear the children were practically clinging to her. She had first attempted to dismiss it as a joke, a prank, but she couldn't lie to the children and knew as well that they would soon understand it was not a game. "Daddy's afraid of certain things . . ." she started haltingly.

Although Jeremy had gone right to the heart of the issue, piecing together what he had observed over the last several weeks, watching Hugh's spastic movements in his office, his outburst in Vermont.

"Is Hugh crazy?" he had asked.

"No, not crazy," Paula had answered quickly, but she didn't even have a chance to put her thoughts into words when Jeremy had groaned. "Come on, Mom . . ." Having already drawn his own conclusions. "Will he have to be put away?" the boy then had asked.

"I don't know."

"Is he going to hurt us?"

"No, dear, of course not—he loves us. . . ." Her answer sounded more than a little ridiculous to her ears.

"Then why did he lock us down here?"

She didn't answer the question. "I don't know . . ." she said distantly, although ironically she knew the true response was the same as what she had just said. *He locked us down here because he loves us.*

The phone rang again. This time it was grabbed on the third

ring. Hugh must have come home, although she couldn't hear him speaking.

"I'm hungry, Mommy . . ." Michelle whined. "How long—" But Paula quieted her as they heard the rattling of the chain and then the opening of the door. All three squinted against the basement light that rushed in. Huddled together on the floor, they must look like refugees, Paula thought.

"The children are tired and hungry and have to go to the bathroom, Hugh—" Paula said evenly, but Jeremy exploded.

"You let us out of here!" He bounded to his feet and charged at Hugh, swinging wildly at his stepfather, trying to push past him. "My sister is afraid. You let us go!" Hugh caught the boy's arms but still Jeremy flailed senselessly, uselessly at him with clenched fists, his arms making giant windmilling circles until he could strike no more and he collapsed against Hugh in tears and exhaustion. "You let my mother and sister go," he sobbed. "You let them . . ."

"I will . . . I will . . ." Hugh said nervously, catching Paula's look. Her face was hard, angry.

"Are you going to let us out now, Hugh?" she demanded coldly. "Are you finished with this—whatever you want to call it?"

"I can't, Paula," he said. "Don't make me have to go into it again. I can't—but I've fixed things upstairs—we can all be together upstairs. Come on."

He let go of Jeremy to reach for Paula's hands and Jeremy bolted, scooting past him, up the stairs. Paula watched Hugh's eyes widen with distress, then he took after the boy. "I'll get help!" Jeremy called as he made a run for it with Hugh after him. Would Hugh kill him? Paula thought frantically. "Jeremy . . . !" she yelled instinctively, but he didn't stop and gratefully she let him go. He was faster than Hugh, he would get away. *But what would happen to her and Michelle if he did?* But she couldn't take the time to think of that now. Now she had to act. The storeroom door was open, the way clear, she could call the police. Holding Michelle's hand, she ran for the steps. She heard the front door opening and Jeremy's calls for help as he burst out of the house.

Then she was up the stairs and in the kitchen. She picked up the phone. There was no dial tone. "Come on . . . come on," she urged. She banged the receiver button but still nothing came. The phone was dead.

And then with a gasp she heard Hugh come back into the house, the slam and snap of the door lock, the muffled grunts of Jeremy struggling against him, and Hugh was back in the kitchen dragging Jeremy by the arm.

"I tripped, Mom," Jeremy cried. "He caught me. I'm sorry . . ." He hung his head in failure.

"You cut the phone lines, Hugh?" she asked.

"Disconnected. Your mother was calling. She wanted to talk to you . . ." He had that same stumbling, fearful look on his face, Paula saw.

"Hugh, why don't we go to my mother's?" she asked softly, disarmingly. "We can call Dr. Grolier from there and talk about all of this. What do you say?"

Hugh's eyes filled with fear at the mention of the psychologist's name. He shook his head. "I can't . . . I don't know what else he's going to make me remember . . . I have to work this out myself . . . have to solve it myself . . . what I did . . . the power . . ."

"You're bonkers," Jeremy said angrily. "And you should be put away until you rot!"

"Jeremy, quiet!" Paula warned. Hugh was a fumbling child. She didn't know what would set him off. Although she knew that acceptance and compliance would keep him calm.

"Please," she said. "Can we all have something to eat? The children are hungry and you must be hungry, too, Hugh."

He nodded. He was.

She opened the refrigerator. "There's some leftover roast. Let me heat it." She motioned the children to the table. "Come on, let's sit down and eat dinner. We'll all think more clearly on a full stomach." She looked pointedly at Hugh and then at the clock. It was eight-fifteen. They had been locked downstairs for more than five hours.

"I have to go to the bathroom," Michelle said defiantly, almost asking for confrontation, as if expecting Hugh to deny her request. She looked at her mother then at Hugh, her hands on her hips. "Is it all right?"

"Can she, Hugh?" Paula asked.

There was a powder room off the kitchen.

"Yes. Of course."

"Be quick now," Paula warned. Hugh watched her go into the bathroom and close the door, then shifted his look back toward Jeremy, afraid the boy might bolt again.

Paula took the meat out of the refrigerator, transferred it to a pot, and put it in the oven. "It should warm up in about fifteen minutes. And I'll make some spaghetti." She reached for the box, then thought for a second of grabbing a knife out of the drawer, menacing Hugh with it. But she quickly rejected the idea as too dangerous. Someone might get hurt. There was a better way to play this out. She would try to act completely normal. There was nothing wrong or different in their lives. They were just sitting down to a late dinner. That way Hugh might relax, either let them go or let his guard down enough for them to get away without danger. And while she playacted at normalcy her mind wouldn't have to dwell on the absolutely absurd nature of the situation—they were being held captive by her husband, prisoners of his obsessive love and psychotic fears!

She tried to make light, happy talk over dinner, but she caught the children's eyes shifting warily toward Hugh. She chattered on about how silly the interviewers were, how asinine the questions, how dumb the jobs, and how she knew she wasn't cut out to work in the advertising world. She had Hugh to thank for that—she smiled at him—making her see the light, and she couldn't wait until tomorrow so she could wake up and start working on her novel. She hoped her voice sounded even, conversational, not at all strained or phony. She studiously avoided Hugh's look, although she stole glances at him out of the corners of her eyes. . . . Was he believing her? Did he know that she was playing with him? Did he think she was making fun of him? But he kept quiet, kept looking at her, warily, yet somewhat more at ease than before, she thought, although wondering, she was certain, about what *she* was thinking, the same way she kept wondering about what he was thinking and what was going to happen when supper came to an end.

If they could only all go to sleep, maybe she could ready the children for school in the morning, get them out of the house.

"Jeremy, Michelle, help me clear the table," she asked. When they were finished she turned to Hugh as if nothing was wrong. "Let's put the children to bed, okay?"

As they all walked upstairs Hugh began to chatter happily. "I wanted to tell you, Paula, I had a good breakthrough on my story today. I think it's really taking shape now. Now that I don't have to worry about—"

"That's nice, Hugh," Paula said dully, cutting him off. She was exhausted.

"I plan on dedicating this book to you too."

"That's good—"

Paula reached the top of the landing first and started when she saw it:

Latches and chains had been affixed to the bedroom doors. That way they could be locked in their rooms overnight while Hugh slept on a cot in the hallway outside the rooms.

"Hugh, you can't," she whispered.

"Please, Paula," he said. "I have to protect you. I'm afraid of the power."

"There is no pow—" she started, but Michelle began to cry. "I don't want to be locked in my room, Mommy."

"Hugh, you're frightening them—"

"*I'm* not afraid of him." Jeremy glowered.

Paula shot a warning glance at him, then turned back to Hugh. "Let them sleep with me. That way we can all be together and safe." *That way her children would be with her.*

He looked hesitant, then decided it would be all right, although he leaned toward Paula and whispered, "But we won't be able to sleep together. I wanted to make love to you."

"Tomorrow, Hugh. I want to be with the children tonight." He looked disappointed. "Just for one night. They'll feel better tomorrow."

The children went into the bathroom to wash up for bed and Paula looked from Hugh to the chains on the doors.

"We're not going to go anywhere," she said softly. "You don't have to lock us in."

"Please," he begged. "Don't be angry with me."

"I'm not, Hugh. And believe me, I really do understand."

"I love you so much. You know that, don't you?"

"Yes," she answered automatically.

"And you won't ever leave me?"

"Never."

"I just know everything is going to be so wonderful for all of us."

"I'm sure."

"Just keep your mother away from us. She doesn't like me

and that's why she's always calling you. She wants to separate us."

A threatened shadow darkened his face. Without completely knowing why, Paula suddenly felt afraid for her mother and said quickly, "Oh, no, Hugh. Don't be ridiculous. My mother adores you and loves our marriage. I can't tell you how many times she's said that to me."

"No, I just don't trust her," he said, seemingly distracted, his lips pursed. "She's like Judith, you know. Judith tried to break us up too. But I put a stop to that. . . ."

It was the way he said it that made Paula ask nervously, "How did you put a stop to it?"

He laughed shortly, inwardly. "I really thought I had taken care of her. I had to keep you two apart because of what she was telling you about me, all those lies about—about the fire, trying to frighten you, get you to leave me. That time when she brought the presents for the children I saw that you were really feeling sorry for her and might want to talk more to her. Well, I . . . I . . ." he said nervously in confession, his hands turning against each other. "I had to make it so you'd never want to see her again. So I . . . I told you I had to take a trip to California"—Paula's eyes started to widen—"then I snuck into the house, pretended to be a burglar, and sprayed perfume so you'd think it was Judith."

Paula's mouth was open in soundless horror, her face flushed red.

"I made it look like she did it so you'd be afraid of her and never speak to her again. But then you called her, Paula, and I knew I couldn't keep you two apart. She'd keep telling you more and more lies until you finally believed her. . . ."

Then Paula chilled in understanding. Judith hadn't been home when she went to see her that day. Hugh had been listening to her call when she phoned the school yesterday. *How many other calls did he listen in on? He must have eavesdropped on the day she phoned Judith. He knew she was going to see her. So what did he do?*

The children came out of the bathroom, ready for bed and safely behind her inside the master bedroom. Hugh lingered at the door. Paula kissed him—obligatorily. His touch and feel were so distasteful to her she almost gagged. But she said the words anyway—"I love you so much, too, Hugh"—because she had to. Then the door was closed and locked behind them and mother and children looked at each other disbelievingly; this wasn't happening to them.

"Come, everyone into bed," Paula said. She flipped off the light and patted her children to sleep. "Everything's going to be all right," she soothed. "We'll be out of here tomorrow, I promise." With Paula securely next to them, they drifted off to sleep quickly, eagerly seeking relief from the nightmare their lives had become.

But Paula couldn't sleep. Not that she had expected to. She gently lifted the covers and climbed out of bed to the window. Perhaps she could sneak out, drop from the roof to the ground and summon help, but she immediately saw Hugh had thought of that too. He had nailed the window shut. There would be no escaping through it unless she broke it, which she couldn't do without alerting Hugh. Perhaps if he left them alone . . . although she suspected that would not be happening soon.

The moonless night was deeply shadowed and she could barely make out the shapes of the trees in the woods behind the house—a dense, lightless acre. Help would not come from that direction either.

She heard the light wrap on the door.

"Are you asleep, Paula?"

"Almost, Hugh." She hurriedly got back into bed; if he came into the room, she didn't want him to think she was plotting anything against him.

"Pleasant dreams."

"Thank you."

"I love you."

"I love you too."

Then the house was silent around her. But still she could not fall asleep. She lay awake in bed staring aimlessly above her, searching for answers to questions she was afraid even to ask.

Because deep down she already knew the answers.

She shuddered because she *knew*.

Chapter 25

HUGH BROUGHT THEM A TRAY OF BREAKFAST FRIDAY MORNing—eggs, bacon, freshly squeezed juice, toast, milk for the children and coffee for Paula, and a single rose in a bud vase. On the tray were the children's toothbrushes, taken from the other bathroom for use in the master one. He sat with them as they ate.

"Delicious, Hugh, thank you," Paula said with false enthusiasm when they were finished. "Now the children have to get ready for school. Look at the time! We're already running late. And I want to start working on my novel. I had some thoughts last ni—"

"No. No school."

"The children have to go to school," Paula said evenly, hoping her matter-of-fact tone would convince him.

Hugh shook his head. "I can't let any of you leave the house. Not without me. I don't know what will happen."

"Well, you can take them and come right back."

"I'm sorry, no, you'll all have to stay here today."

"They can't miss school."

"I . . . I know . . . it'll just be for today . . . I'll think of something for next week."

Next week—there was an entire weekend between now and

Monday—did he plan on keeping them in the room all that time?

Hugh took away the dirty dishes. Paula heard him put down the tray and carefully latch the door again. She looked at the children and shrugged helplessly, although she didn't dare let on how frightened she was feeling. And thankfully neither Jeremy nor Michelle asked any questions, accepting the situation.

Hugh returned a few minutes later with a portable typewriter and Paula's partial manuscript. "You'll have to work down here until I can get you a computer terminal. The typewriter is too loud and I won't be able to concentrate. But next week we'll be upstairs together."

"What about the children, Hugh?" she tried. "If they don't go to school, what are they going to do?"

"They could read, or watch TV. I'm sure we'll work all this out. It's new for all of us. Should they play in here? Will they disturb you?"

"No, we'll be fine in here."

"I'll get their schoolbooks."

After Hugh went upstairs to work Paula explained to the children about his past, feeling they now had a right to know what made Hugh so afraid, and why they were locked in the house. But they would soon be out of there, she hastened to say, and in the meantime there would be no heroics. The children looked at her trustingly; their fate was in her hands.

They passed the morning watching television. It was noon when they first heard, then saw, Marilyn's car drive into the cul-de-sac, then disappear out of their line of sight to the front of the house, and while they couldn't see Marilyn walk up the steps, they heard the ring of the doorbell. Then Hugh's footsteps coming down the stairs, a hoarse "Stay quiet now" as he passed their door.

About fifteen minutes later they heard Marilyn's car drive off, although Hugh didn't come back upstairs for almost an hour after that, bringing them sandwiches for lunch.

"What did you say to my mother?" Paula asked.

"It was simple. I told her that you didn't want her here."

"And what did she say?"

"Oh, I was very convincing." Hugh smiled. "I don't think she'll be coming around to bother us anymore."

When they finished eating, Hugh said, "I've been thinking,

Paula. The children being here with you might be too distracting for you to work. Maybe if they stayed in their rooms you'd be able to get more done on your book."

She didn't want that. She tried to deflect him. "They're not a distraction at all, Hugh. I like them here."

Hugh frowned. "I didn't hear much typing this morning."

"Well . . ." She tried to keep her voice certain. "I wasn't really ready for typing yet. I'm still thinking of my scene now. I've found that if I plan everything out the writing goes much easier. You must work that way too." She didn't want to be separated from the children.

"I do. But I'm sure it would just work better my way."

"Hugh, I don't think so," she said evenly.

"But I want you to have every opportunity at writing a bestseller and you really need concentration for that."

Paula saw Michelle out of the corner of her eye. The little girl was shaking her head; she didn't want to be apart from her mother either. But Paula didn't want to argue with Hugh, not knowing what might set him off. She spoke directly to the children.

"Let's try it for the afternoon. . . ." Michelle started to open her mouth in protest but Paula spoke louder. "And if it doesn't make any difference in my writing, we'll go back to the old system tomorrow. Is that a deal, Hugh?" She winked at her daughter. She was taking care of the situation; it would be all right.

"Okay. We'll take everything one step at a time," he agreed. "And I'm sure by next week your computer will arrive, Paula, and we'll be able to be upstairs working together. Won't that be wonderful?"

"I want to stay with my sister," Jeremy said manfully.

"What if we have to go to the bathroom?" Michelle demanded, her hands on her hips almost brazenly.

"I'll come downstairs from time to time and ask. Okay?" Michelle nodded her head tentatively. "All right, come on now." He opened the door and ushered them across the hall to Jeremy's room, where he locked them in. Paula stood in the doorway of the master bedroom as Hugh came back across the hallway, and with a smile he whispered, "Good writing," and fastened the latch.

She was alone in the bedroom. She looked at the partial

manuscript on the dresser and at the typewriter he had set up for her on the bridge table. Writing was probably the last thing she wanted to do right now. But she didn't know what else to do with herself.

She paced the bedroom, trapped in the house, a prisoner. She tried forcing the windows open but they would not budge. Their family album was inside Hugh's end table, and impulsively she picked it up. There were snapshots taken by Marilyn at their wedding, candid and posed, pictures of the brief honeymoon in New York. And other photos of all four of them together. She looked closely at Hugh's face, full of smiles as he cupped her in his arms or hefted the children, trying to discern a gleam of madness behind his eyes and deceptively innocent boyish expression. Clues. Hints. But it wasn't in any of the pictures, just like he had kept it hidden from her the nine months she had known him.

The sudden noise startled her. Hugh's printer had come on. Connected to his computer, it automatically printed what he had written. The high-pitched typewriter sound carried from his office throughout the house. In a split second the idea came to her. Earlier she had quietly eased open the door and inspected the latch. It was loosely, flimsily fastened to the jamb with plenty of slack to the chain. She thought she could work it off the bar. Now she had a diversion. The sound of the printer would drown out any noise she made as she maneuvered the latch. She could break out of the room, get the children, and steal down the stairs. Or should she do nothing? She hesitated fearfully, her heart pounding with indecision. Wait for someone to help them or for Hugh to let them go? No—Hugh was too unstable. An offhand comment from any of them could set him off. She knew what she had to do.

She ran to the door, gently pulled it open, and peered out through the slit. The brass chain stretched across the door. She stuck her hand through, gained a fingerhold on the chain, and slid it toward the opening. But there wasn't enough slack. Hugh had done a better job in affixing the latch to the jamb than she had thought. If the door was open wide enough for her to put her hand through, the chain pulled too tautly and she didn't have the slack needed to slide it off the bar. If she relaxed the chain, she couldn't open the door enough to get her hand through. It was just out of her reach. *"Damn!"* she said out loud. Upstairs the printer still sounded, a distant jackhammer cry. Hugh usually ran it for about ten minutes at a stretch, the time it took to print out a dozen letter-quality pages.

She had an idea. A nail file. It was long and firm and would extend her reach. She fumbled through her purse, turned it upside down, and scattered the contents onto the bed. There it was! She slipped the door open and sighted along the line of the door, then slid the file through, hooked the chain with the tip, and moved it toward the notch in the bar. Her hand shook excitedly. Her breath was coming rapidly. The printer could stop at any minute and he might hear her.

The chain slipped through the notch and fell free. It slapped sharply against the door, which she immediately swung open. She stepped into the hallway, then gasped in surprise, a sudden intake of breath, her sound masked by the printer upstairs.

Hugh was coming down the stairs from the third floor.

"Paula?" he questioned. His head tilted slightly. "What are you . . . ?" And then his face darkened at the realization of what was happening. "I—I—" Paula sputtered. "I wanted to see the children . . ." She was talking, saying anything, but he wasn't listening to her. His mind was alive, abuzz with the truth. He now knew he couldn't trust her. She had lied to him. Everything she said was a lie. Every time she had told him she loved him, every time she told him she wanted to be with him forever. All lies. She didn't love him. She was going to leave him. Like his father had. And Judith—

Paula was holding the nail file, pointed at him!

His hand clamped around her wrist and forced her arm downward. The file fell to the floor and he kicked it aside, under the cot he slept on.

"Paula . . ." he moaned. "Why . . . ?" The pain was starting behind his eyes. The worst had been confirmed, his fears realized. She was going to leave him alone. He would be all alone. He would never be able to deter her from leaving him. He knew what he had to do. He had no alternative.

Nor did she. She was exposed, defenseless. "Hugh, listen to me," she said desperately. "You have to get help. You're very confused about things right now and I want you to talk to someone. It doesn't have to be Dr. Grolier if you don't want, but we'll find you someone. We'll get you well again, I swear it."

As she talked she edged around Hugh, closer to Jeremy's door. If she could keep his attention, she could free the children. While she held him they could run down the stairs behind him and out of the house.

"This power is a very serious thing, Hugh. And we have to go to someone who can help you understand it—"

"Mommy!" Michelle cried from behind the door. The children were hearing what was going on.

"Quiet!" Paula ordered. She didn't want anything to distract Hugh from her. She was on the other side of him now, between him and the children's door. He was standing motionless in the hallway, staring at her. His expression was alert, wary. She had no idea what was going on behind his eyes. She kept her voice calm, hypnotic, and controlling, the way an animal trainer or a snake handler would.

"Now, I'm going to open up this door, Hugh, and the children and I are going to go out of the house. But we're not leaving you," she stressed. "I'm just going to take the children to school and come right home again and—"

"No!" He shook his head vigorously from side to side.

"Yes, Hugh." She was gathering strength. "That's exactly what we're going to do." Her hand was poised on the latch, ready to slide it off the bar. "And you're going to let us go because you know I want to help you. I love you and I'll never leave you. Never, Hugh, I swear it."

She didn't remember when she had last breathed, the moment was so rifled with tension. But she thought she saw the change in his eyes, a softening, an acceptance. She was getting through to him. He wasn't going to stop them from going. He was finally listening to her. *Thank God,* she sighed silently and started to slide the chain.

Upstairs the printer shut itself off. Without thought they both glanced above them. The moment was broken. Hugh shocked to the sudden silence as if just released from a hypnotic trance. At the same moment Paula slid the latch off the bar and pushed open the door. The children exploded out of the room. But with an involuntary whimper Hugh swept forward and shoved them back in, grabbed for the doorknob, and whipped the door closed. Paula clawed at his hand but he fought her off and grappled with the latch. "Hugh—no!" She huffed and tried to push him away from the chain again but Hugh clamped his hand over her wrist and slid the bar back into place. Inside, the children were screaming.

"You can't . . ." he grunted.

"Hugh, listen to me!" she said sternly, as if speaking to a child. "Stop this nonsen—!"

He caught her arm, pulled it away from the door. "You can't leave . . ." he repeated, a frightened animal cry. He wrenched her arm behind her back and twisted it until her eyes widened and she shrieked in pain. "I don't want to hurt you, Paula," he cried. "Don't make me hurt you." Perspiration had broken out on his forehead. Terror lined his face. But there was no other solution. He knew what he had to do.

With the children locked in the bedroom, he started to steer Paula down the stairs. She kicked at him, tried to free herself, but much stronger than she and driven by an inner fury and terror, he held her arm behind her and when she flailed at him with her free hand he tightened his hold on her, twisting her arm higher, harder, what he had done to the bully who had taunted Jeremy. He hated to hurt her but it was the only way. Paula tried desperately to make a break for the door, but stiffly he dragged her toward the cellar stairs. Above her she heard the children screaming and she redoubled her efforts to break free but still he maneuvered her down the stairs.

Not the storage room again! she panicked. But he threw her roughly against the wall, held her with one hand, manipulated the latch with the other, opened the door, and spun her out of his grasp toward the far wall of the closet. She broke the fall with her hands and used the momentum to propel herself back toward Hugh. But he managed to close the door on her and she slammed into it, swinging at it with her fists, crying out his name again and again. Tears streamed down her face. What was going to happen to her? To the children? She should have waited until he was out of the house, the moment should have been more certain. She had gambled and lost. He was completely out of his senses, gone.

She stepped backward into the room and tripped against a mound on the floor. What? she puzzled. Her eyes hadn't grown accustomed yet to the darkness. But there hadn't been anything else in the room when they had been in there last week.

She knelt down against the object that was shrouded by the blackness of the cellar floor.

Her pupils were already as large as they could possibly be to try to grasp the light that snuck in under the door. It wouldn't seem possible that they could open any wider. But they did at Paula's realization at what was in the room with her, as the object took recognizable shape.

A person lay sprawled across the basement floor, on his side. The back faced Paula, the head rested on an outstretched arm. The face was profiled, lost to shadow, unidentifiable.

There was no discernible movement, no audible sound of breathing.

God no! The words formed on her lips but did not break the air.

Instinctively Paula grabbed for the wrist to check for a pulse.
Was the person dead?
Had Hugh killed him?

Thoughts she would not allow herself even to consider. The person was only sleeping.

Only.

But she knew that didn't make sense as she ran her hand up and down the arm, searching for pulse, trying to will life back into the body.

Nothing.

Horrified, she dropped the arm, which fell limply to the floor, upsetting the delicate balance of the positioned body.

. . . Who? . . . Why?

The body teetered over onto its back.

Gasping at the sudden movement, Paula stood and sprang back. She still could not make out the facial features. She didn't want to know who it was. But in a half second of what she refused to accept as even *possible* she *had* to know.

She knelt down again and put her hand under the lifeless head, raising it. Dried blood tangled the hair stuck to her palm. Reason screamed *pull away, you're touching a dead body.*

She had to know, and there was no controlling her heart, her breath, the gripping in her chest, her head . . . as she strained her eyes to focus, to use what little light—

Hugh's words filled her thoughts at the exact moment the features became dimly recognizable, the faint outline of a nose, the familiar hairstyle.

I was very convincing. I don't think she'll come around to bother us anymore.

And there was no mistaking, no error.

An involuntary shriek rose from Paula's throat as she jerked her hand away from under her mother's head, letting it crack against the concrete floor with a sickening, hollow thud.

Chapter 26

HUGH BACKED AWAY FROM THE STOREROOM DOOR AS PAUla's screams rang in his ears. It hurt him to hear her cry like that. She had to know he didn't want to bring her any pain. She must have found the body of her mother, he considered with perhaps the last portion of his brain still capable of rational thought, remembering he had had to kill Marilyn. She had come back to the house again looking for Paula, to take her away from him. He hadn't wanted to do it, but there had been no other choice. Like with Judith, he had to protect himself.

All for naught. He had done all he could to ensure Paula's staying with him but still she was going to leave. He knew that now; there was no question what her intention was. Anything he did would just buy him time, but he knew he had lost her. She didn't love him. She didn't care about him or his terrible fears of abandonment and loneliness. So it had to be the other way. If he couldn't have her, he would have to kill them both.

But what about the children? The thought still nagged as he started up the basement stairs. *They'll be abandoned by both their parents, just like you were.*

Although the solution came easily. *Not if they died too.*

He could set fire to the house. That way they would all die together and no one would have to suffer.

He kept a gasoline can in the garage for his lawn mower. He could spread the gasoline, set the fire—

The sound of the doorbell broke his concentration. He shocked to the noise, and startled, he stumbled against a step, lost his balance, and pitched forward. He jammed his knee and scowled with pain, but his concern overshadowed his physical discomfort. Who could be here? Using the banister, he pulled himself gropingly up the stairs. His arm twitched involuntarily, an inward, spastic tug, like a puppeteer had jerked his muscles with marionette strings.

Paula must have heard the bell, too, because suddenly the screams intensified, although he knew her cries would never carry outside the house.

The doorbell rang again. Hugh didn't know what to do. He froze at the top of the basement stairs, cocked his head, and assumed a mannequin pose, trying to remain stiff and silent except for the deep booming sound of his heart as it vibrated against his chest, his ears, his throat. Was someone here to try and take Paula away from him? The thought weakened him and he grasped the railing for support. But if he pretended he wasn't home and didn't answer the doorbell, the person would go away. *Damn! Why did this have to happen now?* He chewed on his finger anxiously as he stared at the door trying to will the person to leave them alone.

But then the children began to scream from upstairs. Their cries of "Help" were loud and anguished. They were in Jeremy's room, overlooking the front of the house. The person outside would definitely hear them.

He bolted for the door and threw it open. He didn't have a specific plan in mind, although he had an inkling of what he would have to do. At first he didn't recognize the person standing on the porch. Then it registered.

"What are you doing here?" he cried to Kate Forest. The children continued to scream.

"You told me to come over. Yesterday when we talked on the phone." She raised her eyes. The overhang of the porch hid the children from view. She could only hear them, not see them. "What's wrong?" she asked. "Why are the children screaming?"

Now Paula too. Although her voice was muffled. Only snatches of words came through: ". . . locked in the basement

. . . Hugh crazy, insane . . ." Unclear words, jumbled thoughts, but Kate must have heard enough. His arm twitched but he made no attempt to stop it. He liked Kate, she had never meant him any harm or tried to take Paula from him, but regrettably now he had no other choice.

"Come in. Come in. Hurry."

She hesitated in the doorway, her face wrinkled in question, but Hugh pulled her into the house and closed the door behind her. "I'm sorry there's chaos here. We just had a series of accidents. Michelle hurt herself. And Paula too. Would you see to the children upstairs? I'll be right up from the basement where Paula is."

Kate turned her back on Hugh to start up the stairs to assist the crying children. She didn't see Hugh lift the lamp off one of the end tables flanking the couch. With one tug he pulled the cord from the wall socket, and in the next fluid motion raised the lamp and brought it down on the side of Kate's head. It made a hollow, crunching sound as it connected with the hard matter at the base of her skull. Then he threw down the lamp. He didn't even look at Kate crumbled at the bottom of the stairs. He had other business to take care of.

He went around the house to the garage and came back with the gasoline in a red safety can. He opened the cap and started to spill the contents throughout the living room, staining the carpet, soaking the couch, the drapes, running a trail of the flammable liquid around Kate and up the stairs to the children's bedrooms. He was beginning to feel a little better, more in control. The palpitations of his heart were lessening. The end was nearing, soon it would all be over. There would be no more fear.

The children were still screaming to be freed.

"Quiet," he barked. "Everything is going to be all right. I'm going to let you out in a few minutes."

"I don't believe you," Jeremy challenged through the door. "Let us out now!"

"Just a few minutes." The pungent odor of the gasoline was making him heady.

"What's that smell?" Jeremy demanded. The gasoline fumes had wafted under the door. "Is that gasoline? What are you doing with gasoline in the house?"

Hugh didn't answer. He opened the door to his bedroom and

splashed the gasoline on the bedspread and curtains. When the trail of flames got to the bed the entire room would ignite. The house would be ablaze in minutes.

He was trailing the gasoline back through the living room when the phone rang.

Hugh stopped where he was, hunched over the can, and stared at the ringing phone, which suddenly seemed alive, his enemy. His eyes were wide, fearful of the interruption. The phone rang again.

He didn't want to answer it but its urgency made him nervous. It couldn't be any good, he knew, but still he put the gas can down and lifted the receiver.

"Hugh?" The voice came over the phone and Hugh almost slammed the receiver back into the cradle. It was the last person he wanted to speak to. "Are you there, Hugh?"

"What do you want?" The words were clipped, wary.

"You haven't been back to see me," Dr. Grolier said. "You called that one time to set up another appointment and I phoned you back but I haven't been able to get you. Is everything all right, Hugh?"

Hugh's shoulder twitched uncomfortably. He couldn't stand the sound of that voice. He remembered it from the day he learned all about his father. It grated on his nerves. Dr. Grolier frightened him. He couldn't talk to him any longer.

"Yes, everything is all right. I'm not worried about the power anymore. I'm okay."

"What power?" Grolier asked, concerned. "You sound troubled, Hugh."

He was sweating. His shirt was stained under his arms, sticking to his skin. He wiped his face with his sleeve. He needed to be with Paula *right then.* "I'm all right. Really. Just send me a bill and I'll settle up with you. I don't need your help anymore." His laugh was short, forced. "You're an excellent doctor. You made me all better."

"Do you want to come to the office now and tell me how you're feeling?"

Paula screamed again. His name. Loud. Long. Mournful. He covered the mouthpiece with his palm even though he didn't think Paula's cries would carry over the phone.

"I told you I'm all right . . ." He glanced over his shoulder, almost as if expecting to see her, *someone* coming up the basement stairs.

"Or I can come to your house. Whatever you want. You tell me . . . ." The therapist's voice never lost its cool, professional distance.

"No . . . !"

"What is it, Hugh? I hear something in your voice. There's something bothering you, isn't there? Why don't you talk to me?" But Hugh made no response. "Where's Paula? Is she home with you? If you're not feeling well, maybe she can drive you here. Why don't you ask her if she wants to." Still no response. "I thought you were going to trust me, Hugh. . . ."

Hugh hesitated. His cheek muscles ticked. He licked his lips thoughtfully. Dr. Grolier had brought him pain, but relief as well, as he recalled his calming words after the hypnosis session. He was only a child and not to blame for the accident.

His skin prickled, a crawling, itchy feeling. He swatted at himself to relieve the invisible sensation. He swallowed.

"What's this power, Hugh?" Dr. Grolier asked.

He had never talked with Dr. Grolier about the power. Maybe he should. . . .

Kate moaned and her arm moved. Hugh thought he saw her eyes open, then close again.

"Trust me, Hugh," Dr. Grolier prodded.

Maybe Dr. Grolier *could* help him, he considered. He started to tell the psychologist what was happening. His mouth hung open—"It's this power I have, Doctor, that when people leave me they—" but then suddenly closed with his mind as the realization exploded inside of him. *So what! It didn't matter to Paula if Grolier was going to help him; she was going to leave him anyway. Nothing mattered to her! Not his getting better, not his talking to the therapist, nothing!*

"Hugh . . . !" Grolier said his name sharply as he sensed he was losing him.

Hugh slammed down the phone. He knew he shouldn't have even picked up. Dr. Grolier had only upset him. Besides, there was no other solution; it was time.

He trailed the gasoline down the cellar stairs and emptied the can around the storeroom, turning it upside down to free the last drops. His clothing was soaked with the gasoline, which had worked its way through his pants and was irritating his legs. He searched his pockets for a match but he didn't have one with him. There were plenty in the kitchen. He took the stairs two at a time, ripped open a utility drawer, and took out a box of long kitchen matches. Then he went back down the stairs.

Paula had smelled the gasoline and knew what he planned to do. When he opened the storeroom door she lunged out, desperate to get past him. He caught her in his arms, wrapped them around her chest, and pinned her. She struggled against him, tried to elbow him away from her.

"You can't!" she shrieked. "You can't!"

"I have to do it, Paula!" he cried. "I can't be left alone."

He threw her away from him, down to the storeroom floor. Her mother's body broke her fall. She looked up at Hugh. He was framed in the doorway, his features shadowed and undefined as he faced into the dark storeroom. He had killed her mother and he'd kill her and her children, too, if they didn't get away from him. Her one thought was survival, but she was not strong enough to push past him. She grabbed hold of herself. There was another way.

"Hugh, let's go back upstairs," she tried softly. "We can forget about all of this and be together again. What do you say?"

He shook his head. He didn't believe her. "You don't want to stay here. Neither you nor the children. You want to leave me."

"Hugh, you're wrong. I love you. And I know this power is troubling you and I want to help. Believe me. Then once you're not bothered by the power anymore we can be together again . . ."

His father had left him, Judith had left him. And Paula was going to leave him too. Everything she was saying was a lie, a masquerade for what she really felt. They would get upstairs and he would never see her again.

"Don't believe you," he croaked. "You want to leave me. You don't love me." She and Dr. Grolier had probably even conspired against him.

"You're wrong. And is it better to die than to trust me?" Even though she was shivering, she tried to keep her voice steady. Stay strong, she ordered herself, for the sake of the children. "You have to trust me, Hugh. You just have to," she begged with all of her heart.

"How can I trust you?" he cried. "You broke out of the

room. If you loved me, you would have stayed in there. For *me!* Because you knew how I felt."

"I was afraid for you, Hugh. I had to get you help."

"No." He shook his head. "I don't believe you." Inside, he was burning up. The pain knotted his forehead, blurred his sight. His fists clenched and his eyes closed tightly, his face compressed and gritted. He didn't want to listen to her, to the psychologist, to anyone. He opened his eyes and saw Paula through a filtered mask. He couldn't talk to her anymore. It was too late for any more talk. *All this talk was just making him hurt more.* He touched the match to the box and Paula screamed, "How can you kill us, Hugh? How? *How?*"

Her sudden intensity unnerved him and stopped his hand, poised above the matchbox. "Can't be left alone," he sobbed. "The power . . ." He was a frightened, babbling child.

"You say you have a power," Paula challenged. "But you killed your children and now you're going to kill all of us too. What kind of a power makes you kill a family you love?"

"No!" he rasped. "The fire that killed John and Danielle was an accident. Don't say I did it. That's a lie."

"A lie, Hugh? How can you say it's a lie? Look at you. You're soaked with gasoline. There's gasoline all over the house. You're holding a match, about to start a fire. Just like you started the fire that killed your children!"

"No!"

"Just like it, Hugh!" she repeated loudly. "There's no difference. You killed them then and you're going to kill us now."

"Accident . . . !" The word caught in his throat as he spat it out. He covered his ears with his hands so he wouldn't have to hear any more. But still she pressed.

"No accident, Hugh. *You* did it. Judith was right. All those times she accused you of being there and setting the fire, she was right, wasn't she? *Wasn't she?*"

Paula knew she had nothing to lose because she had already lost. Hugh stood in the doorway holding a match in one hand and the box in the other. To strike the match was to kill them all. But instinctively something told her she was on the right track. Hugh didn't really know what he had done that night on Cape Cod. The same way he didn't remember the car crash. Dr. Grolier had yet to bring out of him that he had set the fire, but there was now no question in her mind what he had done and again repressed; that was his pattern. But would this knowledge stop him from what he was doing? Or if she helped him remember what happened that night, would it fill him with such remorse that he would kill them to escape the inevitable, overwhelming guilt?

But she had no alternative, although she tempered her accusation. "How can it be an accident, Hugh?" she asked softly.

She looked into his face. She couldn't see his eyes, but his head was tilted toward her and his arms were lowered. He looked vulnerable, and Paula thought of rushing him but rejected the idea. *This* was her approach. He was at least listening to her now. Because even he had to admit the evidence was strong. "What happened that night, Hugh?" she repeated. "Tell me. Tell me what happened on Cape Cod when your children died. What did you do?"

He shook his head weakly. "I . . . I don't remember."

"You saw Judith's note," Paula prodded, trying to recall the story the way Hugh had told it to her. "What did the note say?"

She saw his strain, the contracting of his posture as he remembered. "That . . . that she was taking the children to Cape Cod. She said she had to think about our marriage. I was smothering her."

"Then what did you do?"

"I called her. And she told me she wanted to be away from me for a while." His look was pained, his voice thick. "She was leaving me."

"Then what?"

"I . . . I . . ." Hugh's head wobbled weakly on his neck, making little nervous circles. He was looking around, searching inside of himself, suddenly being confronted with what had been the worst night of his life. "I can't remember," he cried out in frustration.

"You were afraid of being left alone. So you went to her," Paula pressed calmly, evenly. "You drove to Cape Cod."

"No." He shook his head violently; he didn't want to hear.

"You drove there. Why, Hugh? Why did you go there? To talk to Judith? Try to convince her to come home? Why did you go to Cape Cod?"

"I . . ." He ran his hand through his hair. "I don't remember . . ."

"Yes, you do. You can remember. You can. . . . You drove to Cape Cod, followed her. You were upset. Frightened . . ."

He moaned, low and mournful. "No . . . don't . . ."

"She had left you. Judith had left you and you wanted to bring her back. I know you can't remember now, Hugh. I know it's painful and like what happened with your father you don't want to, but think, Hugh, try to remember. *Try.* Remember how you felt when you found the letter Judith left you, when you talked to her and knew that she wasn't coming back? You had to do something, you had to go to her, talk to her, do something to get her to come back. So you got into your car—"

"No." He was crying, swaying, suddenly afraid of what he might remember, his subconscious mind refusing to subject itself to pain.

"Work with me, Hugh. Focus in on that night. You can remember it. It's important. Perhaps the most important night of your life. . . . Try to remember what you did. . . ."

As Paula repeated her instructions, her voice took on a melodic quality, a calm intensity. It was like Dr. Grolier was talking to him, taking him backward in time, leading him to remember the night his father was killed. But now he wasn't regressed to the event; instead he was being charged to search his memory. "It's there, Hugh . . ." Paula said softly, yet forcefully. She was in control for the first time in days. "Go to it. Dig it out. Allow yourself to recall that night. I know it's hard but you can do it. . . ." Hugh's appearance seemed to change. His eyes narrowed, his forehead tightened, his face compressed in anguish as he struggled to reach deep inside himself. He remembered finding the letter Judith had left him, making the phone call, hearing her terrible, terrible words that she was leaving him. A moan escaped his lips.

But that was when a curtain of darkness shut him out from any further recall. He couldn't get past it, and while one part of him fought to keep the curtain closed, another part struggled to pull it open. He was at odds with himself, dizzied, and almost lost his balance.

The picture was out of focus. Intellectually he still couldn't remember what he had done. Emotionally, though, he knew the memory was going to hurt like hell—*he felt it*—and knew it was why he had repressed it then, and why his mind refused to release it to him now as well.

But Paula pressed. She lost track of time, her concentration was riveted only on him because right now there was nothing else, repeating her words hypnotically, trying to penetrate layers of defenses, years of thick protective netting. It was important he remember that night and he could, *he could,* she continually stressed.

And then the curtain parted and Hugh remembered driving.

It was late November, a misty, cold night; tourist season had been over for months, the wintry Cape cruel and foreboding. The windshield wipers flicked back and forth monotonously; the oncoming headlights formed mesmerizing stars, flared and distorted by the drizzle. Hugh was upset, confused, almost detached from his physical self, blinded to everything except his knowledge that his wife had just left him. The choking anxiety that clogged his head was familiar—he had felt this way when his father was leaving him. And the horrible memory that his father had died spurred him to drive faster. Because his thoughts had confused, blurred into one another and became *my father left me and thus he died. To leave me is to die. And now Judith and the children left me so they* might *die.*

Which increased his desperation to get to them so they wouldn't die.

He arrived in Eastham and pulled off the highway and onto the back road that led to their vacation house. Few people lived year-round along the stretch of road and there were no lights except his headlamps slashing the night and fog.

He parked his car well before the house and approached it on foot so he wouldn't startle Judith. The rain had stopped but the air was raw and he zipped his windbreaker up to his neck. When he got to the house he stood at the edge of the woods looking in. The lights were on and he clearly saw Judith and the children inside. They were playing some sort of game but he couldn't make out what. Although it didn't matter. He could see that they were all fine and having a good time. *Without him.* And it hurt him to see them like this. He felt very disconnected from them as the evening drew on, becoming more and more alienated from his family. "We don't need you," they seemed to be saying, laughing at him, mocking him, rejecting him. Rage welled inside of him, consumed him, and chest-wrenching anger burned in a need to punish those inside the house.

And twisted his thoughts into a bizarre, psychotic two-plus-two-equals-five:

Judith and the children no longer *might* die. *Because they left him, they* had *to die.*

He had to kill them.

And filled with satisfaction, he waited until they went to sleep. A night-light burned near the bathroom, the only light in the cottage. Silently, Hugh used his key and snuck inside, carefully made his way into the kitchen, where he turned on all four burners and blew out the pilot lights. All of the windows were closed, the night too nasty to keep any of them open. The house would soon fill with gas. His plan was to asphyxiate them.

He went back outside, where he stood watching at the line of woods. The night was dark and starless; it was almost frightening being outside all alone and he grew anxious, fidgety. *They had to die!* and he could no longer wait for the gas to kill them. He had to hasten their deaths.

He broke a window and threw a lit torch into the house. The explosion rattled the clapboard cottage, shards of glass blew outward, and the fires were instantaneous.

He heard the children's screams from inside, saw Judith running out . . . and turned and disappeared into the trees.

He could barely recall the drive home. Only waking to the ringing phone, and the police telling him about the fire and deaths. That was all.

Until now . . .

He looked madly from Paula to the match in his hand, and couldn't get rid of it fast enough. He collapsed on his knees in front of his wife.

Chapter 27

PAULA HELPED HUGH UP THE BASEMENT STAIRS, THE BOX OF matches left harmlessly behind on the tiled floor, soaked in a puddle of gasoline. Her heart pounded furiously in residual terror and relief. Thank God she had cracked Hugh's armor and sent his defenses reeling, opened him to his past.

They had to get upstairs and out of the house. His knees were wobbly and he was leaning on her as if all his support had been removed, muscles and bones weakened beyond help. He was shuddering; he couldn't warm himself, his body racked by sobs as torturous images raged through his mind, unleashed memories, visions of horror. He was seeing and hearing what had been buried in his unconscious—the fire, the cries of his children, Judith's frantic efforts to save them, a cacophony of sounds—screams, and the crackle and hiss and roar of the flames, and a kaleidoscopic wheel of sights—bold colors, dark shadows, twisting images. "I killed them . . ." he muttered almost incoherently, overwhelmed by thunderous guilt.

For her part, Paula murmured soothing, comforting words . . . she loved him and would never leave him . . . they'd go right to Dr. Grolier's office, he'd help Hugh like he did the last time . . . things would be all right. She kept talking, repeating her words over and over to keep him diverted. Right now all she wanted was to get the children out of the house and away from the terror of their confinement, as well as the very real possibility of the gasoline fumes being ignited by one of the heater pilot lights in the basement. As long as they were in the house they remained vulnerable.

The frail figure startled them both as they reached the top of the basement stairs. Kate's body was heaving and tears streamed down her face, contorted in pain from Hugh's blow. Blood trickled down her neck and stained her dress from where the lamp base had broken the skin. She was gripped by a searing mental anguish as well, perhaps worse than her physical suffering. Filled with confusion. Loss. She had been betrayed; the man who meant more to her than life itself had struck her down. Her pent-up emotions came tumbling out.

"I love you, Hugh," she sobbed. "Ever since I first met you, I've wanted you so much. That's why I came here today—to tell you. I've wanted to so many times—but you said you were married and I was afraid of rejec—"

"Not now, Kate!" Paula said sharply, cutting her off, not wanting anything to disturb Hugh's delicate state.

Upstairs, the children had heard the sounds in the living room and were screaming again to be let out. Alarm stabbed through Jeremy's voice. "There's gasoline up here, Mom!"

"I'm coming . . ." Paula called up to them, then hissed, "Kate, please go."

But there was no stopping Kate. She smiled at Hugh through her tears, a desperate, pathetic yearning clouding her eyes. "I need you to love me in return, Hugh. You have to . . . I've been waiting . . . I'll forgive your hitting me. Let's just go and be together . . ."

Hugh's face was creased as if he'd never seen her before. Her words to him made no sense, had no meaning. His voice was weak. "I love Paula . . ." he said blankly, his tone stating the obvious. "Not you . . ." Then his expression filled with fear—*Paula couldn't think he loved anyone except her, not now!* "I don't love you, Kate," he said more firmly. "I never did. It's *Paula* I love." He gripped her arm tightly.

Kate shook her head violently at the impact of Hugh's words. Her chin braced against her neck as she seemingly tried to escape from them. Her hands went stiffly to her ears, then lowered. "No—no—" There was a long pause between her words, which were more gasps of horror and realization, a cry of denial as she tried to fend off a mounting, frightening reality. It had taken so long to declare herself and her illusions were being dashed, her fantasy destroyed, disintegrated like so much dust. The scenario was all wrong. In her mind she just had to express her feelings and she would take Hugh from Paula and they would love each other forever. Rejection was not in the picture. It had to be a mistake.

She ran to Hugh and tried to throw her arms around him, but with a worried look toward Paula he fended her off, pushing her aside. "Kate, no—get away—"

"Don't say that!" the younger woman spat out, still not accepting her dismissal. Her eyes stared unblinking as she looked at Hugh dumbly, trying in vain to somehow piece together what was happening. Because it couldn't be so. "I've been waiting . . ." she croaked out the words. "I can't live without you, Hugh . . . I won't . . ."

"Kate, please leave us," Hugh whispered hoarsely.

The children were screaming for her and Paula couldn't take any more time to deflect Kate. The woman had to be ignored.

"I'm going to get the children now, Hugh." She leaned him against the couch so he wouldn't lose his balance and fall to the floor. "I'll be right down. Then we'll go far away from here."

"Yes," he answered dully with a mechanical nod. But there was fear in his eyes as they darted from Paula to Kate—"I love you, Paula, and you'll help me?"—the crying need of a condemned man in his voice.

"I swear, Hugh," Paula said. She kissed him quickly in reassurance and started out of the room.

"No!" Kate shrieked as she stood alone, isolated, the rejection too much for her fragile psyche. It was a venomous, inhuman wail, a desperate sound without beginning or end as reality crashed around her and icy terror gripped her. The hopeless cry of the damned. Until now there had been fantasy, expectation, now there was nothing. "I love you, Hugh!" Her eyes flared and filled with hatred and knowledge—*It was because Paula was still there!*—then firmed with resolution. *There were solutions to problems! There were always solutions!*

With a screech she threw herself at Paula, hitting her with the full weight of her body. Unprepared and startled, Paula was thrown off balance. She went flying into a display case that held one of Hugh's antique typewriters, taking the wooden base hard in her chest. The crunching sound was audible. Paula gasped at the sudden pain and struggled for breath. A rib had cracked, she knew.

"Hugh . . . !" There was pain and fear in the word as she slumped to the floor.

"Paula . . . !" Hugh's face had gone ashen, his cry strangled. Paula was hurt. He started toward her. Kate grabbed his arm.

"Leave her, Hugh. Come with me."

He tried to break Kate's hold on him but she held firm.

"You know it's me you want. Forget Paula." Tears laced her voice, and *uncertainty* suddenly. Things weren't right.

Then Hugh wrenched his arm free of Kate and ran to Paula.

"The children, Hugh," she gasped. "Go upstairs and get them. Bring them down here."

"I can't leave you—"

"The children, Hugh!" she yelled. "Go and get them."

Paula was still there. That was the problem.

Hugh hesitated for only a second, then sure in his mind it was all right, he started toward the stairs. He didn't see Kate standing alone, her chest heaving as she struggled for breath—

There was a way to make it right, there was still another solution. The children were upstairs, Paula was incapacitated. . . . If it wasn't for Paula and the children, Hugh would be hers!

—and reached into her purse.

Paula saw her.

"Kate, no!" she gasped in a mixture of horror and disbelief as Kate struck the match. She made a half lunge back toward the other woman but was too late. Hugh was on the stairs as Kate dropped the match to the floor. Immediately ribbons of flame shot out in every direction wherever Hugh had trailed the gasoline, past Hugh and up the staircase to the bedrooms where the children were still trapped.

Hugh spun around on the third step. "Paula!" He reached out toward her but fire separated them.

"The children, Hugh!" She tried to struggle to her feet. Pain racked her body.

"This way, Hugh—" Kate cried. She could barely contain her excitement. "Come out of the house with me." She ducked around a row of flames and grabbed Hugh by the arm to lead him to safety.

"Paula—" he shrieked. For one second he couldn't see her through the flames.

"Hugh, the children—"

Kate yanked on his arm almost triumphantly. "Leave them. We can get out and be together."

But Hugh didn't hear either Paula or Kate. His only thought was *He had to save Paula! There was nothing else. No other sound. No other distraction. Just Paula.*

He pulled away from Kate to go to Paula but lost his balance on the stairs. Arms outstretched and in almost slow motion he slipped off the step and with a cry that bespoke his fate tumbled forward into the fire. His gasoline-soaked clothing exploded into flames which quickly spiraled upward to his face and hair. He screeched with the most intense agony as his skin became liquid fire, instantly blackened beyond hope, a human pyre. He whirled around the room, all sound and terror, flailing his arms wildly, fanning the flames even more. He tried to reach the doorway but within seconds the fire entered his mouth, consumed his throat, and cut off all sound forever.

Kate and Paula stared mutely, in stony horror, too overwhelmed even to scream as Hugh succumbed to the flames and dropped to the floor.

"Mommy!" Jeremy's terrified voice came above the rush and broke the moment, snapping Paula free!

My God! The children!

Her husband was dead, although the thought barely connected because she still had to do now what had been ahead of her all along.

But now there was fire.

And her rib—

She was on her feet. Pain ripped her chest, and she could barely breathe, from the cracked rib and the flames and the heat. But she had to get to Jeremy and Michelle.

Clutching her chest to keep the rib in place, she started up the stairs past Kate, who had dropped to her knees next to Hugh, whose face was already charred beyond recognition. The younger woman's eyes were wide, and thoughts were filling her mind. About Hugh. About Paula. Her love was dead and Paula had killed him!

"Get out, Kate, you'll die!" Paula screamed, but didn't know if she had heard or not.

But Kate wasn't her concern.

Flames opened up before her. The fire blazed on the second floor and Jeremy and Michelle were shrieking in terror. They banged on the door, still latched from the outside. Over the crackle of the fire Paula heard her children's screams. Only distantly she thought of Judith, who had also heard her children crying through the flames but wasn't able to save them. But Paula was determined to save hers and knew she would die sooner than lose them. Filled with purpose and unconscious of the danger and her own pain, she raced up the edge of the staircase, hugging the wall. A gasoline-stained line of the rug burned beneath her and flames wrapped around the wooden banister. Her hair was singed and her skin reddened from the heat, starting to blacken. She held her breath to avoid inhaling the choking smoke, fumbled with the latch, and pushed into Jeremy's room, slamming the door shut behind her.

"Mommy!" Michelle cried. Hugh hadn't poured gasoline in the bedroom, and although flames were outlining the door and smoke was pouring in underneath, they still had several seconds. But fire had closed off the staircase and their escape route. There was only one other way out.

Jeremy's bedroom overlooked the sloped roof overhang of the wide front porch, which ran the length of the house. Acrid gray-black smoke was already rising from the first-floor windows as the living-room drapes ignited. In the distance she heard sirens.

If they could get out onto the roof, they could wait for help.

But the windows were nailed shut.

Damn Hugh! she cried to herself.

She would have to break the window.

Jeremy's baseball bat was in the corner of the room. Ignoring the pain in her chest, she hefted the bat. "Stay back now!" she ordered, and with unbearable agony swung it. The bat connected with the glass, shattering it, leaving a gaping hole. But they would get badly cut going through. Another swing was needed. She lifted the bat. But the pain raged through her, forcing her to drop it.

"Let me." Jeremy raised the bat and swung at the window, cleaning out the glass.

Paula pulled a chair under the window for them to climb on.

"Up now, onto the roof," she ordered hoarsely. "And stay low. Keep your balance. We can wait for help out there."

Jeremy was the first one on the chair and through the window. Then Michelle was helped outside by her mother and brother.

Paula put her foot on the chair. Holding her breath to minimize the pain in her chest, she shifted her weight and stepped up. That's when she felt the tug on her leg. Something had grabbed her!

She screamed in surprise and twisted around.

Kate was there. "He loved me!" she shrieked in a hoarse voice. "You killed him. Now you have to die!"

Her hands grabbed firm hold of Paula's leg and she tried to pull her off the chair. Sucking in her breath, Paula kicked out with her other leg, catching Kate in the face, snapping her back, breaking her hold. With a moan Kate slumped to the floor, her jaw broken.

Paula barely glanced behind her as she girded herself and hoisted her body through the window. Only a few more minutes, she told herself, and they would be safe.

"Low now," she ordered the children. With all fours on the roof, they would maximize their stability and keep their balance. *A few more minutes. Just a few—*

Then Kate leapt through the window, insanity raging across her face.

Paula sprang aside to put distance between herself and her children. With a lunge, Kate was on top of her, trying to wrestle Paula to the edge of the roof, throw her over. The drop was ten feet to a concrete walk. Paula tried to secure a hold on the window ledge but Kate grabbed at her wrists and tried to pull her fingers free. Their feet slipped on the shingles as they struggled for footing. Jeremy beat at Kate, tried to push her away, to no avail. Blinded to everything else, she had only one purpose. To kill Paula, then the children.

Her madness gave her the upper hand. With a chop she broke Paula's hold on the windowsill and started to pull her toward the edge. Paula flattened herself on the roof, stretched her body, and screamed from the crushing pain in her chest. She could barely catch her breath to defend herself; a deep inhalation caused her tremendous pain. Arms extended, her fingers clawed at the shingles, pulling them up. Her nails were broken, her fingers bloodied. With strength borne from madness, Kate pulled. Paula's feet slipped over the rain gutter and dangled in the air. Then her knees. Soon her center of gravity would be over the edge and she wouldn't have the strength to save herself.

Then Paula saw her chance. In a sudden move that caused her pain enough to see stars, she rolled over and swung her fist at Kate's face. She connected cleanly. The momentum unbalanced Kate and sent her reeling. In a frozen moment, she teetered at the edge, held out her hand toward Paula, and with a shortened scream went over.

Paula struggled to her knees. "Oh, God . . ." She gripped her chest. Her sudden movement at striking Kate had broken the rib. She prayed a lung had not been punctured. Although *she* didn't matter anymore—only the children. "Come on . . ." she hissed. Jeremy and Michelle were hunched on the roof above her. Grabbing at Michelle, Paula helped the little girl inch her way carefully down the roof to the edge. Flames shot up around them. "Are you okay?" she called, her voice barely carrying over the rush of the fire. "Try not to inhale." The smoke could kill them as fast as the heat and flames.

Jeremy nodded tensely, too overcome by the heat of the fire to utter a word. Michelle was already rasping as she struggled for air.

But Jeremy's bedroom was now ablaze behind them, the shingles on the roof, the wooden structure. To wait for help would be to die. So close to safety, yet still so far. The sirens were louder but the fire trucks were still not within sight. They were out of options and Paula knew they had no choice but to jump. And pray.

They had a chance. They were just above a row of bushes that might cushion their fall.

The children knew what they had to do. But then a bush beneath the house burst into flames and quickly spread to the entire line of shrubs. Paula couldn't let the children land on the burning hedges. Then the wind shifted for a second and through a break in the smoke Paula saw that at the very end of the house there was soft ground still untouched by fire. They were only ten feet from the ground, a safe enough distance for a calculated jump, perhaps, if the impact was smooth and flawless. Anything short of a ten-point landing might result in a broken leg, a ripped tendon. Or worse, she thought as she looked at Kate's motionless body sprawled out on the concrete. Holding Michelle with one hand, and balancing herself with the other, Paula slid them both across the roof, which had become alarmingly hot.

"I can't breathe, Mommy—" Michelle cried.

"Hang on, baby, okay," Paula yelled over the roar of the flames. "We're almost there. We're going to make it."

Their faces were blackened, their lungs filled with the noxious smoke. Fire lapped over the roof line; the decorative cedar shakes that sided the house were now ablaze. But then they were at the corner. Hoping she wouldn't lose her balance and tumble them both over awkwardly, Paula stood and grabbed Michelle's hands, and holding on with the last of her ebbing strength, she dangled the child low over the edge. There were daggers in her chest. She had to contort her body to keep the rib steady. "Keep your knees bent," she barked instructions, "then get up and run away from the house. Or crawl if you have to"— she envisioned broken, dangling limbs—"just get far away." A sudden wave of smoke blocked her view as she let the child go. She couldn't see if Michelle had landed safely. She had to hope because she hissed, "Jeremy—go!" as the flames ballooned around them.

Then Paula stood. A gust of wind blew the flames onto the roof and caught her dress as she jumped. Her knees absorbed the shock of her fall but her clothing was on fire and her rib broke the skin. Terrified as never before in her life, her instinct was to run and flail her arms but she was trapped by pain, which ironically saved her life. Because hands grabbed her and wrested her to the ground. A jacket was thrown over her, smothering the flames. Then she was scooped up and carried away from the burning house. Had she run, she would have died.

"The children?" she croaked hoarsely to her benefactor, gasping to inhale.

"They're all right. Don't worry. And you will be, too, I promise." The man laid her down on the grass. "I'm Dr. Grolier," he said. "I knew there was something very wrong with Hugh when I spoke to him. I came right over." He looked at the scene grimly. "Just in time I see." Only then were the fire engines turning into the cul-de-sac.

Paula's eyes were slitted from the smoke, but they didn't fail to open wide with the purest of joy as she saw Jeremy and Michelle come running toward her. And she barely felt the pain from her burns or her rib as she grabbed their hands.

Then as Paula was laid on a stretcher and carried to the waiting ambulance, the house disappeared behind an awesome wall of flames that weakened the timbers and brought the structure crashing to the ground.

Paula squeezed her children's hands. They had survived by only seconds.

But they had survived.

Imagine yourself finally settled into your large Victorian home. Life in your charming, quaint New England village is a dream come true...until the dream turns slowly into a nightmare. And you must confront evil forces *you don't even believe in*...and cannot stop.

Just like the families in these 3 novels of horror and suspense. By the *master* of supernatural terror,

DUFFY STEIN

_____	**OUT OF THE SHADOWS**	16826-0-05	$3.50
_____	**THE OWLSFANE HORROR**	16781-7-10	$3.50
_____	**GHOST CHILD**	12955-9-19	$3.50

Dell

At your local bookstore or use this handy coupon for ordering:

DELL READERS SERVICE—DEPT. B1055A
P.O. BOX 1000, PINE BROOK, N.J. 07058

Please send me the above title(s). I am enclosing $_____ (please add 75¢ per copy to cover postage and handling.) Send check or money order—no cash or CODs. Please allow 3-4 weeks for shipment.

Ms./Mrs./Mr._____

Address_____

City/State_____Zip_____

John Saul

No other book and no other novelist will prepare you for the nightmares he has in store.

☐ COMES THE BLIND FURY	11475-6-20	$3.50
☐ CRY FOR THE STRANGERS	11870-0-70	3.95
☐ PUNISH THE SINNERS	17084-2-79	3.95
☐ SUFFER THE CHILDREN	18293-X-58	3.95
☐ WHEN THE WIND BLOWS	19490-3-24	3.95

Dell DELL BOOKS B1055B
P.O. BOX 1000, PINE BROOK, N.J. 07058-1000

Please send me the books I have checked above. I am enclosing $_____(please add 75c per copy to cover postage and handling). Send check or money order—no cash or C.O.D.'s. Please allow up to 8 weeks for shipment.

Name _____

Address _____

City_____State/Zip_____